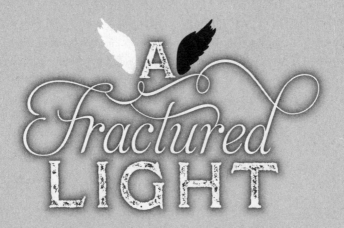

A Fractured LIGHT

JOCELYN DAVIES

HARPER TEEN
An Imprint of HarperCollinsPublishers

HarperTeen is an imprint of HarperCollins Publishers.

A Fractured Light

Library of Congress Cataloging-in-Publication Data
Davies, Jocelyn.
  A fractured light / by Jocelyn Davies.
    p. cm. — (Beautiful dark ; bk. 2)
  Summary: "In the aftermath of Devin's shocking betrayal, Skye learns
that Asher has been using her for the Rebellion. She wishes she could
forget about both sides, but as war between the factions looms, Skye is
forced to make a choice about where her heart and loyalties truly lie"
— Provided by publisher.
  ISBN 978-0-06-199068-7
  [1. Angels—Fiction. 2. Identity—Fiction. 3. Supernatural—Fiction.
4. Good and evil—Fiction. 5. Colorado—Fiction.] I. Title.
PZ7.D28392Fr 2012   2012011525
[Fic]—dc23   CIP
                                                             AC

Typography by Erin Fitzsimmons
13 14 15 16 17 LP/RRDH 10 9 8 7 6 5 4 3 2 1

First paperback edition, 2013

To Shelbs (laugh, worry less)

Praise for A FRACTURED LIGHT

"Angst, simmering undercurrents of violence and war, and tortured love abound, leaving readers with another cliff-hanger ending full of possibility."
—ALA *Booklist*

"Points to plenty of action in the final book." —*Kirkus Reviews*

"Davies delivers a main character who defies expectations and chooses her own path, refusing those blatantly offered. Readers will once again be left breathlessly waiting to see how Skye tackles the challenges set before her, but will find themselves confident that she will find a way to save the day—and herself." —*SLJ*

"Surprising discoveries are made in this sequel. There's no way you'll be able to pass up the last installment." —*New York Journal of Books*

"An awesome read with a killer ending! I can hardly wait to read the final installment in this series. I have a feeling it's going to be incredible!"
—*Mundie Moms*

"I am in love with this series. I just finished this installment mere moments ago and I am already anxious for the next novel." —*Reading Lark*

"I love how the story would take a turn somewhere unexpected and give you moments of jaw-dropping goodness." —*Zach's YA Reviews*

Praise for A BEAUTIFUL DARK

"Jocelyn Davies has done a fantastic job at creating a story with an appealing lore, a beautiful setting, and some fascinating characters. Normally for me it's the characters that hook me with the story, but this time around it was Jocelyn's writing that lured me in." —*Mundie Moms*

"This takes the whole fallen angel thing to a completely different level! It will make you wish you were snowed in so no one could stop you from reading beginning to end in one sitting!" —*The YA Sisterhood*

"This book is amazing! Five stars! Two thumbs up!" —*Good Choice Reading*

"*A Beautiful Dark* brings in just enough mythology, emotion, and heart-wrenching moments to hook paranormal fans. A book just as beautiful inside as it is outside." —*Confessions of a Bookaholic*

Also by Jocelyn Davies

A Beautiful Dark

A Radiant Sky

I am hovering on the edge.

It's the dead of winter, and snow covers the slopes like it is trying to bury us. I can hear the sound of my classmates' voices echoing off the mountains as they laugh and horse around. I can see my best friend, Cassie, down on the bunny slope, shrieking as she falls for the thousandth time, and our friend Dan laughing as he helps her up. A few feet away from me, on the top of the mountain, Ian pulls his goggles down over his eyes. I feel drawn to the ledge, tempted by the chasm below.

I am always torn. Between control and chaos; passion and tranquility. Between what's fated and what I want. Part of me longs to take the plunge, to dive off headfirst and let the feeling of control evaporate on the wind. And part of me wants to be in a place where I'd never have to worry about that choice—or any choice. Where peace and calm are the only things I'd feel. After a lifetime of trying to erase the hurt of my parents dying, of Aunt Jo and my devoted friends helping me put the pieces back together again—maybe that is where I belong. Maybe I deserve some peace, after all.

But when I take a step back from the ledge, the adrenaline fades away, and all that's left inside me is an empty coldness. I don't feel the hurt anymore. But I don't feel happiness, either. There is a voice in my ear, whispering: Make a choice, Skye. You can't stare off the edge of this cliff forever.

In the dream I have every night, I have made up my mind. Every time, I am about to jump. To let the pain rush back in but also every other feeling that comes with it—love and grief and joy. I want to fly down that slope and never look back. I want so many things. The desire is what prevents me from being able to exist in a perpetual state of calm.

And so I align my skis. I get ready to push off down the mountain.

But someone always stops me. An icy blond angel, his face calmingly familiar and yet terrifying all at once. His wings are so blindingly white I have to close my eyes. And while they're closed, the cold steel of a blade plummets straight through me. The pain rushes in as the sword comes out. I can't make a choice between chaos and control, because it's already been made for me.

I am taken away into the clouds.

I have the dream every night. And I never wake up to the relief that it's only a dream. Because for days, I don't wake up at all.

The first thing I noticed when I opened my eyes was the gray light surrounding me like a film of gauze. I winced and squinted, trying to focus my vision, but the light was so bright that my head began to throb. I closed my eyes again, and I took a deep breath.

That was good. I was breathing now, at least. It meant I wasn't dead.

When I opened my eyes again, I tried harder to focus, struggling to make sense of where I was. The cold seeped in around me, and I tried pulling my cream-colored jersey-knit comforter up around my chin. A threadbare fabric brushed my skin instead.

This isn't my blanket. Panicked, I looked for something familiar, some touchstone to show me that I was in my bedroom. But everything around me was strange and unknown.

I'm not at home.

Slowly things began to crystalize. Images and shapes snapped into place; lines sharpened and space defined itself. The light was falling softly through an open window. I could just make out a couple of brushstrokes of color, brown and green smudged against a white sky. Treetops. Colorado in winter.

A stray slant of light fell across the faded quilt that covered me. I wiggled my toes and watched the movement cause ripples in the light thrown across the bed. So I wasn't paralyzed. I tried my fingers, too, and then my neck. I blinked several times and then opened my mouth, stretched it wide, and closed it. I could move, but my muscles and joints felt stiff and unused. How long had I been lying here?

As I turned my head, I caught a glimpse of something metal on a wooden nightstand next to my bed, and my body tensed. Instantly my mind flashed to the woods in the darkening gloom of evening, to the glint of metal hurtling toward me. My heart was pounding, and my throat was suddenly dry. I didn't know if my reaction was caused by my memory or my imagination.

What happened to me?

"Wake up," a female voice whispered, using the hushed tone meant for hospitals and libraries. "Come on. Go sleep downstairs on the couch. You must be exhausted."

Straining to see where the voice was coming from, I honed in on a young woman standing in the far corner of the room. Long chestnut hair hung in a thick, glossy braid down her back. *She isn't talking to me*, I realized.

Then a second voice yawned in response. A guy's voice. "Mm-hmm. How long was I asleep?" I tried to see around the woman without moving the muscles below my neck, but that was harder than I'd thought it would be, and I gave up. I could just make out a battered snow boot splayed out behind her. Whoever she was talking to was sitting in a rocking chair in the corner. Something about his rough, scratchy voice was familiar. I felt a spasm in my chest.

"Has anything changed?" His voice was hollow, like he already knew the answer.

"No," she said. "And if you want her to get better, you have to let her rest."

"I'm not bothering her if I just sit here, am I?"

"It's not just her I'm worried about. You need rest, too. How are we supposed to protect her if we're exhausted? Come on, I just slept. It's your turn."

"But I . . ."

"You're not doing her any favors if you fall asleep again.

With all that's coming . . ."

"I don't care about what's coming, Ardith. I care about what happened. If I could just go back to that night—"

"Asher, listen to me—"

Asher. At the sound of his name, something silvery and light coursed through my veins. My face felt hot and cold at the same time.

"You can't," the woman said.

I wished I could sit up and call to him across the room. But my body wasn't cooperating.

"I just want her back," he said quietly, and I was struck by how different he sounded. So serious and somber. I couldn't detect the smallest hint of the usual sly wink in his voice.

Thousands of tiny stars pricked across my vision. Something terrible must have happened to me to make Asher this worried. But what?

"We all do," the woman said. "We can't win this without her."

"Not because of the *fight*, Ardith."

"I know." The woman's shoulders tensed. "Once upon a time someone said that about me. He risked his life to get me back. And look what happened." Even from my bed in the corner, I could tell these words were full of meaning. I wondered what the story was. They'd clearly known each other for a long time.

"That was different," said Asher darkly.

"It was the same. Passion is our way, but love can drive an angel mad, Asher. It can disrupt the heavens, change the outcome of a war."

"Isn't that the point?" Asher exhaled loudly and kicked his boot out in frustration. He was hundreds of thousands of years old, but he looked and acted just like a seventeen-year-old guy. "I thought we're all about falling in love and changing the world. Isn't that what makes us Rebels?"

"Ordinarily, yes," she said. "But these are strange and dangerous times. The truce between the Order and the Rebellion ended the minute Astaroth destroyed Oriax. Now we have to look out for ourselves first."

"A little hypocritical, isn't it?" He snorted.

Ardith stared at him. "Maybe," she said. "But there are repercussions now that we couldn't have known. We're not the Gifted. We can't divine fate."

"I won't let go of her," Asher said, his voice hard. "When she wakes up, she'll join the Rebellion. You'll see. She'll help us."

"Yes," she said. "In the meantime, go to bed. I started a fire down in the fireplace."

Asher sighed, dropped his head into his hands. "I hope this works."

Ardith placed a hand on his back. "Me too," she said.

She moved out of the way then, and I could see him perfectly. I was reminded instantly of the first time I saw him, leaning up against the wall outside of Love the Bean on the night of my birthday. His hair was so dark, his eyes such a magnetic black that he didn't just look at ease at night—it seemed as if he was a part of it. The moonlight shone on his high cheekbones, and he had a playful, arrogant glint in his eye.

Now his eyes were sad, serious. There was no hint of moonlight, no cocky challenge. His long-sleeved thermal shirt and jeans looked wrinkled and slept-in, like he'd been wearing them for days. His dark hair had grown a little longer and looked wild, like the worry was causing it to stand on end. Something had changed him.

Wind rattled the window frame, and I swallowed back a lump of jealousy when Ardith turned around. She was stunning, with dark brown eyes and flawless olive skin. I closed my eyes before she could see me awake.

"I want to stay here tonight," Asher said. "In this chair. You take the bed."

Ardith sighed. "Okay. But if she wakes up, remember what they said. Don't talk about what happened. She's going to be in a precarious state, and it could be dangerous if the memories come rushing back too quickly."

"Yeah, yeah, I know." He let out a long breath. "What are we going to do? Even if this works, we can't take her back to the Rebel camp."

"No," Ardith agreed. "If she does wake up, her powers will be much too unstable. They'll collide with so much chaos. It could destroy us. Or her," she added.

"They were right. She's a ticking time bomb. A weapon waiting to happen."

"But eventually"—Ardith paused—"*soon*, I hope, she'll be more controlled. Asher, the memory will trigger powerful emotions in her. You know what she's capable of in that kind of state. You were there. You have to stave off those memories for a while. If they come rushing back suddenly, it may be too much."

"She can handle it."

"I mean for us."

There was another pause. I was dying to open my eyes, but held back. My heart was in my throat, and I was so afraid that in the silence they would be able to hear it beating faster, hear my breath coming in short, uneven gasps.

"I remember when I felt the way you do now," Ardith said quietly. I pictured her putting a gentle hand on Asher's back.

"It wasn't your fault," Asher said. "What happened to Gideon. It was mine." He took a breath, and everything in the room seemed to breathe in with him. "I love her."

"I know," she said. "And there's nothing I can say to stop it from happening." I heard the swish of material, and a door squeak on rusty, ancient hinges. The sound of footsteps going down the stairs. And then, suddenly, it was quiet in the room. So quiet I really could hear the beat of my own heart. Not Asher's, though. That didn't exist.

I opened my eyes.

Asher was still sitting with his head in his hands. His back rose and fell softly with each breath.

I couldn't get his words out of my head. *I love her.*

I couldn't pretend to sleep anymore. I couldn't just lie there and not say anything. *I love her, I love her, I love her,* coaxed my heartbeat. I struggled to sit up.

The rickety bed creaked under me.

Asher's head snapped up at the noise.

And our eyes met, a flash of darkest lightning, blinding me to everything but the only two things in the world that mattered:

I was alive.

And Asher loved me.

We opened our mouths at the same time. I closed mine immediately, but Asher's remained open. I felt tears spring to my eyes. *Be strong, Skye. You're alive. You can do this.*

Asher let out a strangled noise and jumped out of his chair.

"Skye!" he choked, pushing his hair out of his eyes. And then he was beside me, around me, scooping me up in his arms and pressing me tight against him. "It worked," he said into my hair. "I thought—I didn't know what to think. It's my fault. I . . ."

My face felt wet, and I realized tears were streaming down my cheeks.

"Did I die?" I asked. My voice came out croaky and hoarse.

He laughed, a soft murmur that sent a thrill through me. "No, you didn't die. Just scared us for a bit, that's all." He pulled away and looked me square in the eyes. "I knew you'd make it."

"Aunt Jo always says I'm nothing if not a fighter," I said croakily.

"Too true," he said, a grin spreading slowly across his face. He let his thumb slide across the freckles on the bridge of my nose. "You're a lot of awesome things."

I put my hand over his, and it slid down to cup my cheek. He was staring at me like I was something precious he had almost lost.

"What . . . what happened to me?" I asked.

"We can talk about all of that later."

"But—"

"Right now, just rest," Asher said soothingly. "We'll talk when you're feeling up to it."

"I'm feeling up to it," I argued, struggling to sit up straighter in the bed.

He put a hand on my shoulder to steady me and looked at me seriously. "You really don't remember?"

I shook my head, wincing a little at how stiff I felt. Asher pulled back so that he was looking down at me.

"You're alive, Skye," he said. "You're safe here. Those

are the important things."

"Way to avoid the question." My gaze swept past him, to the open window. "Are we in Colorado?"

"Yes," he said. "But, Skye—"

"What is this place?" I asked.

"We're in a cabin. But listen, once you start asking questions—"

"What kind of cabin? How did you find it?"

"Let's talk about it when you've got all your strength back," Asher said. "I don't think the Order will be able to find you here."

I paused. *The Order.* How could I forget that group of angels who could control fate and the Natural Order of the world—including human lives? They believed in living by rules no matter the cost. Their messengers were called Guardians, sent to Earth to carry out their master plan. They had no free will.

According to the Order, no one did.

Asher grinned at me and raised an eyebrow. "And if all else fails," he said, "they'll have to get through me before they can lay a finger on you." The familiar flash of mischief crept back into his eyes. "Only *I* get to do that."

I grinned at him challengingly. "Oh, yeah?" It was hard not to feel safe with Asher. He exuded confidence, and in that moment, I believed him when he said he wouldn't let anything hurt me.

I wondered if my mother had felt the same way with my father. If that was what had led her to believe he was worth risking everything for. My parents had been angels, something I'd only just found out on my seventeenth birthday. My mother was a Guardian, and my father, a Rebel. But by the time they'd given birth to me, they'd already been cast to Earth as mortals—the punishment for loving each other. Now they were dead, and I had powers raging within me that no one seemed to be able to understand. Least of all me.

You'd think the Rebellion would be dangerous, with their staunch belief that revolutions and destruction led to rebirth and renewal. But, as I looked into Asher's dizzying black eyes, I knew that he was right—being safe from the Order was the better option. Something about the Order's calculated control felt even more dangerous. I had an eerie feeling that there was a specific reason I was scared of them now, too. It had to do with why I was here, with how I'd ended up in a coma in the first place. I could almost remember. . . .

I just needed to get Asher to give me a few details.

I looked up at him, and his magnetic grin drew me in

the way it always had. Heat flushed my cheeks. *Asher*. I remembered him so clearly. The emotional memories were as strong as a physical one, a scent or a touch or a song. I had fought against opening up to him for so long.

It had been a battle between us: who could be wittier, more playful, more guarded. I didn't want to admit that I was different enough to be special. And he was supposed to protect me, watch out for me, help me to determine my powers, and ultimately guide me toward the dark and the Rebellion.

It didn't feel like that long ago that I had sat, curled up with him on my deck in River Springs, Colorado, a wool blanket wrapped tight around us, snuggled in our Adirondack chair as the moon rose brighter in the sky.

The whole point of the Rebellion is so that we can live by our own rules. That's the entire reason we jumped. I know you're stuck between two choices, and you don't exactly have a conscious say in the matter. Your powers will take over when it really counts.

But I have a choice, Skye. And there is nothing that I've ever wanted more.

And then, I'd kissed him.

But everything after that was a blur. There had been sirens. Someone I loved had gotten hurt. Aunt Jo was off in the woods, far from home. And something had come between Asher and me. Something that had landed me here.

I knew it had to do with the Order. They had been trying to control my fate for seventeen years. Why stop now?

But I'm safe here, I thought as my heart began to beat faster. *At least from any bodily harm. And I'm with Asher.*

His hand was still warm as he cupped my cheek, and I put my hand over his again. A tiny buzz of electricity thrummed and grew stronger where our skin touched. My powers always seemed to generate heat whenever I felt emotional; it was the angelic Rebel blood running through me. I moved his hand down to my neck, as I reached up with my other hand to pull him toward me onto the faded quilt.

"I'm so glad you're back," he murmured as he let me pull him close, his fingers winding themselves through my hair. His lips were dry from the sun and wind but were warm against mine. They tasted salty, from my tears and maybe his, and I wanted more. I wanted as much of him as I could have.

And then a memory coursed through me.

He'd been carrying me. Cold feathers brushing my cheek and hair. My eyes were closed, but I could feel the wind rushing past me and smell the winter sky.

His hands were fire on my neck, trailing down my body, finding their way over my jeans and under my sweater. I pulled him even closer to me, tangling him up in the quilt. My limbs were still stiff from my being asleep for so long, but I wasn't in pain anymore. I was alive.

"Stay with me, Skye." As we flew higher, he grasped me tightly in one arm and pressed a hand over my wound with the other. "Don't die. You can't die. Not yet."

Asher's fingers were searing hot against my skin, and the soft fabric of his thermal shirt grazed my stomach as he drew my body closer to his. He rolled on top of me and the weight of him felt comforting, like gravity was pulling me back down to Earth.

I couldn't break my lips from his. My fingers trailed against his neck and over the rough edges of his jawline. He'd saved my life; he must have. The heat running through my veins threatened to consume me until I combusted in a pop of spark and ash. We were together now. There was nothing standing in our way anymore.

The air brushing past us had smelled like pine needles and clouds, and something else. Something black and acrid.

Smoke.

"Skye!" Asher cried suddenly, pulling away from me sharply and batting at my legs with the quilt. I looked down and drew in a breath. The hems of my jeans were smoking, bursting into tiny flames.

Flames.

Asher whipped the blanket out from the tangle at my feet and smothered the fire. But I couldn't feel anything. I could only sit there, bolt upright, numb, staring at him as he made sure the last of the flames were out. Ardith had been right—my powers were unstable. I was dangerous.

My heart was pounding furiously. And not because of what had just happened.

But because of what I suddenly remembered.

In the clearing far below me, a wall of fire rose from where I'd fallen. A black spiral of smoke curled into the air.

"Skye, are you okay?" Asher was right next to me, but his voice came from a million miles away as my heart lurched. "The fire's out," he said. "It's okay. Are you hurt?"

"Skye!" a voice called. "I have to warn you!"

"Hurt?" I asked, as if searching for the meaning of the word.

Warn me? I stood there, immobile, rooted to the ground like a tree. "About what?"

"From the fire," said Asher, still trying to catch his breath. "Your powers are still as out of control as ever, it looks like." He paused to grin devilishly. "Was it because of me?"

A cold blade, icy and sharp, plunged through my stomach.

My dream. The flash of metal on the nightstand. The blood blooming out across my shirt like a watercolor rose.

"Asher," I gasped, reaching for my stomach. He looked alarmed.

"What is it? What's wrong?"

I was surprised at how sudden the pain was when it came on.

"I remember. I remember it all."

"Skye, calm down," Asher urged. His eyes searched mine. "You don't want to get too agitated. We have no idea what could happen. What you could *do*."

But I ignored him. I remembered now. And the truth was even more terrifying than I could imagine.

"It was Devin," I said. "He tried to kill me."

The little room in the cabin in the woods was suddenly much too warm, and I could feel a faint rumbling beneath us as I struggled to steady my breathing. Asher noticed, too. "Shh," he said, like I was some wild animal who needed to be soothed. "Stay calm. You're okay, remember? You're safe. You don't want to cause anything else to happen."

Eyeing him, I felt around my midsection for a wound where Devin had stabbed me. But there was none. No bandages or tenderness. I lifted my sweater a few inches and looked down. The skin on my stomach was smooth. It looked the same way it always had. There was no evidence that I'd been stabbed at all.

"He did—didn't he? I remember . . ." I winced and

brought my sweater back down. "He stabbed me." I whispered the words, afraid, however irrationally, that saying them out loud could somehow make it happen again. "He stared me right in the eye while he did it."

Asher's face clouded over.

"Why?" I asked, panic and confusion and a deep, aching sadness welling in me. "Why would he do that? I thought—he said—he loved me."

"As if I needed a reason to hate him more," Asher muttered, avoiding my gaze. I immediately regretted saying anything. The Order and the Rebellion would hate each other until the end of time, and Asher and Devin were just pawns in the great rivalry. They couldn't look at each other without the air between them turning at least ten degrees colder.

"I didn't say I loved him back," I said quietly.

"I know." He continued to be fascinated by a knot in the wooden planks of the floor, his hands balling into fists at his sides.

I took his hands in mine and slowly uncurled his fingers. He looked up at me, something in his eyes softening. "Did you save my life?" I asked.

Asher's face turned a brilliant shade of red, and I could feel his fingers trembling slightly. "I don't know, I mean . . ." I grinned, and he suddenly seemed to snap out of his embarrassment. "You bet I did," he said, some of his old cockiness returning. "And I'm taking full credit. I was able to get you here just in time, too. The fact that you didn't die immediately from that sword is a credit to your human blood. If you were a full angel, you'd have died in a heartbeat." He frowned. "I'm sure the Order is real thrilled about all this. They thought they'd eliminated you as a threat."

"Well, they were wrong," I said.

"Glad to see the coma didn't knock out the fighter in you." Asher smiled and leaned back in his chair.

"What happened to Devin? After we left?"

"Don't know." He crossed his arms over his chest, watching me. "Maybe he burned up in the fire? That would be a happy ending to all this."

I thought about the golden-haired angel who'd been my friend. He'd been more than that—the only one I could turn to when I was feeling alone and scared and had no one to trust. And he'd been prepared to betray me all along. Rage simmered just below the surface of my skin. But still, I couldn't quite wish him dead.

I leaned back on the pillows, suddenly exhausted.

"So how long was I out? Aunt Jo, my friends—will they be worried?"

"It's been a couple of days."

I stared at him blankly, trying to suppress the panic.

"Yeah," he said. "They're probably pretty worried."

"Does Aunt Jo know I'm all right? Have you heard from Cassie?" Asher's face twisted uncomfortably. He looked almost guilty. "What?" I said, the panic building. The last time I'd seen Cassie, she was in a coma, in the hospital. "What about her? Have you talked to her?" Suddenly the thought of life without my best friend caved in on me. I could do a lot of things. I could create fire and cause a flood and had angel blood running through me. But I couldn't live without Cassie. "Asher, is she okay?"

He looked down and shook his head. "I couldn't . . . I didn't know how without revealing myself. I couldn't just call your aunt on the phone and say, 'Hey, Skye is in a coma! But I can't tell you how it happened or where she is, so don't ask!' Imagine if all I could say was 'Trust me'? Come on, Skye. Look at me. Even *I* don't trust myself." He looked up and spread his arms wide, showing off. The rumpled shirt. The faded jeans. The scuffed-up boots and the devilish grin. If I was Aunt Jo, I wouldn't have trusted him with my life, either. It had taken forever for me to trust him myself.

"I guess."

"That and . . ."

"And what?" I asked.

"They wouldn't let me. The elders. They forbade me from contacting your family and friends until we knew what would happen to you."

"How could they do that?"

"The truce is over. All bets are off. Just because the Rebellion doesn't control your fate doesn't mean they don't want things to go their way."

An uneasy anger took over me. "They need me, don't they? They need my powers."

Asher stood up and gripped my hand.

"You're so important to this fight, Skye. I wish you knew just how important you are." His eyes glittered, serious. Suddenly I wondered if we were talking about the Rebellion anymore.

Asher put a tentative arm around me. "Hey," he said. "It's going to be okay." I leaned into his chest and felt another rush of emotions at the familiar scent of cinnamon and cloves. Spicy and sweet. It reminded me of so many things: the time we got stuck in the ice cave on the ski trip and he showed me how to create fire in the palms of my hands; the magical night on the snowmobile with the tiny balls of fire that floated around us like lanterns;

and the night I realized how badly I wanted to be with Asher, that I couldn't do it alone. That I needed someone. I needed *him*.

I snuck a glance at his dark eyes. He needed me, too.

It struck me that as long as I was with Asher, maybe I *was* home. I was safe here. The Order couldn't hurt me. And my powers of the dark were way stronger than those of the light. Ever since the two angels had descended on my life, I'd been so against making a decision. Everyone had a plan for me, something that they wanted from me. But maybe I knew what I wanted.

Maybe I'd already made a decision.

We had to be quiet. The cabin had no electricity, and when we lit a fire, Asher closed the dusty curtains to make sure no one could see us from the woods—in case anyone from the Order was watching. They couldn't just rely on the Sight anymore. As Asher reminded me, my powers were blurring the destiny of everyone around me. They'd have to resort to other methods.

It took a few days before I really started to feel better. I was exhausted constantly, and Asher and Ardith took turns watching me from the chair as I drifted in and out of sleep. Jealous as I had been when I first saw her, I couldn't help but like Ardith. When Asher was asleep and she watched over me, I'd try to get her to talk.

"How long have you known Asher?" I asked one night. The moon hung high in the black sky, shining light across the floor of the small bedroom. I was curled on my side, the quilt pulled up under my chin, and Ardith sat in the rocking chair across the dark room. Every time she rocked forward, her face would emerge from the shadows.

"A long time," she said. "Since we were very young. We used to beg to be sent to Earth on missions like our parents. And each time they told us, 'Not until you're older.'" She smiled at me. "Then when we were older, we wanted to be young again. The things we've both seen." She shook her head. "We wished we'd never asked."

I hesitated. A shadow passed in front of the moon, and I couldn't see her face anymore.

"Why?" I asked.

"Being a Rebel, it's not easy," she said. "The constant chaos. Reacting to the Order's plans. It's not easy being a Guardian either, but that I do not know firsthand."

"It must be hard having only those two options. Dark and Light and nothing in between."

A wry smile cracked her face.

"You of all people should know how that feels, Skye."

It was true, but the more I thought about it, the more it didn't seem right. There had to be a middle place. Otherwise, how did someone not lose her mind? How would *I* not lose my mind?

I lay awake for a long time, thinking and watching the pattern of moonlight shift on the wood floor. When I looked up, I realized Ardith was asleep. It seemed strange to me that an angel would need sleep, but then I remembered what Asher had told me. *When we're on Earth, we take on human form, human desires, human needs.* I wondered what they were like when they weren't on Earth. What were *angel* needs?

I was feeling restless. Quietly, so as not to wake Ardith, I pulled back the blankets and crept out of the room. I shifted my weight slowly on the old wood floor, careful not to step on any creaky planks as I tiptoed down the hall and crept gingerly down the stairs. I kept close to the wall and peered into the large main room of the cabin. Asher sat hunched forward on the couch near the fireplace.

But there was no fire burning within it.

Instead, it had risen from the hearth into the air itself. Orange and red and yellow and blue flames crackled above him in the dark room, casting shadows that danced on the walls. As I watched, the flames fanned out in a circle, and he sat below it, his head in his hands. What was he doing?

Asher's back rose and fell rhythmically, with each breath. He looked so controlled, like he was doing everything in his power to breathe steadily. Given to following his every mood and whim, Asher wasn't exactly good at self-control. Watching him now filled me with a strange sense of awe. I wondered what he was controlling.

As I stood there, his breath hitched and his chest spasmed slightly. As if he couldn't hold it in anymore, a strangled noise escaped him. *Oh, no,* I thought, realizing too late that I was watching something I shouldn't. I went to move, but my foot hit a loose floorboard that squeaked beneath me. Asher's head shot up, and we locked eyes. I gasped.

The storm that swirled in them threatened to over-power me. It was a look that I'd seen only once before, the night we'd gotten into a fight on my roof. What he'd said to me that night came rushing back as if he'd said the words yesterday.

"Do you know why I joke all the time?" He stood up as if he'd been wound up and sprung. His eyes glinted in the moonlight. "Do you know why I've been keeping things all light and devil-may-care? Because if you knew—if you really knew what was happening—inside of you, within the Order, within the Rebellion, if you knew what the angels are saying, what's waiting for you,

you would be sobbing, Skye. You would be paralyzed with fear. That's why I tease you. I'm doing it for you. Because if I didn't, you wouldn't make it. You wouldn't last another week."

Asher tore his eyes away from mine. The fire fell to the ground abruptly, turning to smoldering ash as it hit the floor. I took an involuntary step backward into the shadows, pressing myself flat against the wall.

He never showed me when he was worried or upset. That's what he'd been trying to tell me that night on the roof. What I was seeing now was something I wasn't supposed to. Some private moment that Asher hadn't wanted me to see. Something he tried, every day, to hide from me by covering it up with wisecracks and banter.

It was fear. Asher was afraid.

Before he could say anything, I turned and ran back up to my room, snuggling deep under the quilt until morning. He didn't come after me.

When I woke in the morning, sunlight was streaming through my window. Birds chirped outside, and if I closed my eyes and just listened to the music of the woods, I could almost imagine being back in my bed at home. My homesickness was an ache growing inside me.

I turned to see if Asher had come up to my room in the night, but the rocking chair was empty. In fact, everything was strangely silent and still.

In the hall, the quiet was deafening. No hushed conversations came from downstairs. No low tones. I was alone in the house for the first time.

So I explored. In my little bedroom, in addition to the bed and the rocking chair, there was a low wooden chest of drawers. The drawers stuck a little from disuse, but I managed to get them open one by one. Inside were bits of evidence that the cabin had been inhabited once. An old cable-knit fisherman's sweater was folded up in the bottom drawer. I pulled it over my head, and the heavy wool fell in baggy folds around me. It was a man's sweater. But even though I was swimming in it, and even though it had belonged to a stranger, something about it felt comforting. I rolled up the sleeves and kept pawing through the remaining drawers, but they yielded nothing more.

Next to the bedroom was a rusty bathroom with a warped mirror hanging over a chipped, white enamel sink and a toilet with an old-fashioned hanging chain. I stared at myself in the mirror, like I had done a few times since I'd been here. There was a bruise under my left eye and a giant scratch across my cheek. I ran my finger over it, remembering that my anger had caused the earth to rumble in the clearing and a tree to fall. Asher had swooped in to save me just in time. I'd been mad at him for keeping the Rebellion's plans from me. He'd lied to me, but as I thought about the night before, I realized he had done it to protect me. To keep me sane when everything in my life was changing. He was doing it because he loved me. That was a crime I could never hold against him. It was nothing like what Devin had done.

As my finger trailed over the dried blood and puckered skin, I could feel something in me changing. I glanced up to meet my own gaze in the mirror, and my eyes flashed—a bright, metallic silver. My heart beat faster and I gripped the edges of the sink, but when I blinked, they were gray again. I turned the handle of the faucet to try to wash my face, and the pipes gave a low, rusty hum, but no water came out.

I would go back to exploring. I would try to forget about what could be making Asher so afraid. I had been powerful in the woods the night I'd almost died, and I could still feel it in me. Maybe I could start learning how to protect *myself*.

There was one more door upstairs. I opened it to reveal an old cupboard with rows of tiny drawers, like an apothecary's cabinet. The sort of strange closet that would get built into an old cabin like this. A thrill welled inside me as I thought about what things I might find in these drawers. I pulled the sweater tighter around me and stood on tiptoe to open the top drawer.

Nothing.

I moved on to the second drawer. It was empty, too. When my hand touched the tiny handle on the third drawer, sudden heat scorched my skin. I pulled away instantly, but I knew there had to be something in there. *Something my powers are reacting to*, I realized. Slowly I went to reach for it again.

"Skye?" Ardith called from downstairs. "We come bearing breakfast!"

I stared longingly at the little drawer, vowing to come back to it later. "I'll be down in a second!" I called.

Asher was rummaging through the kitchen cabinets as I came down the stairs, while Ardith was chopping some root vegetables—carrots and beets and parsnips. I wished she wasn't there so Asher and I could talk about what had happened.

"I take it you guys weren't out hunting?" I joked.

Asher's back muscles tensed, but he didn't turn around.

"What are you looking for?" I asked, trying to keep up the lightness in my voice.

"Found it."

Asher turned around, an ancient can of coffee and a tin coffee press in hand—the kind Aunt Jo and I took camping with us. He looked up at me, his eyes soft and hopeful. Almost like a peace offering.

"Coffee!" My body shook like an addict at the thought of a cup. I yelped and threw my arms around him.

"Hey, let go," he said, laughing. "You're only delaying

the coffee-making process."

I backed away quickly. "Oh, no. Sorry, sorry. Go ahead."

He grinned. "Can you break off a few icicles from the windowsill? There's no running water."

My snow boots sat by the door, so I slipped them on and made my way outside into the frosty woods. I hadn't been out of the house yet, and I had to bring a hand up to shield my eyes from the bright sunlight. The light bounced off the row of icicles hanging from the window ledge, throwing tiny rainbows onto the snow. I squinted, remembering how Asher had caused an icicle to fall from a tree branch, not far enough away from Devin's head. The memory stirred up something in me, and I felt myself grow hot underneath the heavy sweater. My cheeks burned, despite the frigid temperature outside.

No, this is good, I thought. *Use this.*

I focused all of my energy on one of the icicles hanging from the top of the window frame. As I stared hard, it began to glisten brighter, shining in the sun the way ice does when it's finally beginning to thaw. A drop of water splashed to the ground below and turned to ice. Then another, and another.

As I watched, the base of the icicle weakened. It snapped from the sill, and I reached out my hands to catch it.

Surprised, I looked up through the window. Asher was staring at me, a strange, thoughtful grin on his face. When he caught my eye, he quickly turned away.

One by one, I caught the remaining icicles as they fell. Inside, Asher created a fire on the stove and melted the icicles in a dented tin camping pot. Then he made coffee and poured it, steaming, into three chipped blue-and-white ceramic mugs.

Ardith, Asher, and I had breakfast at the big farm table. Asher grinned at me tentatively over the lip of his mug.

"Now that I'm feeling better, will you tell me more about that night in the woods with Devin?" I asked. "How did you find this place?"

Asher's face suddenly grew serious, and he glanced at Ardith, who nodded slightly.

"You were losing a lot of blood," he said. "I knew I didn't have time to take you to the Rebel camp, and I didn't know what your powers might cause once you were there. You'd just destroyed an entire clearing in the woods—just because you were angry. It was terrifying."

"Wow." I was capable of doing something like that? It seemed so impossible.

"I was frantic, and soon I saw this cabin below us. I knew I had to get you here, to save you."

"He summoned me," Ardith said, continuing on. "I've never seen him so shaken up. I spun Rebel protections around the house. Fog and rain, heavy snow. To block us from sight."

"I kept you warm," said Asher. "It took a few days, but the bleeding finally stopped and you woke up."

"Thank you," I said. "Thank you both, so much. I owe you my life. I don't know what would have happened if . . ."

"You would have died," Asher said simply. "The Order's plan would have worked."

I shivered as I thought about how badly the Order wanted me dead. What kind of a threat did I really pose to them? Asher and Ardith had said I was a weapon, but what did that really mean? I brought my hand up to my stomach without thinking, running my hand over the wound. But again, the skin was smooth.

Wait a minute. A wound as deadly as the one Asher said I had doesn't just heal on its own so quickly. I should have had a big, ugly gash to show for what had happened. Neither Asher nor Ardith had the power to heal. It wasn't a Rebel power. That was something only the Guardians could do.

So what weren't they telling me?

My mind flashed to Devin. He had that power. He'd tried to get it to manifest in me, too. But my one small attempt to revive a withered flower had been in vain.

Devin had healed my broken ankle on the ski trip. Surely he was capable of healing a stab wound. He cared about me, right? He'd told me so in the clearing after he'd pulled the sword from me. *Falling in love with you was one more thing I couldn't help.* His blue eyes had been full of anguish. What if he had had a change of heart, regretted what he did? Did he still care about me, enough to save my life?

Don't be stupid, Skye. I mentally kicked myself. *He tried to kill you, just a few days ago. It's over.*

It was true. Devin had been a friend when I needed a friend the most. He'd risked a lot for me, too. And he'd betrayed me worse than anyone else could have.

I pushed the memory to the very back of my mind as Asher reached a hand across the table and covered mine with it. His fingers were still warm from holding his coffee mug—or maybe it was just him.

"Want to take a walk?" he asked. "Are you feeling up to it?"

I looked up at him and tried to relax. I trusted that Asher would do whatever he had to do to keep me safe. I had to stop questioning everything.

"Sure," I said.

We bundled up in all the layers that we had with us. Despite the cold, it felt good to be outside. Ardith stood in the doorway summoning snow, strengthening the elemental protections around us. It fell in heavy waves, making it hard to see. Snowflakes clung to my lashes and sparkled in Asher's hair.

"That's a good look for you," I said, taking his hand.

He grinned at me sheepishly and self-consciously brushed his hands through his hair. We kept walking. Neither of us said much. There was so much I wanted to say, but I couldn't think of where to start or how to form the words. I just squeezed his hand tighter. Eventually the snow made it too hard to see, and we slowed to a stop.

"Okay," he said. "I don't know what else to do to find our way back. Don't tell Ardith." He winked and took both of my hands in his, holding them up palm to palm. "Close your eyes," he said. "Focus your energy." He closed his eyes, then opened one of them again. "Like you did with the icicles earlier."

I did. I thought about Asher, the palms of his hands resting against mine and how good it felt. How much I cared about him. What he was willing to do to save my life. Before I knew it, I felt a gentle warmth on my face.

I opened my eyes. A soft glow surrounded us, forming a protective shield that kept the snow from getting in our eyes. I peered ahead and could see a ball of fire just in front of us. "It will guide us back through the snow. Come on."

We walked back, again in silence. The little orb of fiery light led the way. After all of the drama of the past few days, I was grateful for the chance just to walk, side by side, with Asher. To let him hold my hand as if it were all that mattered in the world.

Because with all that was coming, I knew the feeling wouldn't last.

We spent the rest of the day inside with the curtains drawn, a roaring fire in the fireplace. I was surprised at how easy it felt just to hang out with Asher and Ardith, listening to stories from their childhood with the Rebellion.

"The elders could never keep us in line." Ardith laughed. "Little Rebels causing mischief every chance we got."

"We were terrible," Asher said, grinning at me. "They used to tell us stories about the Rogues to shut us up."

"What are Rogues?" I asked.

"Rogue angels," Ardith said, then more slowly, "Rogues," as if the secret to the word might be hidden somewhere in the word itself. "It's just a legend."

I leaned forward on the moth-eaten couch. "What?" I asked. "Tell me."

"They've been telling this story to Rebel children to keep them in line for generations," Asher said. "The Rogues are the children of Rebels and humans. They're even more unpredictable than we are because they hold no allegiance. Not to the Rebellion—and definitely not to the Order."

"In the legends, they hold a grudge against the Rebellion," said Ardith. "Rogues live on Earth, indistinguishable from humans. They know what they are, and they can recognize full angels—Rebels and Guardians. But they can't distinguish other Rogues. And we can't recognize them." She shivered. "They lead a confused, lonely life. Often have trouble settling down and being happy. They used to tell us that the Rogues were constantly trying to find a way into the Rebellion camp—someplace they were never allowed. That they would come for us in the night, and kill little Rebel babies as revenge and out of jealousy. The poor, tortured Rogues. They had no true home."

"Earth wasn't their home?" I offered.

"But they never really belonged there," Asher said. "When we got older, the legend was more that they were trying to start their own faction. One that adhered neither to the Rebellion's ways nor to the Order's. A new way of living."

"But those were just stories," Ardith said, standing. "That never happened. If they were planning a new movement, as far we know, they never succeeded." She walked toward the kitchen. "I'll see what else we can eat," she said.

When she was gone, Asher put his arm around me, and I snuggled deeper into him. It was hard to believe that just a few days ago, I'd almost died. Sitting here around the fire, I could have forgotten that the Order was out to kill me. It was true that we didn't have running water or heat or electricity, but I felt safe and happy here. And not just from the Order, either—from all of my troubles at home, too. I shrank under the weight of what I might face going back there.

Everything I'd left behind was a mess. Cassie was unconscious in a hospital bed—or worse—because the Order was afraid I might tell her my secret. She and Dan had finally gotten together after a whole lifetime of friendship, and now he might be alone for good. Aunt Jo probably thought I'd run away or something. And Ian wasn't exactly my biggest fan right now, not after I'd ditched him for two mysterious strangers—one of whom had tried to kill me.

Did I want to go back there and face them? And then a more chilling thought occurred to me: Did my friends even want me? I hadn't been there for them at all since my birthday, not really.

"I missed you so much," Asher whispered into my hair, stopping my thoughts. "You have no idea how much— how scared—"

"I was, too," I whispered, looking up at him. The fire reflected in his almost black eyes.

"I thought I was going to lose you," he said.

I brought my hand up to his face and smoothed a stray hair. "But you didn't," I said. "I'm here. I'm yours."

He took my hand in his. "Can I . . . ask you something?" His voice shook slightly.

"Of course," I said. "Anything."

He paused and took a breath. "Join the Rebellion," he said. His voice was barely a whisper. "We'll fight the Order side by side. Whatever's coming, we'll face it together. We'll be unstoppable. Fierce."

I sucked in my breath.

"Will you do it?" he asked.

I stared at him. *He saved your life*, I thought. *You owe him everything.* But even if I hadn't owed him anything, how could I say no? I pictured us together, partners in all this chaos. No matter how much I loved my friends, there were secrets I couldn't tell them, things that kept us apart. I'd tried to confide in Cassie, and it had only landed her in the hospital. I could never tell her the truth now—I couldn't tell any of them. Not Cassie, or Dan, or Ian, and especially not Aunt Jo. The truth would only hurt them.

The world pitched forward as I realized it.

I'm alone.

Asher squeezed my hand, a gentle reminder that I hadn't answered the question.

But I don't have to be.

He smiled at me hopefully. "What do you say? I need you, Skye."

In my heart, I knew that it was time to make the choice I never made in my dreams. The one I had never made in River Springs. And I finally knew what the answer was.

"Yes," I said, knowing that the decision, once it left my lips, would be impossible to take back. I smiled, and for the first time since I'd woken up, Asher looked alive again, confident, like we could take on anything in the world as long as we were together. "Yes, I will."

It was an almost moonless night. I couldn't sleep. Ardith had taken couch duty downstairs, and I waited for Asher to doze off in the rocking chair before silently slipping out of bed and out of the room. The closet door at the end of the hall beckoned to me. I wasn't sure quite what it was that compelled me about this cabin, but I felt connected to it somehow, like I felt connected to the sweater I'd found earlier. I wondered who had lived here, and why they had abandoned their home.

I opened the door as slowly as I could so that it didn't squeak. The cabinet of drawers stared back at me.

I started where I'd left off, opening each drawer slowly, quietly, and then closing it again. The first row was empty. So was the second. When I got to the third row, I felt the same scorching heat jump off the knob as before. Gingerly,

I used the sleeve of my sweater to grasp the knob and pull open the drawer. Inside was a tiny, moleskin notebook. My hands trembled slightly as I picked it up.

The first page was dated March 6 in the year I was born.

Guardians haunt these woods, watching us. I know they know. It's only a matter of time.
We have to act quickly. There are too many of them. We need more recruits.

What? It sounded like something Ardith or Asher could have written this morning, as if they'd been keeping a secret journal during their time here. But the date at the top of the page made that impossible. Could it be that this notebook belonged to someone, years ago, who knew about the Order? Someone who—like me—was being watched?

As quietly as I could, I riffled through the remaining drawers but turned up nothing. I tucked the notebook into the enormous sleeve of my sweater and tiptoed back into the bedroom. When I was sure Asher was sound asleep, I hid it under my pillow.

My discovery felt important. A clue—but to what mystery?

I climbed into bed, and my sleep was peppered with feverish dreams.

I was being chased.

Crouching lower into the wind, I let my skis propel me faster. The snow beneath me was hard and icy, and it was almost impossible to keep myself from slipping in every direction. I veered wildly back and forth, certain with every passing second that he was going to catch up. I didn't know what would happen when he did, but my whole body shook with fear at the thought.

The figure in white was gaining on me. He was remarkably controlled, every movement precise, like he was merely running on the ground. He laughed, and I could have recognized that voice anywhere.

"Well, hey there, Skye," it called out to me.

It wasn't a *he* at all.

It was Raven, the stunning, deadly Guardian who'd first told me just how far my powers could reach. That I was blurring my own destiny and the destiny of those around me. That Devin was changing because of me. Raven, who'd cut the brakes on Cassie's car when Devin had told her I'd come close to revealing my secret. Raven, who had told the Order just how big a threat my powers were to them. Because of Raven, Devin had tried to kill me. And yet I'd almost forgotten about her.

"The last time I saw you," she called, "you were about to die." Even yelling over the wind, her voice was sickly sweet and dripping venom.

Now we were neck and neck, flying down the slopes.

Flying, I realized with a start, as my feet left the ground. Her great white wings expanded behind her, sparkling like icicles in the harsh sunlight. I was suspended in the air, my own set of wings flung wide behind me. I couldn't see them, but my heart lurched at the shadow they cast. What color were they? Pure, feathery white—or blackest black?

"You think about him still, don't you, Skye?" she yelled, gaining on me.

The freezing air whipped at my face, which was numb from the blowing ice and snow.

"I don't!" I yelled back. And then, "What do you want from me?"

"Come." Her voice carried on the wind, sharp as a razor's edge.

"I'm not following you anywhere!"

She moved closer. I could feel her just behind me now.

"I can protect you," she said, more urgently, the tone of her voice changing slightly. It wasn't a threat. It was more . . . a plea. "You know as well as I do that the Rebellion doesn't care about your safety. They're just going to use you as a weapon against us, anyway. I can get you home, and I can get you there safely."

Home. I ached for it. I missed Aunt Jo, missed my friends, wanted desperately to have my old life back. Was she really trying to help me? Could I trust her?

"No!" I yelled back, trying to make my voice as steely as possible.

"Fine, suit yourself. But I have to warn you."

Warn you. I have to warn you. My blood pounded in my ears, and I braced myself for whatever was coming next.

"You should know. He's in River Springs, waiting for you. They all are. Tons of them. If you're going back there, you should know what you're getting yourself into."

"Why are you telling me this?" I asked. What ulterior motive could she possibly have?

"I may be a Guardian," Raven said, "but there are laws that I'll never understand." She pulled up alongside me. "Don't get yourself killed," she added. "If it's going to happen, I want to be the one to do it, 'kay?"

I continued for a moment in silence, breathing hard.

"Careful there, Skye!" Raven shouted as she veered, suddenly, left. Her voice was shrill and mocking. "Don't fall now!"

And then as if her words were a direction I had no choice

but to follow, I fell, tumbling forward through a gaping hole in the side of the mountain and into what looked eerily like the snow cave that Asher and I had fallen into during the avalanche, the first time he'd shown me how to create fire. A figure in a black snowsuit stood hunched in the corner, his back to me.

I was flooded with relief.

"Asher!" I tried to catch my breath. The figure turned around, pulling down the hood of his jacket. The light reflecting off the snow caused his blond hair to blur into a halo around his head.

Devin.

I wasn't at all prepared for the wave of emotions that overtook me when our eyes met. He looked so helpless, like he had that night in the clearing. Not at all like the evil monster he'd become in my head. "Skye," he said. "I missed you."

"How can you say that?" My voice was shaking. "How can you talk like you didn't try to kill me?"

"I'm sorry. It wasn't me. It wasn't." He reached out his hand. It was trembling ever so slightly, as if he was willing it not to. "Take it," he said. "Take my hand."

"No." I couldn't. Not after what he'd done. "I will never trust you again."

"You will," he said. "The Gifted can see it. They know you will."

"Then prove it!" I yelled. My voice rose above the howling of the wind and snow. "Prove to me I can trust you!"

"You know the Rebellion isn't the place for you. You have too much chaos in your life already. You want order, Skye. You want rules and serenity. You know I can give you that. You'll look for reasons to trust me again."

I paused, the wind whipping my black hair in every direction. We stared each other down. The ice glistened on the walls around us.

"You're lucky this is just a dream," I said. "If this were real life, I'd hurt you, just like you hurt me."

"Are you sure it's just a dream?" he asked. His voice was low, level, calm as always.

"Yes," I said. "I've had this one before. In a minute, you're going to warn me."

"Warn you? About what?"

"You know," I said through gritted teeth, waiting for it, bracing myself, "what you have to warn me about."

And just like that, a searing pain sliced through my stomach, and the walls of the cave became wings, writhing and alive, white as the snow and stained with my own blood.

I woke up gasping, clutching my stomach. I wondered if a day would ever come when I wouldn't be afraid of dying.

I thought about home. I was afraid to find out what had happened to Cassie. Afraid to face Aunt Jo. And since turning seventeen, I'd been afraid of my powers—terrified of becoming as powerful as everyone said I would be.

But I didn't want to be a person who was governed by fear anymore.

I was going to have to go home.

I lay awake in bed as the sky changed from inky night to stormy gray. Thunder churned outside my window and lightning flashed silently across the clouds. I knew, somehow, that my fear was causing the storm. I didn't know how to calm myself down, to shut off my mind—or my powers. They all just blended together. The turmoil of being me.

When the sky was light enough to count as morning, I turned from the window to the door. The rocking chair was empty. Asher was gone.

As quietly as possible, I got out of bed and tiptoed to the top of the stairs. There were voices coming from below, and I held my breath so I could hear them.

". . . have to leave here." Asher's voice was low and insistent. "What if she told them? It's not safe."

"But where do we go? We can't take her back to the Rebel camp. She'll destroy it; she's too wild. Uncontrollable."

"You saw her with the icicles. She's learning. . . ."

"No, it's too risky. But if we take her home—"

"There are Guardians everywhere," Asher said darkly. "It's not safe anyplace."

I couldn't believe they were talking about what to do with me, like I was just some doll they could pack up in a suitcase and carry away. Like I had no say in the matter. I thought we were done with all that. But it looked like I was wrong.

If I was really as powerful as they said, then it was time I took control of my own destiny once and for all. I pounded down the stairs. Asher and Ardith looked up, startled.

"I'm feeling better," I said loudly. "I'm ready to go home now."

They shared an uneasy glance.

"We were just talking about that," said Asher.

"I don't think there's anything to talk about," I said, trying to sound more confident than I felt. "I need to see Aunt Jo. I need to find out what happened to Cassie. I need to finish school and get into college." I was getting more worked up by the second. The cabin was growing warmer. Asher glanced around nervously. "I can't stop living my life just because of who my parents were. Because of *what* they were. I can't just abandon everything I love and everything that makes me *me*."

"It's not just your parents," he said to me, passion building in his voice. "This is who you are, too."

"But I don't—"

"Your powers are a gift. You've been given greatness. You'll see. Once you learn to control it—and you *are* learning—"

"I didn't ask for this!" I yelled before I could stop myself.

"No one ever does." Ardith's voice cut across the room like glass. We both turned to look at her. "You can't abandon the life you've always known, Skye, we know. But you can't abandon the life you've been given, either. It's not the powers you were born with that will define you. It's what you make of them. That's what everyone's waiting to see."

My powers. Everyone said I had the potential to be more powerful than any Rebel or any Guardian. They all wanted to see just what I was capable of. But I just wanted to be me. I just wanted to be happy. What was so great about what I could do? As far as I could tell, my powers were impossible to control.

I looked down at my hands, cupping them in front of me like I was holding water from a river.

Okay, powers, I thought. *Do your thing.*

Nothing happened. I closed my eyes, and tried to remember what Asher had told me back in my room in Colorado.

"Just pretend that everything inside you is lots of unfiltered electricity. Imagine what you want to do with it. And then imagine flipping a switch—and turning it on."

He paused, and I opened my eyes and looked at him. His eyes were searching mine, impossibly deep. I had to control myself. "The Gifted," he said, "start small. They focus on nuances. A whisper of a breath. A hair out of place. They manipulate each and every small thing on this earth. And every little thing has an effect on something else. Just think of what a big change can do: it could sway the path of someone's life, the outcome of battles, the course of history."

I swallowed, hard, mesmerized by the look in his eyes.

"It's our job, as the Rebellion, to stop them from controlling what they have no right to control. You could help us do that."

I tried to stop the energy roiling inside of me like storm clouds. My wild, impossible-to-control feelings for Asher. My anger at the Rebellion for wanting too much from me, and at the Order for trying to control me. My fury at Devin for betraying me, and frustration at my friends for never being able to understand. And most of all, my fear of all of this—of being the powerful blend of light and dark that would sway the outcome of a war. Of becoming Great with a capital G. Being Great wasn't going to bring my parents back. It wasn't going to make me closer to my friends. And it really wasn't going to make it any easier for me to let myself trust anyone.

A gentle warmth began to bloom in the palms of my hands. I opened my eyes.

Entirely on my own, I had created fire. I held it in front of me like it was an offering to Asher and Ardith. They looked at each other.

"I need to go home," I said.

"Okay." Asher relented. "Okay. We'll take you home. But we're going to need—"

"Gideon," said Ardith, quietly. "We're going to need Gideon."

We'd officially made a decision, and Asher and Ardith kicked into gear.

"We'll fly you home," said Asher. "No one can see us unless we reveal ourselves to them. We'll be able to get you back there safely."

"I'll summon Gideon," Ardith said. "He can go ahead and secure the area, and we'll meet up with him there."

"You sure you want to do this, Skye?" Asher put both hands on my shoulders and looked at me pointedly. "Home won't be like it used to. It's not the River Springs you knew and loved. It's not yours anymore. It's the Order's. Guardians will be everywhere. You have to be aware, everywhere you go." His eyes were serious and deep as he searched mine. "You're on borrowed time."

I took a deep breath. "I know what I need to do."

Asher nodded. "Okay," he said. "We'll go tonight."

Ardith went off to contact Gideon, and Asher took my hand. "I almost don't want to leave this cabin," he said. "There's something about it—"

"I know."

"It's like our little place. Where we can just . . ."

"*Be*," I finished.

"Yeah." He pulled me toward him and wrapped his arms around me. I lay my cheek against his chest. "I just want to protect you, Skye. All I want is to keep you safe. But I also want to see you be as awesome as I know you can be, and if that means going back to River Springs and all the things that might come between us, then that's what we have to do. But . . . can I just show you one thing before we go?"

"Of course," I said.

I looked up into his eyes, and the air grew suddenly misty and cold. Now that we'd stopped talking, a deafening roar crashed in my ears.

"Asher, what—" I turned around to take in my surroundings, and my jaw dropped. "Where are we? How did you do that?"

We were at the top of a huge cliff. Water spilled down

over the side in huge, driving waves, pounding into a whirlpool below.

"Do you like it?" Asher asked.

"It's unbelievable," I said, letting the mist fall against my face. "It's gorgeous."

"This is what I did while you were unconscious."

For just a second my heart stopped. "You what?"

"Before you woke up," he said, eyeing me, tentatively gauging my reaction. "I couldn't sleep. When it was Ardith's turn to watch you, I would come out here in the woods, at night. I needed to do something. To feel like I could control *something*. The thought of losing you . . ." He grazed his thumb along my cheek.

I squeezed his hand. "You made this for me?"

"I made it because I didn't know what to do with myself. I was struggling with so many . . . feelings, I guess, and I had no idea what to do with them." He paused and looked around, surveying his work. "I could have kept going, but you woke up. And then I needed to be with you."

"I . . . I don't know what to say."

He had told me he loved me, but it wasn't until this moment that I really knew what that meant. The water crashed around us, wild, impossible to control. He shrugged. "Don't say anything." He gestured at the waterfall, the cliff, and the jagged rocks below. "Come on," he said, taking my hand. "This way." We wended our way down a path in the side of the cliff that took us to the bottom. Asher held back branches for me when they hung too low, so they wouldn't snap back in my face. Something had changed while I'd been unconscious. Asher had certainly never held back during our training or treated me in any special way. Now, it was almost as if he was afraid of breaking me. All of a sudden, I was fragile to him. Something that needed protecting.

My heart felt like I'd swallowed it. I wanted so badly to stay close to him, so he'd never have to worry about losing me again.

"Asher?" He'd disappeared. I was alone on the path, mist from the whirlpool fogging my vision and making it hard to see.

"In here." His voice rang out over the din of the churning water. I stepped cautiously through the curtain of mist, finding my footing on the slippery stones. The small path opened up into a dark cave. Asher stood several feet away, his back to me. When I walked up beside him, the view took my breath away. We were in a cave behind the waterfall, staring out through the velvety sheet of water.

I slipped my hand into his.

He turned to look down at me, happiness radiating from his face.

"You and me, Skye," he said. "We're partners."

"For always," I said.

He put his arms around me, and I leaned into him.

"You're going to be so powerful, once you learn to control all of this," he said quietly. "You could have powers greater than any other Rebel. That's why we have to be so careful about what to do now." He paused, his eyebrows knitting together as he stared out over the raging pool. "They're in awe of you. And some of them are afraid."

"Are you?" I whispered.

He didn't say anything, but his arms tightened around me.

"I don't know how to feel about all this," I said, watching the waterfall as if it held all the answers. "I don't want them to be afraid of me." *Or you*, I thought. For some reason, it reminded me of something Devin always used to say about the Order. *A place with no fear.* I hated how he kept creeping back into my thoughts, whether I wanted him there or not. I was grateful that Asher's powers didn't include the ability to read my mind. Though I had a hunch he suspected I thought about Devin. Every now and then, like now, as he gazed out at the water, his eyes grew dark with storm clouds. And when they did, I knew he was thinking of ways to get back at the icy blond angel for coming so close to stealing my life.

I didn't want to be there when he finally found a way.

"I'll keep you safe," Asher murmured to himself.

Safe. He'd said the word so many times, I wondered which of us he was trying to convince.

That night, we flew. Asher gripped me in his arms like he had the night he saved my life. Ardith coasted on black wings, silently, beside us. The wind rushed in my ears.

Soon, the dark clouds gave way to a scattering metropolis of lights below us. And then, the lights thinned out, and we began to descend.

My feet hit the ground hard, and as I looked around to get my bearings, I realized we were on Main Street. The moon hung low in the sky, casting the dimmest of light on downtown River Springs.

The air was cold, and it reminded me so much of the moonless night when I had turned seventeen.

The air had a brutal edge to it as I stood outside of Love the Bean.

The sky was dark. The street, deserted.

Snow from a recent storm had frozen over in the subsequent days' chill, leaving the roads and the sidewalks in town slick and hazardous.

Asher and Ardith stood on either side of me.

"We won't reveal ourselves yet—unless we need to," Asher said reassuringly.

The wind sliced at my neck where it was exposed beneath my hat, and I scanned up and down the street for signs of life.

In the window of Into the Woods Outdoor Co., a light was on. I felt tears well in my eyes.

I was home.

A white mist swirled around me, dense and damp. It caught in my eyelashes, and when I blinked, it trickled down my cheeks. I opened my mouth and the mist tasted salty on my tongue. *Just like tears*, I thought.

Where was I? It wasn't Main Street anymore, yet I knew this place. I'd opened my eyes to find myself here before.

I took a step forward, and the ground gave easily under my feet, soft and grainy. The mist began to clear for the first time. A black sand beach stretched out before me, trailing off into the distant mist. The dark sea lapped at the shore, constant, insistent. It was trying to tell me something.

But what?

I tripped on something and fell to my knees. Panic tore at me blindly, but it was only the hem of my dress, dirty and soaked, that had gotten tangled beneath my feet. *My dress?*

It was long and gauzy white, grazing my ankles. For a moment, I was shocked to be wearing something so beautiful. And then, the shock gave way to sadness as I realized that I'd ruined the barely-there fabric. The dark sand and seawater stained the hem and at my knees where I'd fallen.

Nothing perfect ever lasts, I found myself thinking.

I stood up, collecting the folds of the beautiful dress in my arms to keep from falling. I leaned forward into the wind, into the mist, as I took one step and then another. And then my feet hit something solid.

My heart beat fast, and I swallowed the wet air, bending to see what I'd stumbled upon. *Feet*, I realized. *Those are feet.* The mist drew out with the tide, and now that my vision was clear, dread descended on me. I was looking down at a body. It lay unmoving on the beach, but I couldn't make out the face.

And then the mist returned, like the ocean was sucking its breath in with me, and the whiteness expanded into the sky, until it eclipsed everything else.

When I opened my eyes again I was inside, lying on a worn velvet couch, staring up at Ian.

"Hey," he said, his freckled face expanding into a huge grin. "You're awake."

"Ian?"

"Welcome back," he said breathlessly. "But give a guy a break, Skye. I already thought I'd never see you again, then I have to go and find you passed out in the street?"

I looked up, alarmed that he really was angry with me, but the grin was still plastered across his face. Before I knew what was happening, I was smiling and laughing and holding back tears while Ian scooped me up in his arms and held me against his chest.

"Oh my god," he said, laughing. "I didn't know if I would ever hear that laugh again."

"I didn't know if I would ever see those freckles again!" I cried.

He smiled and brought a hand to his face in mock self-consciousness."What, these things? My mom says I'll grow out of them by the time I graduate. She says then I'll be ever so handsome."

"No! Don't you ever grow out of them," I said. "They're the most reassuring sight in the world." Under his freckles, Ian's cheeks turned red.

"Oh, man, Skye," he said, taking my hand in his. "You're really here, aren't you? I'm not just dreaming this?"

"I'm here," I said. I raised an eyebrow. "Ian, have you been dreaming about me?"

"Every night." As with most conversations Ian and I had, I knew he wasn't exactly kidding when he said things like that. I let my hand fall from his, and he noticed. "Sorry," he said quietly. "Are you still, you know, with . . . ?"

"Yeah," I said, dropping my voice, too. "Asher."

"Asher. Right." He looked up at the clock, probably just to avoid my gaze. Then he looked back at me. "You know, he wasn't out there on the street when I found you. No one was. You were just lying there, passed out, alone. What happened?"

He'd been there, of course. *We won't reveal ourselves yet.* They were here, watching everything. Asher would never leave me. But I couldn't exactly tell Ian that.

"Skye," Ian prodded. "I'm serious. What happened? Are you okay?"

"I don't know," I said, suddenly really tired. I thought about all the questions that were awaiting me now that I was back. "I was awake and then . . . I was here." I paused. "Maybe it was exhaustion. I was traveling. . . ."

"Traveling," he repeated.

"Yeah."

"Do . . . you wanna tell me where you were?"

I looked up at him again. There was a steaming mug of something delicious-looking on the coffee table next to him. *Oh, Ian.* He was always there for me when I needed him. Not for the first time, I wished I could be there—*had* been there—for my friends in the same way. But, no matter how hard I tried, I didn't see a way that I ever could.

"I do want to tell you," I said finally.

"But?" His smile was lopsided, a little sad. He knew me that well.

"I can't. I'm so sorry. I wish I could."

"Hey." He took my face, suddenly, in both his hands. I was caught off-guard, and my body responded before I was ready. There was something so aggressive, yet gentle, about his sudden forcefulness. So unlike Ian. "You never need to apologize to me." His green eyes flashed with an intensity I'd never seen in them before. "I know you need your space. And I know that, when you're ready, you'll tell me everything."

I felt the tears well up in me again, and for a couple of seconds, I couldn't say a word. Finally I whispered, "Thank you."

In another surprise move, he bent and kissed me on the

forehead. Something had changed about him while I'd been gone. He was the same Ian, but different. More confident or something. I could still feel his lips on my skin after he pulled away.

My mouth dropped open as I realized that I liked it.

"So," Ian said, letting his hands fall to his sides and standing. He began to busy himself straightening up the Bean. We were the only people there. It must have been after closing already. "Am I the only one who knows you're here?" I stood and followed him behind the counter as he opened the cash register and counted a stack of bills.

"Yup," I said, hoisting myself onto the counter next to him. He double-checked the till to make sure he'd swiped it clean of money, then put the stack of bills down on the counter and ruffled through them nervously.

"You talk to Cassie?"

I straightened, fully alert now.

"She's awake?" My heart was in my throat.

Ian smiled—a weary, relieved smile—and for the first time I noticed how tired he looked. Like he'd been through a little bit of hell.

"She's awake," he said. "Bruised and battered, you know. It looks . . ." He coughed. "It looks not so great. But she's alive. She's going to be fine." He nodded, as if confirming this fact to himself.

"Oh my god," I said, jumping off the counter and throwing my arms around him. I buried my face in his neck and let the warm scent of cookies and lattes wrap itself around my heart. The comforting scent of home.

"I don't know what I'd have done if . . . if she hadn't . . ." I couldn't finish.

"Yeah," Ian said quietly, running his fingers softly—almost tentatively—through my hair. "She was lucky. We all were."

He put his arm around me tighter, and I let the stability of his presence in my life comfort me. He had always been there for me, and he always would be.

No matter what I did to him. No matter how many times I told him no.

"Been home yet?" Ian asked, pulling away.

"Not exactly," I said with a sheepish smile.

"Wanna see her?"

"Yes," I said, too quickly. "Definitely."

"Cool," he said. "Just give me a few minutes while I close up."

Ian went off to the supply room, and I wandered around the coffee shop. The last time I'd seen it so empty was the day after my birthday party, when Cassie, Dan, and I had helped Ian clean up the mess. I shivered as I remembered the bitter cold air that had blown through the broken windows on that gray day.

As if brought back to that actual moment in time, a chilly breeze brushed my hair into my eyes, and I turned to see where it was coming from. The window in the back was open, the one by the couches that the four of us had sat on that very afternoon, our feet up on the coffee table as we surveyed the work ahead of us. I walked over to close it, but as I did, something caught my eye. Something that stood out against the drab, walked-all-over carpet and worn plush cushions of the couch. A single white feather was blowing lightly in the breeze.

My heart dropped, and the wind rushed in my ears as my knees gave way. I sat down on the low coffee table, hard. *A white feather.*

They'd warned me, hadn't they? There would be Guardians here.

And not just Guardians. Devin, too.

I knew what to expect. But suddenly I wondered if I was ready.

Falling in love with you was one more thing I couldn't help. Had he meant those words? How could the Order make someone such a hypocrite? How could he feel that way and still do what he did to me?

I couldn't understand it.

I felt like I was wearing headphones with the music blasting at full volume. Above the rushing in my ears one sound struggled to get through.

"Skye!" My head snapped up. Ian stood over me, looking concerned. "Are you sure you're okay?" He went over to close the window, and I took that opportunity to shove the feather into my jacket. "Ready to leave?" I nodded. He cocked his head to one side. "Skye," he said, his voice already making me feel better. "No one blames you, you know. For leaving. For any of it."

I nodded grimly. I wished I could tell him that I hadn't just left. That I would never abandon him, or Cassie, Dan, or Aunt Jo like that. They were my family. But there were so many things I could never tell him. "I think maybe I should just go home first. See Aunt Jo. If word got to her that I saw Cassie before I saw her, she'd never forgive me."

"Good call," said Ian. "You're a way better person than me." He clapped his hand on my back. "Come on, let's get you home."

As we drove, Ian and I fell back into our old banter.

"So what's been going on since I've been away?" I asked.

He glanced over at me. "Are you pumping me for gossip?"

"I feel so out of the loop!"

"Well, I'm not as good at this as Cassie, so bear with me.

You'll have to get the full scoop from her tomorrow."

"Pleeease?"

"Okay, okay. Well, you know about Cassie and Dan, I guess, right? How they're . . ."

"Together?" I asked hopefully.

"Sickening." He laughed. "Ever since she left the hospital they've been surgically attached."

"Yay!" I said, clapping my hands, so excited, suddenly, to be surrounded by all the little normal things that I loved about my life.

"I think we have different definitions of 'yay.' I lost a bro this winter, Skye." He bowed his head. "A true bro. One of the good ones."

I laughed. "Hey, eyes on the road. So what have you been doing with yourself while that's been happening?"

Ian glanced in his side-view mirror and switched lanes evasively. A police car passed us in the opposite direction. My stomach tightened involuntarily, as I remembered the sirens on the morning of Cassie's accident.

"I've been finding ways to have fun." He focused on the road as we neared my driveway and didn't elaborate.

"That's such a guy thing to say," I muttered. "You're no fun." He grinned and wiggled his eyebrows at me. There was a mischievous look in his eyes that he was not going to tell me about. Something had shifted between us, as quickly as a cloud passing across the sun, but I didn't know what. "Home, sweet home," he said. "Ready to face the wrath of Aunt Jo?"

"Ugh," I said. "No. But I'm going in anyway."

"You can do this." He patted my knee gingerly, like I might slap his hand away at any moment. "She'll just be so relieved that you're home. She's been frantic."

"Way to make me feel better," I joked halfheartedly.

"Just call me if you need anything," he said. I got out of the car, and leaned down to stick my head in the window.

"Thanks, Ian," I said. "I'm glad I saw you first."

"Me too." He grinned. "Just don't tell Cassie. She'll kill me for not bringing you straight to her."

I zipped my lips and threw away the key.

"Our secret."

He nodded and peeled out of the driveway.

The light from the kitchen windows spilled out into the front yard as I stood and stared up at the house. It used to be home. It still was, I guessed.

I took a deep breath and made my way inside.

The front hallway was dark but for a faint light from the kitchen. It took me a moment to get my bearings before walking toward it.

What was I going to tell her? Where had I been?

The kitchen was deserted and still. The sink was clean and empty, the counters were spotless, the cleanest I'd ever seen them. The floor was so shiny that I could see my reflection in the polished wood. Was Aunt Jo out on a trip with Into the Woods? My stomach sank at the idea of coming home only to find myself alone again—like I'd been right before I'd left.

In all my life, I'd never known my adopted guardian to be such a neat freak.

Something was wrong. Something didn't feel right at all.

But then I began to notice small hints of life here and there. A wet tea bag resting on a spoon on top of the microwave. A book with an envelope holding the reader's place. Some neat stacks of papers on the kitchen table, with the topmost page pulled slightly askew, as if someone had been looking at it recently and hadn't put it neatly back in place. I walked over to the table and picked it up.

My birth certificate.

Heart pounding, I riffled through the rest of the papers on the table. Xeroxes of my passport, Social Security information, and my adoption papers were sorted and stacked into piles, along with paperwork from the River Springs Police Department for filing a missing persons report.

I started when I heard a voice, and seconds later Aunt Jo came into the room talking on the phone.

". . . about five five, black hair, gray eyes, a champion skier, sort of intense, but once you get to know her—" When she saw me, she stopped. She clicked the phone off and it fell from her hand and clattered to the floor.

"Skye," she whispered. Her eyes filled with tears. There was such a mix of emotions on her face: sadness, relief, anger, regret.

"I'm . . . ," I started, not sure what I was about to say.

"Oh my god," she said, running to me and squeezing me

in her arms. "Oh, Skye, Skye, Skye," she repeated, rocking back and forth. "Are you okay? Where the *hell* have you been? You are in a world of trouble, young lady, but I'm too happy you're home to be angry right now."

"I'm so sorry," I said, burying my face in her hair and letting her hold me. "I'm so, *so* sorry. I missed you so much." For the first time, I realized just how scared I'd been that I'd never see her again. She pulled away, looking me over as we both sat on the floor in the middle of the kitchen. She squeezed her hands up and down my arms as if checking for broken bones.

"What happened to you? Do you even know what you put us through? Do you have any idea how worried we were?" She wiped her eyes. "I should have been here. I should have said something, told you, I should have—"

"Aunt Jo," I said. "Stop the crazy talk. It's not your fault!"

"What happened?" she asked again, running her fingers over the cuts and bruises on my face. "My god, look at you. Are you okay? Do you need to go to the hospital?"

The time for that had definitely passed.

"No," I said. "I'm fine. Really. Just tired. I missed my bed."

"Of course," she said, pulling me in for an air-sucking

hug again. "Of course. You don't have to worry. You're home now. You're safe."

But how could I tell her the truth? I wasn't safe. The white feather told me all I needed to know. I may have been back in the house I grew up in, with Aunt Jo there to take care of me and make me my favorite meals. But everything about home was going to be different from now on. "Safe" couldn't have been farther from how I felt.

Upstairs, I took a shower—my first shower in days. I let the hot water spill over me, washing away the dirt and the knots in my hair. Washing away every trace, every memory of what had happened in the woods that night. I let every betrayal, every thought of Devin swirl down the drain. Steam billowed up around me and I let myself get lost in it.

After I wrapped myself in a big plush towel and padded back into my room, I took my favorite T-shirt and boxers out of a drawer and put them on my bed.

"Skye!" Aunt Jo called from the hallway. Her voice was nervous and didn't sound right. "Everything okay in there? Do you need anything?"

"I'm fine!" I called. "I'll be out in a second!" I turned to my full-length mirror and let the towel fall to the floor around me. My stomach was smooth and unmarked, as if I'd never been stabbed at all. I couldn't believe it. I ran my fingers across my skin, but they felt nothing. Goose bumps prickled my arms and legs, and suddenly I had the creepy feeling of being watched. I quickly stepped into the old flannel boxers and pulled the T-shirt over my head. It felt like forever since I'd put them on, and I relished the feel of the soft cotton. I finished brushing my hair, pulling it up into a knot on the top of my head.

Suddenly I winced, pitching forward. The room seemed to spin and fade away into darkness. When I looked into the mirror again, I had to grab the dresser with both hands for support. A dark wet spot was blooming from the center of my shirt. Frantic, I lifted it, and what I saw made me scream out loud.

There was a gaping stab wound through my stomach, seeping blood onto my hands, the dresser, the carpet. My vision ran red with it. "Jo!" I yelled. "Aunt Jo!"

"What is it?" She came bursting into the room, and everything came back into focus. The light returned, and my dizziness cleared. "Skye?" she asked, coming to me. "Are you okay?"

"I—" I looked down at my hands, the carpet, my stomach. There was no wound, no blood. Everything was the way it had been. "It's nothing," I said. "I'm—I'm sorry. I thought . . ."

She looked at me with an expression I couldn't read.

"Are you sure you're okay?"

"Yeah," I said. I had to stop dwelling on what had happened. I was home now. It was time to move on. "I'm fine."

"Come downstairs," she said. She looked so helpless, like she was running through a mental checklist of all the things she might have done to drive me away. "I made you something. We'll talk."

We sat across the table in the kitchen. Aunt Jo had whipped up my favorite snack while I was in the shower, and the warm, fresh-from-the-oven cinnamon cookies now sat, cooling, on a plate between us.

"I'm not going to push you," Aunt Jo said. "You're a good kid, Skye, and I trust you. You know that, right? I trust you to make your own decisions and not get influenced by a bad crowd." She twirled the plate nervously in her fingers. "But I need to know where you were." She paused. "And you're definitely grounded."

"But I—"

"No buts. That's not negotiable. I was worried sick about you. What was I supposed to think? Do you even understand how selfish it was to disappear like that?"

"I guess not," I said hoarsely. This was the worst—getting yelled at, feeling guilty for something that had been beyond my control. I wanted to yell, "*None of it was my fault!*" But I held it in for my safety—and for Aunt Jo's. Who knew what the Order would do to her if I told her the truth?

I was sick of everything being *out* of my control. Anger burned through me as I clenched my fists under the table.

"So. Where were you? Not even your friends knew. Were you with those guys? The two you were telling me about?"

I wondered, for a moment, if I could get away with telling her an *abbreviated* version of the truth. The idea of continuing to lie to Aunt Jo—someone who had always treated me like I was her real, blood daughter—made me feel sick.

"There's a cabin, in the woods. It's not too far from here. I . . . discovered it. On a hike." I swallowed. "I was scared." And that, at least, was the truth. "I was standing there in the hospital with Cassie, and it looked like she might not . . ." I found myself getting choked up. "It looked like she was going to die, and it felt like my fault. Like I wasn't there for her when she needed me this semester." Aunt Jo murmured something to herself. "But it felt like everyone needed something different from me. And I didn't know how to handle it all. Like everyone had a different idea of what my life should be. I had to get away."

"Skye," she said softly. "What happened to Cassie was *not* your fault. One thing has nothing to do with the other." I wished right then that I could have told her everything, but that's how Cassie had gotten hurt in the first place. If I broke down and told Aunt Jo, I'd only be putting her in danger, too. And after seeing Cass in the hospital that day, her face bruised and her arms and legs in casts—that was something I couldn't face.

I just had to handle this on my own.

Not on your own, a voice in the back of my mind whispered. *You have Asher now. You have the whole Rebellion on your side.*

"A cabin," Aunt Jo mused, breaking me out of my thoughts. "What kind of cabin?"

"Kind of old. There was one of those toilets with the chains and weird closets with lots of little drawers. But someone was living there much more recently: there was coffee from at least the nineties or something."

Aunt Jo got a funny look in her eye. "I know that place," she said. "I put that coffee there. Into the Woods has been trying to buy it for years, to use as a trail stop." A small smile spread across her face. "How funny that you ended up in that cabin. That's really where you went?"

I nodded.

"Thank you for telling me," she said. "I'm not happy that you felt you had to run away for a few days instead of talking to me about it—"

"You were never here!"

"—but I understand that I was gone a lot. Jeez, Skye, I was just about to say that. I'm so sorry I left you alone for so long. I'm here now, and I'll be here when you need me. Just talk to me, okay?" She eyed the cut on my face. "Believe it or not, your old Aunt Jo was a teenager once."

"Please," I snorted.

"All I'm saying is, I may know what you're going through better than you think."

"Fine." I slowly let my fists unclench under the table. "I'll try."

"Good, but for now, you should go to bed," she said. "You look exhausted." She stood up and walked toward the door. When she got there, she turned around. The light from the stairs cast a fuzzy halo around her blondish-gray hair. There was something in her eyes that I couldn't figure out.

Things were definitely different between us now. First Ian, now Aunt Jo.

I realized that the look in her eyes—it was worry. Fear. It was different from the looks she'd given me earlier in the winter, each time she was about to go away and afraid of leaving me alone. No, this wasn't about what might happen to me. It was, I realized, about what *I* had done— or might do.

It was the same way Asher had treated me at the cabin. Like I was something fragile and yet unpredictable, something extremely precious.

I glanced at the window, wondering if he and Ardith— and Gideon now, too—were out there. Watching. Keeping me safe.

When I turned back from the window, Aunt Jo was still staring at me.

"You look older," she said. "You know that?"

I thought about all that had happened to me since I'd turned seventeen.

"Yeah," I said. "I guess I am." There were dark circles under her eyes and the lines in her forehead looked deeper than I'd remembered. She looked older, too.

"G'night," she said.

"Night, Aunt Jo," I whispered back.

I couldn't really remember what it felt like to be with my mom, but if I'd had to guess, I figured it probably felt exactly like this.

I stayed in the kitchen for a few minutes longer after Aunt Jo went upstairs, absently nibbling on a cookie. The spicy sweet taste reminded me of everything from before. Suddenly my stomach flipped, and I didn't feel so great. A shiver ran down my spine as I remembered that time in the kitchen, at night, alone, when Raven had first confronted me. Was she out there right now? What if they all were? Waiting in the bushes and behind trees. Poised to attack the first chance they got.

I stood up quickly, turned the light off in the kitchen, and sprinted up the stairs to my room.

It was freezing in there, and it took only a second to figure out why: my window was wide open. I rushed to it—but instead of closing it automatically like I might have a month ago, I stuck my head out the window and looked up toward the roof.

"Asher?" I whispered. "Are you up there?" I heard a rustle of feathers in response, and then he appeared in my window.

"Hey." He winked, his eyes glittering with mischief. "Want a hand up?" Grinning, I threw on a hoodie and sweatpants. I put my hand in his, and he pulled me up with him to the roof.

"Nice look," he said.

"Shut up," I replied. He put his arm around me, and I sank into the warmth of his body. All the tension I'd felt talking to Ian and Aunt Jo melted away, and I knew, right then, that this was home. Being with Asher. That was all that mattered.

As long as we were together, everything would be fine.

"They're out there," Asher said under his breath, looking out at the field below. "Do you see them?" I looked down at the field.

"Who?" I said. "I don't see anything."

"Shh," he whispered. "Be still. Look again."

This time, I did think I could make out some movement in the dark. Was I imagining things, or could I catch a glimpse of feathers among the trees, a flash of moonlit white against the night?

"Guardians," I said in a low voice.

"Waiting."

"For me." I paused as I really let the weight of it sink in. "Asher, what if I see Devin at school tomorrow? What if I see Raven?" He tightened his arm around me protectively.

"Trust me, Skye, they'd never stage any kind of attack out in the open. At school like that, with everyone watching. Believe it or not, right now, school is the safest place to be."

"I can't believe it," I said, shivering. "Hey, do you have anywhere to be tonight?"

"You mean other than right here?"

"I just thought, with Ardith and Gideon here—"

"Skye." He stopped me. "I'm pretty sure protecting you is my top priority right now."

"Good," I said. "Look. I know this is stupid and embarrassing, but would you . . ."

"Yes?" He grinned.

"Um, sleep with me tonight? Just sleep, I mean. I hate saying this, but . . . I just don't want to be alone."

Asher raised an eyebrow. "Just sleep?" A smile tugged at one corner of his mouth in the most infuriating way.

I tried not to blush. It would only egg him on more. "Okay, you know what? Never mind. I'll take my chances with the Guardians."

"Oh, stop," he said, helping me up. "I would love to just sleep with you, Skye." He walked to the edge of the roof, then turned around, shaking his head. "Are you going to be this scared every night? Because I'll have to check my calendar . . ."

I pushed him lightly. "Just don't get used to it."

We climbed back through my bedroom window. Asher took off his shoes and crawled into bed with me, pulling the covers tightly around us. I fit so perfectly in the crook of his arm. We were safe as long as we were together.

I turned off my bedside lamp, and we lay in the darkness.

"What's the story with Ardith and Gideon?" I said sleepily.

"I'll tell you tomorrow," he whispered. "Go to sleep."

As we dozed off, I thought I heard him mumble, "Never leave me." Though it could have been "I'll never leave you." I wasn't sure.

In the morning, I woke up before my alarm, as prepared to face school as I'd ever be. Asher was gone.

He always left before I was ready.

That morning, I relished the familiarity of waking up in my own bed—but only for about five seconds. I was up and out of there like a shot. The exhaustion I'd been feeling since waking up in the cabin had melted away, replaced with a determined energy. I was back in River Springs, and I had things to do. I had to face my life again.

I reached for my jeans but hesitated. Remembering how ready-for-anything I'd felt the night of Cassie's show at the Bean, I pulled on an off-the-shoulder sweater dress, tights, and motorcycle boots. A little blush, some mascara, tinted lip balm, a necklace or three, and a scarf, and I was good to go. My eyes blazed silver in the mirror. I didn't even worry that they might not be normal again by the time I made it to my car. Somehow I knew they would be. I had to start trusting myself.

If I was going back to school, nobody was going to mess with me today.

"Whoa," Aunt Jo said as I stomped through the kitchen in my heavy boots. "What did you do with Skye? And are those my boots?"

"I'm practicing mind-body consciousness," I said, biting into a toaster strudel. "Look the part, act the part."

"Just be nice to your teachers." She tried to hide a smirk as she refilled her coffee mug.

"I am affronted!" I yelled, heading to the hall and zipping up my parka. "I am always nice!"

"Well, be *extra* nice today," she called after me. "Offer to do extra credit or something. Get yourself back on track."

"Yeah, yeah," I mumbled. "See you later." I hesitated in the doorway, remembering what it had felt like to come home to an empty house for weeks on end. "You'll be home, right?"

"For sure I'll be here. And you're coming home *right* after school."

"Got it," I said. "Love you!"

"Ask the next time you borrow my things!" she called after me.

Oh, how I'd missed my car. The way it hugged the curves of the mountain roads. The way the piercing cold wind whipped at my hair. I always kept my windows open, even in the most freezing temperatures. Maybe because it made me think of skiing.

Or maybe flying.

I was early, but I wasn't going right to school. I was going to pick up my best friend.

The closer I got to Cassie's house, though, the more nervous I grew. What if she thought I had abandoned her? What if she never wanted to see me again? Suddenly, even though I felt sort of guilty for thinking it, the idea of Cassie hating me forever was so much worse than the thought of her dying.

I pulled around a tight bend and the grayish white side of her house came into view. The front yard had the same slightly askew, lived-in vibe it always had. Toy trucks and an overturned bucket of little green soldiers littered the frosted ground. As I parked alongside the curb, I noticed that the car parked directly in front of mine belonged to Dan. My heart beat double time. I hadn't expected to find Dan here, too. I was hoping to have my reunions one at a time, in bite-size pieces.

Oh, well, I thought. *Here goes nothing*.

Good thing I'd worn my tough-girl boots.

The breeze was unseasonably warm today, the morning sky clear and bright, and even though it was still winter, I had a feeling I knew where to find them. Instead of ringing the front doorbell, I walked around through the side gate to the backyard.

Cassie and Dan were sitting side by side on the swing set with their backs to me. Dan was holding her hand, leaning in close to whisper in her ear. She giggled and swatted at him stiffly. Suddenly I panicked. They didn't want to see me. Why would they? Whether I meant to or not, I had abandoned Cassie, and now there was no room for me in her life. She had Dan.

I took a deep breath.

"I better not feel like the third wheel all the time, now that you guys are couple of the year," I said loudly. Dan whipped around so fast he almost fell off the swing.

"Skye! Holy crap, really?" He bounded over to me, grabbed me off my feet in a huge bear hug, and twirled me around.

"Ow." I choked. "You don't know your own strength."

"Sorry," he said, putting me down gently. "It's just— you're back! We missed you!" He turned to Cassie, as if she was going to chime in. But she still had her back to me.

Oh no, I thought. *She's mad. This is it. She thinks I abandoned her, and I'll never be able to tell her the truth and I'll have to find a new best friend and—*

"Skye?" Cassie said breathlessly, and it sounded so normal—so like *us*—that she may as well have been about to say, *This gossip isn't going to spill itself!* She tried awkwardly to turn around. "Is that really you? Shit, ow, wait—" She gripped the chains of the swing. "Dan! Crutches?"

"Oh, right, sorry." He ran to her and picked the crutches up off the ground. Slowly he helped her lift herself onto them and turn around.

Cassie's cascading reddish-blond waves had been hiding a neck brace, and her right leg was locked in a huge blue cast that went all the way up to the middle of her thigh. She looked up at me, and our eyes met. Half of her face was bruised, which gave her sort of an angry look.

I swallowed.

"Cass?" I said. "Oh my god."

"Oh, whatever," she said, a small smile lighting up her face. She was secretly into the fact that she looked like an invalid, I realized, as I broke into a smile, too. It was definitely dramatic looking. I bet she was getting tons of attention for it.

"You're totally milking this, aren't you?"

"What? No," Cassie said, her smile widening like she really wanted to say, *Who, me?* "But listen, you're going to have to come to me, because it's effing impossible to move with this stupid cast on." Before she even finished talking, I ran across the yard and threw my arms around her. "Ow," she cried. "Ow, neck brace, neck brace!" But she was laughing. We both were.

Cassie pulled away and gave me a once-over. Her eyes looked glassy, but I knew she'd die before she let herself cry in public.

"Dan?" she said sweetly. "Can you get me that thing?"

Dan looked at her blankly. "What thing?"

She rolled her eyes. "You know, that *thing*. The thing I use to scratch inside my cast?"

"Oh, *that* thing. 'Course, babes." I was surprised by the tenderness in his voice. He bent and kissed the top of her head. She smiled after him as he walked away, then turned to me.

"*Babes?* You guys say *babes* now?"

"Don't change the subject," she said, pointing her index finger at me accusingly. "Where the hell were you? I woke up and you were gone. And I thought something terrible must have happened to you, because there's no way you would have left me there alone." A tear brushed down her face, but she stubbornly ignored it. "So tell me that's it, right?" she said. "You were kidnapped? You were abducted by aliens? A tribe of hot nudist boys whisked you off to their native land, where they hailed you as queen?" She looked hopeful.

I swallowed. Face to face with Cassie, the story I'd told Aunt Jo about being scared felt flimsy and stupid. Cassie would never buy that. I was the strong one. I was the one who was supposed to be cool and levelheaded and unemotional. I was good in a crisis. I didn't panic and run away. Cassie, of all people, would know I was lying.

"I don't . . . have . . . a good reason," I said. She stared at me, and the silence hung between us. I couldn't keep lying to her like this. I opened my mouth to tell the truth, but something flashed in the woods behind her yard.

Guardians.

My head snapped up, and I glanced behind her toward the trees. Was it my imagination, or could I see a streak of white disappear behind an evergreen? It was a reminder that I could *never* tell Cassie the truth—no matter how much I wanted to. "I was scared," I said quickly, trying to sound convincing. "I guess . . . I guess I didn't handle it well."

"That's *it*?" She hobbled backward on her crutches. "Oh, gee, Skye, you think?" Well, thank god one of us was scared. It couldn't have been me, you see, because I was the one *in the coma*!"

I glanced behind me, nervously.

"What do you keep looking for?" she asked. Suddenly recognition dawned on her face, and her jaw dropped. "I know that look. That's the same look you had plastered to your face in the cafeteria all winter, and the look you had when we were waiting for the bus to the ski trip." Her eyes widened. "You're looking for them, aren't you? Asher and Devin? *They're* the reason you ran away!"

"What?" I cried. "No way!"

"Don't play this game with me, Skye. The jig is *so* up. You left me. For a *guy*."

"I didn't, I swear!"

"You know, Skye, I'm boy crazy. I can accept that. But I would never put one of them ahead of you."

"Uh," Dan said, coming up behind her with a long instrument that looked like a deconstructed hanger. "Standing right here."

"Not you, Dan," Cassie said. "The other ones."

"*What* other ones?"

Cassie turned to him pointedly. "The ones who came

before." She raised an eyebrow. "Catch my drift?"

"It's rare that I do," Dan said.

"Aunt Jo may have bought the whole 'I was scared' line," she continued, wheeling back around. "But I know you better than that. You really want to stand there and tell me that's why you left?"

No, I thought desperately. *I don't.*

"You weren't even shaken up after that avalanche almost killed you," Dan added.

"Well played, babes," she said to him, holding out her hand so he could slap it five. "So are you going to tell us the truth?"

My throat went dry. Every fiber of my being fought against telling her. There were Guardians everywhere. And the last thing I needed was to put my friends in danger. Most of the time, they were all that was keeping me sane.

"You're right," I said. The words were out of my mouth before I could think about what I was going to say next. "The night of your gig—of the party—Asher told me that he wanted to, um . . ." I paused. How could I explain this? "Be my boyfriend. He said with all the drama at home and him and Devin fighting and everything, he wanted to take me away. There's this cabin in the woods not far from here. We went there for a couple of days." I paused again. "Just spent some time away from everything. I spent most of it worried about you," I added, glancing at her. Cassie was frowning at me, listening intently.

"Skye, that is the"—she propped a hand on her hip—"*best* story ever! How romantic! Now I get why you couldn't tell Aunt Jo. She'd flip, right? Wow. Are you grounded? In the name of love? Did you drive here? Where's Asher?"

I grinned. I should have realized the way to distract Cassie sooner.

"I really was scared, though," I said quietly. "That part was true."

"Eh, I know." Cassie sighed. "I was scared when I woke up and saw myself in the mirror." She pointed at her eye. "Purple is not a good color on redheads!"

"I was scared, too," said Dan. "My first and only girl-friend almost didn't wake up. Can you imagine any other girl wanting me after that?"

"Aw," Cassie cooed. "Of course they would. If I had died, you'd be all wounded and mysterious and nursing your broken heart. Girls love that crap. They'd want to put you back together."

"Really?" Dan asked hopefully. Cassie hobbled over and put her arm around him.

"You bet," she said. "But let's not test the theory, okay?" Dan leaned in really quickly for a surprise kiss, and Cassie lost her balance. She toppled over her crutches, fell to the ground. "Dan!" she yelled. "Ow?"

"Sorry, sorry," he said, rushing to help her up again.

"You know what, on second thought, those girls can have you."

"You love it," Dan said.

"Not as much as you do," she crowed. They were kissing again.

"Guys?" I said. "I'm back now, remember?"

"Mm? Oh, right, Skye. Sorry," Cassie said, breaking away sheepishly.

"Come on," I said. "I'm driving. I don't want to be late my first day back."

Cassie leaned on Dan's shoulder, and we made our way to the car.

"So," she said as I pulled out of the driveway, "you may have left just in time. I heard that Devin has a new girl-friend."

"*What?*" I wheeled around involuntarily.

"Oh my god, watch the road!" Cassie and Dan shouted at the same time.

"God, sorry," I said. I glanced casually in the rearview

mirror as we turned on to the main road. "What do you mean?"

"Well." Cassie took a deep breath, her eyes glinting mischievously.

"Um, have you been gossip starved or something?"

"I'm only getting started. There was a chemical contamination at River Springs High, right? And they had to shut it down, for like a month or so. They merged with us until it's safe to reopen." She met my eye in the mirror. "Some cuties, Skye," she whispered. "That's all I'm gonna say."

"Again, sitting right here," muttered Dan.

"I'm in a relationship, not blind, okay?" She gasped. "And now Skye is, too! We can double-date!"

"Yay," said Dan with mock enthusiasm.

"Cass, what about Devin? Finish the story."

"Right. Anyway, he has a new girlfriend, or maybe they were even *already dating*. She came in with the RSH students. Her name is weird. Some hippie name. Sparrow or something."

The wind grew suddenly colder as it whipped through the open windows.

"Raven?"

"Yes! That's it. Anyway, she must have been really popular at RSH because she doesn't talk to anyone at

Northwood. Just Devin and some kids from her school."

Guardians.

"Whoa, Skye, you okay? You look like you've just seen . . ." But Cassie's voice faded out, along with the houses and the swings and the tall evergreen trees ticking past. My grip on the steering wheel loosened. The wind around us picked up, lifting dead leaves into the air and surrounding us in a tunnel of wind and leaves. Suddenly I was in a dark room, with thousands of tiny lights illuminating my way. Someone's hands were on my waist, and out of the darkness, a face took shape. First I saw the ice-blond hair. Then the blue eyes. And then I realized I was staring up at Devin. I drew him closer.

"Have you thought any more about what I said?" I asked. His hands on my waist guided me to the right, and then again to the right, and I realized we were dancing in a slow circle. There were lights flashing around me. Was it lightning? As we danced, I grew aware that we were being watched.

"Yes," he said quietly. His voice was low in my ear. "I have." The music was faint, and I struggled to place the song but I couldn't.

He looked down at me, but he was already fading, and the darkness was fading, and the lights were growing dim.

I opened my eyes to Cassie screaming and Dan leaning across me, grasping the steering wheel.

"Are you okay?" Cassie's voice rang out, and her reddish hair wisped into my vision. "What's wrong with you?"

"Oh my god." I exhaled, grabbing the wheel and righting it. We swerved momentarily before straightening out again on the road.

"Skye, pull over," Cassie said stonily. "Dan, you're driving."

"I'm fine," I muttered, pulling the car to the side of the road. "The change in altitude coming back here just hit me hard, that's all."

But as I switched seats with Dan, I couldn't stop my mind from racing. That wasn't one of the dreams I'd been having. Those dreams always ended with Devin stabbing me. Those dreams ended with blood staining my vision red and my life flashing before my eyes.

In this one, we seemed to be having a normal conversation. We were dancing. We were—

It wasn't a dream at all. It was . . . a vision. Some manifestation of powers in my mind's eye. Like the vision of walking on the beach in my beautiful dress, of finding the dead body—it couldn't have been real. But what were they visions of? What did they mean?

As I sat up, a white feather smacked into the windshield before it tumbled off and was sucked away by the wind.

In the blink of an eye, two things were suddenly clear to me:

The first was that I had to figure out what part of me was causing these strange visions. What if I was alone in the car the next time one of them overtook me? If Dan hadn't grabbed the steering wheel, I'd have wrapped my car around a tree. I had to figure out how to control them. If they were in any way related to my powers, maybe I could teach myself how.

And the second thing I realized? Devin and I were going to have a reunion.

Standing in the parking lot staring up at school felt both the same and like being in another world. I had been away only for a little more than a week, but it felt like a lifetime had gone by. The big stone arches had always felt vaguely gothic to me, and now, as I anticipated what might be waiting on the other side, they felt downright foreboding.

"Are you ready for this?" Cassie asked. "First day back?"

"No," I said. "But that's never stopped me before."

We pushed through the big front doors, and the typical din hit us hard as we walked in. I kept my head up and my eyes straight ahead, trying to feel confident with Cassie and Dan by my side. A few unfamiliar faces turned from their lockers to watch me as I made my way through the hall. Their blond hair flashed in the harsh lighting. My heart beat fast. There were so many of them. Ardith turned from her own locker to nod at me reassuringly as I passed.

I couldn't help notice that other kids I'd known for years eyed me, too, whispering in small groups. I wondered what kind of rumors had been circulating about me while I'd been gone. I could only imagine the pregnancy speculation, the talk of drugs. Running away with my delinquent boyfriend. I wondered if anyone had set them straight or if my reputation had been established as a total badass. I wasn't sure which I preferred.

Next to me, Cassie stiffened on her crutches. "Let them stare," she muttered. "Nosy bitches."

At the stairs, Dan hung a left. "See you guys at lunch," he called. We turned the corner, and I could see Asher leaning against my locker at the end of the hall, his arms crossed, staring down some freshmen girls who passed him in a giggling cluster. As we walked up, he uncrossed his arms.

"Did you hear I knocked you up?" he asked, his eyes wide. "You already had the baby *and* gave it up for adoption. Wow. We work fast."

"That's me," I said, tossing my hair over my shoulder

and spinning the combination on my lock. "To-tal badass."

"Hey, Asher." Cassie grinned, opening the locker next to mine. "Looking good."

"Cassie," I whispered.

"You two have a nice mini break?"

Asher laughed. "News really travels fast around here, huh? Did *you* start that pregnancy rumor?"

"Please," said Cassie. "That rumor was the work of an amateur. If I had started one, it would have been *way* more interesting." She shifted on her crutches. "Hacks." Someone opened the locker door next to hers, whacking her arm. "Ow!" she said loudly. "Hello! Invalid here!"

The locker door closed, and Cassie was face-to-face with a guy I'd never seen before. He had dark, perfectly messy curls, and was wearing jeans and beat-up sneakers, wire-rimmed glasses, and a faded T-shirt in some kind of stoner-skater-mathlete look. A *hot* skater-stoner-mathlete. Cassie's eyes widened involuntarily.

"Oh," she said in a small voice. "Hi." She may have been smitten, but my stomach clenched. Was he a Guardian? He didn't have blond hair. . . .

"Guys," Asher said. "This is my friend Gideon. He's one of the RSH transfers."

"Hey," said Gideon. He smiled at us. Next to me, I

could almost hear Cassie gulp.

"Hi," I said. "I'm Skye."

"I know," he said. "Asher's told me all about you." His smile seemed genuine, and I felt instantly that I could trust him. But there was a playful quality to his voice that made me think Asher had told him about more than just my powers.

"Oh, really?" I made a face at Asher.

"All good things," he said.

"That's what I'm afraid of." I turned back to Gideon. "I wish I could say the same, but Asher's been very tight-lipped about *you*." Gideon glanced at Asher.

"Oh," he said as we closed our lockers and began walking down the hall. "Well, we'll get to know each other soon enough." He grinned at me knowingly, and I was startled to realize there was something dark in the depths of his eyes. He may have been smiling, but Gideon had something bottled up deep inside him. I knew that look, because I saw it every day in my own mirror. "Later," he said and peeled off into a classroom on our left.

Cassie, Asher, and I continued to homeroom. As we paused outside the door, all I could think of was the first time that I'd stood between Asher and Devin. The look in their eyes could have cut diamonds as they glared each other down. I'd been so innocent then. I had no idea, standing in that hallway on the first day of the semester, how much that feeling of being caught in the middle would continue to haunt me.

"Come on, Skye. You made it this far," Cassie said. She nudged me reassuringly with her elbow and hobbled in ahead of me.

"I'm right behind you," Asher whispered into my ear.

I took a deep breath and walked through the door.

Cassie was making her way to our usual seats by the window. Ardith sat at the front of the room in a floor-grazing skirt and boots, her armful of bangles jingling softly every time she moved. She caught my eye and winked at me in the most imperceptible way. At the front of the room, Ms. Manning eyed me coolly.

"Skye," she said. "Welcome back. We have some recent additions to the class, so you'll find your usual seat is currently occupied. You can take a seat in the back, where I've brought in extra chairs."

I cast my eyes toward my usual seat behind Cassie, and my heart lurched. As if in slow motion, a sheet of glossy blond hair swung to one side, and I found myself meeting Raven's piercing glare. I knew it was just in my head, but I could have sworn I almost saw the shadow of wings beating menacingly behind her. Trying not to shake, I turned toward the back of the room.

Ms. Manning had indeed brought in extra desks, and the back row was crowded. I spotted an empty seat and made my way toward it, focused only on getting away from Raven. I could feel Asher moving right behind me, shadowing me, focused on another empty seat in the back row. He must have noticed Raven, too, because I heard him take a sharp breath. But after that, I wasn't concerned about what Asher was doing anymore.

Because in the seat next to mine, sitting stick straight and watching me intently, was Devin.

His eyes, as always, were the bluest blue and so hard to read. I had no idea how he felt to see me, but as I sat in the empty seat and tried not to look over, I was overtaken by a rush of emotions. Fear, panic—and something else. Something harder to define. I felt trapped in my own confusion.

On my right, Asher threw his arm around my shoulders possessively. Devin didn't even flinch.

It was starting again.

When the bell rang to signal the end of homeroom, Asher stood up with me. Devin stayed seated, avoiding all eye contact with either of us. At the front of the classroom,

Ms. Manning held up her hand for me to stop.

"Stay and chat for a minute, Skye," she said. "I'll give you a late pass for your next class."

I hesitated. Asher glanced from Devin, still sitting in the back of the room, to Ms. Manning and back to me. He raised a questioning eyebrow.

"Go ahead," I said. "I'll see you later." Glancing back at Devin again, he clenched his jaw and left. Ms. Manning cleared her throat.

"Devin?" she said. "Would you come up here for a minute?" Devin looked up, carefully avoiding my gaze. He slung his backpack over his shoulder and walked to the front of the room. I felt something electric thrum in the air between us, but he stared straight ahead. Every fiber of my being wanted to run, to get as far away from him as possible. Ms. Manning sat on her desk, facing us.

"Do we need to talk about this?" she asked. My pulse quickened. *It's like she's reading my mind.*

"What do you mean?" I said slowly.

"Those are some interesting rumors circulating about you. I heard you had Devin's baby last week."

"What?" That was a new one. So I guessed people had noticed that we used to hang out.

I glanced at Devin, but he stayed remote and resolute.

"That is clearly not true," I said.

"I didn't think so," she said. "But at any rate, you need someone to catch you up on the work you missed last week. You two are friends, right? Devin, I thought you could spend study hall with Skye. Fill her in on what we've covered." My heart raced. *No.* I couldn't be alone with Devin.

"Devin and I don't exactly . . ." I struggled for the words.

"We used to be close," he said suddenly, breaking his silence. It felt like years since I had heard his voice, and its calming effect washed over me immediately. "But we're not anymore." He kept his eyes trained straight ahead, never once looking at me. My pulse quickened, but I said nothing.

"Well," Ms. Manning said, "in that case, all Skye needs is a tutor. Nothing more." She scribbled down something and handed each of us a late pass.

We left the room one after the other. In the empty hallway, Devin finally looked at me.

Maybe it was the shock of eye contact after all this time. Maybe it was fear. The hallway faded. *Oh no*, I thought. *It's happening again.* I was having a vision.

In a flash, Devin's body was pressed against mine, backing me into the row of lockers. But it wasn't cool, smooth metal that I felt behind me. The floor had prickled up into frosted grass, and I was leaning against a tree under a canopy of night. Devin's blue eyes flashed intensely as he let his hands trail down my arms. His lips were so close to mine. I could feel the feathery touch of his breath as it grazed my neck, leaving a trail of tiny shivers in its wake.

He's going to kiss me, I thought. *I want him to.*

Then the hallway came rushing back, and Devin was still standing there, several feet away from me. He gave me one long look. If he had been capable of expressing any kind of emotion, I might have understood. His eyes might have been mournful, or guilty, or apologetic. Instead, his features were still as calm and Zen as ever. Impassive. His face was empty.

Then he turned and walked down the hall away from me.

I realized I'd been holding my breath, and now I struggled to catch it. Behind me, the sound of boots on the linoleum floor drew closer as Devin disappeared around the corner.

"Hey," Ardith said, her bangles jangling softly as she came to a stop. "Come on. I'll walk you to your next class."

Neither of us said anything, but I knew she'd seen the moment between me and Devin. I got the sense that she knew exactly what I was feeling, and I was grateful that she didn't try to talk to me about it. I knew she wouldn't tell Asher. I don't know how I knew, but I did.

For once, it was nice to have a friend who really understood. Even if she wasn't human.

I couldn't focus for the rest of the morning. I kept replaying the vision, absently touching my neck when I thought no one was looking. His eyes haunted me, lifeless, empty.

At lunch, I found Cassie, Ian, and Dan already sitting around our usual table in the cafeteria. I grabbed my typical lunch—a turkey sandwich and an apple—and slid in next to them.

"You're *so* famous," Cassie said, beaming. "Or should I say, *infamous*?"

"And just think, we're in your inner circle." Dan grinned. "I feel so lucky."

"Privy to all your secrets," Ian joked.

"I know." I smiled and unwrapped my sandwich and took a bite. "I kinda like it," I added through a mouthful of turkey.

As the four of us joked, I glanced around the cafeteria. People did seem to be glancing over at us more than usual. The table where the skiers—my former teammates—usually sat, was no exception. Ellie, in particular, was eyeing us. When she caught me glancing over, she turned to Meredith Sutton and whispered in her ear. They both looked up at Asher, who was waiting in line. My hands curled involuntarily into fists under the table.

Ardith strolled up then, her tray hovering tentatively above our table. "Is it okay . . . ," she said softly, "if I . . . ?"

Dan blushed. Ardith was clearly the most stunning girl in the room, with her glossy chestnut hair and flawless olive skin. Dan wasn't the only guy staring at her. "Of course," he said, moving down on the bench so that Ardith could squeeze in. As she was about to sit, someone hip-checked her from the side, and her tray went flying forward, spilling buttered pasta all over the cafeteria floor. Suddenly Ardith went from soft-spoken and earthy to angry goddess. She turned on the person behind her, eyes flashing and hair spiraling out in a fan. The guy was one of the new kids from RSH, tall, with a lean, wiry build and shoulder-length blond hair.

"Do you have something you want to say to me?" the guy asked.

"Only to watch where you're going," she spat. By the salad bar, Gideon and Asher looked up from their trays and tensed. Two of the other new kids walked up behind the blond guy, flanking him.

"Is there a problem, Lucas?" one of them said.

"Your friend needs to watch where he's going." Ardith's tone was shockingly tough.

"I think he was watching just fine," the other said. I thought, for a moment, that I detected a slight lilt to his voice—almost like an accent—before it faded away into the din of the cafeteria.

Dan stood up and moved to her side.

"Hey," he said. "Are we all cool here?" He was making his voice deeper, and Cassie coughed back a laugh. Before he could say anything further, Gideon and Asher were there, and Dan fell back.

Gideon stepped forward, eyeing Lucas. "I think you guys better get out of here," he said. Lucas glared at him but took a step backward.

The tension in the air was thick. To the rest of the cafeteria, it looked like the new guys clearly felt they had to stake their claim on the school or else. But I knew the truth. They were Guardians, and this was our first warning.

It's only a matter of time. That's what the notebook had said, right? Not for the first time, I wondered who had written it.

Lucas made an *I'm Watching You* gesture to Gideon, and he and his friends turned and stalked toward the soda machines.

The Rebels looked livid.

Dan sat back down at the table and stared at his stack of fries.

"You gonna eat those?" Ian asked.

"What? Oh, yeah," Dan said. "Help yourself."

Cassie's face clouded over. "Oh my god, Dan, really?" Dan looked up.

"Really, what?"

"I get that you think she's hot, but you don't have to be all obvious about it!"

"What? I didn't even say anything."

"No, but I can *tell*. It's, like, oozing out of you."

"Oozing? Really?"

"Shut up," Cassie said, standing up and shoving a fry into his ear. Ian and I burst into laughter. "I've got things to do after school today," she said crisply. She grabbed her crutches and huffed off.

"Cass, come on!" Dan scrambled after her, leaving his fries untouched on the table. "Don't be like that!"

"Oh, so now I'm like *that*!" Cassie's voice trailed after her.

"His loss." Ian grabbed a fry off Dan's plate.

No matter how much we try to keep things around us from changing, I realized, standing up and walking my tray over to the conveyer belt, *the universe tends toward chaos.*

"Let that be a warning to you," a cold voice said, low in my ear. I turned around, and found myself face-to-face with Raven. "Your little Rebel boyfriend can't protect you all the time," she said. "So you better start learning to protect yourself. Because wherever you go, whatever you do, we're watching you." She turned to leave, winking at me over her shoulder just before she pushed through the cafeteria doors.

As I walked through the crowded halls, my hands were shaking so hard that I had to grasp the handle of my book bag to keep them steady. I felt so distant from every other student pushing past me. The thought occurred to me that I might never feel like one of them again.

I kept pushing and didn't even realize that the bell had rung until the hall cleared out and I found myself walking alone.

Devin was already sitting at a table in the library by the history stacks. He looked up when I walked in, then looked back down at his notebook. I slid into a chair across from him.

My heart beat uncontrollably. I didn't want him to sense

my panic, but it was hard just to breathe. Even so, the longer we sat there in silence, the calmer I began to feel. It was his Guardian presence, the serenity that always radiated from him. I'd forgotten what that felt like. I closed my eyes, and realized that my hands had stopped shaking. When I opened them again only a second later, Devin was looking at me. He closed his notebook.

"I'll let Ms. Manning know this isn't going to work," he said, looking away. "She'll find someone else to tutor you." Then he stood up, shifted his backpack from one shoulder to the other, and walked out of the library without once lifting his eyes.

I stared after him, watching the door swing on its hinges.

I drove Cassie and Dan back to Cassie's right after school, leaving them to sort things out. By the time I pulled out of the driveway, they were kissing, so the effects of their lunchtime fight must not have been very lasting. I headed home, letting relief overtake me when I pulled into my own driveway. I threw my backpack down by the front door and collapsed onto the porch swing. A breeze blew in from the mountains, bringing another tantalizing hint of spring. Maybe winter would thaw soon. The sky would stay lighter longer, and the nights wouldn't feel quite so dark.

My arms and legs felt restless, and there was a burning energy inside me. I couldn't go into town, and no one had gone over the catch-up homework with me. I felt like if I didn't get up and do something, my restlessness was going to eat me alive. If this had been a normal winter afternoon, I'd have been at ski practice. But I'd quit the team, too scared of how my powers might manifest if I lost control on the slopes.

I needed to move.

As if the energy was guiding me, I got up off the porch swing and jogged inside, calling a hello to Aunt Jo, taking the stairs two at a time to my room. Not waiting for a response, I threw off the sweater dress and boots and dressed in leggings and a sports bra, a long underwear top, and a fleece vest. I bent to lace up my sneakers. I hadn't been for a run in a long time. But I had to do *something*.

My breath formed clouds of steam in the gray afternoon light as my feet pounded against the ground. I pushed myself up the trail in the woods, pumping my arms and breathing in short, regulated breaths the way I did when I was skiing. It felt amazing to be working my body again, to be so in control of it.

Halfway up the trail, a clearing opened up into a view of the valley below. I stopped there to rest and stared out over the mountain panorama. The light began to shift, and clouds moved in, tempting me.

Focus your energy. Find the switch.

The clouds took the shape of rolling waves, resembling the sea. I rocked back and forth on my heels, and the clouds rolled back and forth with me. I crouched low, and the clouds descended on the valley, so thick I couldn't see a thing. I stood up, and they wisped out into a fine mist, swirling around me. I closed my eyes and wished for snow. When I opened them again, snowflakes floated from the sky, catching on my eyelashes.

It didn't let up. More snowflakes followed as I jogged back down the mountain, coating my ponytail and soaking through the sleeves of my shirt. By the time I got back home, it was flurrying, accumulating on the ground, a soft layer of white drowning out every other thought but one: I had done this.

I vowed to go for another run again the next day. I was grounded, after all. I had all week.

When I walked into the kitchen, shaking snow from my hair, I stopped short. Aunt Jo was sitting at the kitchen table with Asher. The two of them were stiff and awkward. Aunt Jo's eyes were narrowed suspiciously. They looked up when they saw me.

"Skye," Aunt Jo said. "Asher just came by to drop off a book you left at school."

"Oh," I said, still breathing hard from my run and marveling at the awkwardness I'd stumbled into. "Thanks. Come on, let's go upstairs." Asher smiled politely at Aunt Jo, and followed me upstairs to my bedroom. I closed the door behind us.

"Wow, I don't think she likes me," Asher said, falling onto my bed. "That's a first."

"How could she not like you?" I asked. "Didn't you charm the pants off her like you do everyone?"

"I tried," Asher said, bewildered and annoyed. "It didn't work."

"Huh." Maybe she thought he'd been with me at the cabin. Maybe she still blamed him for my running away.

"Hey," Asher said, a slow smile tugging at the corners of his mouth as if noticing me for the first time.

"What?" I grinned.

"You look kind of sexy in those running clothes."

"These? This spandex is like a million years old."

"I so don't care. Come here." He reached out his hands to pull me toward him, and I leaned down for a deep, intense kiss as he ran his hands up my legs. Even through the fabric, my skin prickled at his touch. I still had the energy from the clouds pulsing through me, and I felt alive, connected to the earth, to Asher's spicy scent. As if sensing this, he pulled me on top of him on the bed, deepening the kiss with his hand on the back of my neck.

"Wow," he whispered. "What's gotten into you?"

"I just feel good today. Is that so bad?" I batted my eyelashes against his cheek.

"Bad? Hell, it's amazing."

I glanced out the window behind my bed. The stars were moving in the night sky, twinkling on and off, rearranging themselves.

I'm doing that, I thought. I watched them move in different directions, trying to control the pattern of stars. I frowned and stared hard. I had to focus my thoughts. I could do this. I could control this. The stars came together, pulled to the center of the sky as if by some great magnetic force. They formed letters. They were spelling something.

Asher pulled me back down before I could see what.

"Hey," he said. "You okay? Where did you go just then?"

Suddenly I heard footsteps in the hall. *Aunt Jo.* I broke away quickly. Asher groaned.

"Man," he said under his breath, "that *sucks*."

We sat up.

"I'm sorry," I said. "She's . . . been strange since I've been back. Or maybe I've just been used to her being away all the time."

When he didn't respond, I glanced over at him. But I wasn't sure that he had heard me. His eyes had zoned in on my dresser.

"Skye," Asher said suddenly, "what's that?" He stood up abruptly, crossing the room in two strides. He picked up the white feather I'd found at Love the Bean.

"Nothing," I said, reaching for it. He swiftly lifted it out of my reach. "I found it last night."

He let the feather fall from his hand to the floor. The shaft was broken in three places, the fringes bent and mangled where it had been crumpled in his fist.

"That's a Guardian feather," he said. "And that's what I do to Guardians."

"You know," I said, heating up, "I do have Guardian blood in me. I can't change that."

"You're not a Guardian. You chose the Rebellion." He paused, his voice softening. "You chose me."

"I know," I said. "I did. I do! But my powers aren't just dark. I can feel it."

He squinted at me. "You can use that for good."

"I need to understand it. You can't teach me that. No

matter how hard you wish you could." He sighed and turned toward the window, his back to me. I wanted to go to him, but I stayed still. "You can't destroy me if your job is to protect me," I snapped. "So mull that one over."

He raked a hand through his hair and turned, looking at me. He looked apologetic and annoyed at the same time, but at least he wasn't angry anymore.

"I'm sorry." He breathed out. "I just— I see him. In homeroom. Walking down the halls. In the cafeteria. In the library." Had Asher seen us together in the library? It's not like we were doing anything, but still, the idea of him thinking I was warming up to the Guardian who had tried to kill me made me uncomfortable. "And I get so angry. He still looks at you. What right does he have to look at you? I just want to kill him. And I will, Skye. I will. As soon as I get the chance."

"Asher—" I said. "Stop." But he was already brushing past me out of the room. I didn't follow him. Instead, I picked the white feather up off the floor, and brought it over to my dresser.

I started when I lifted my gaze and saw my reflection in the mirror. The girl who stared back at me had silver eyes, flashing in the early evening light. Intense and bright.

Powerful.

That night, Aunt Jo and I ate dinner at the kitchen table in tense silence. I knew she didn't like Asher—that she didn't fully trust me anymore, no matter what she said. And she knew I knew. I believed that she loved me and that she was glad I was back. I believed that I'd scared her when I was gone. At least . . . I *wanted* to believe it. But something felt different between us now.

Why did Aunt Jo distrust Asher so much? He was the one person—the only person, really—who I trusted now. Was she picking up on something I somehow couldn't see?

Before bed, I took the notebook I'd found in the cabin out of my sock drawer.

> *Guardians haunt these woods, watching us. I know they*
> *know. It's only a matter of time.*

How come there wasn't more written in it after that first page? That couldn't have been the only entry. Unless— the Guardians had attacked before he or she could write more? What if the owner of the notebook hadn't written any more—because she or he hadn't lived long enough? Slowly I thumbed through the rest of the notebook. I hadn't noticed it before, but several pages had been ripped out, leaving jagged, torn edges. So maybe there was more, but the writer didn't want anyone to find what he or she had written. What if the pages contained something important? Or dangerous? Something the owner needed to keep hidden, in case a Guardian found the notebook.

Unless . . . the owner of the notebook hadn't ripped out those pages. What if someone else had? Someone who had found the notebook before me.

Were the pages destroyed? Were they hidden some-where?

Maybe there was still a chance that I could find them. And it felt so important that I did.

I woke up to the sound of thunder. It ricocheted off the walls and shook the floor, so loud it felt like it was coming from inside my head rather than from outside. I pulled on dark skinny jeans, rain boots, and a lightweight sweater, and headed down-stairs. The weather had been unpredictable since I'd been back, right along with my erratic moods. Yesterday it had been snowing, and today it was pouring. Once I learned to control my powers, maybe I'd be able to control what kind of weather I inflicted on people. I'd have to work on that.

Ardith met me at the door with an umbrella. "I can't do anything about this rain," she said, frowning. "You are more powerful than you even know. Give me your keys. I'll drive. You concentrate on aiming the lightning away from us. Sound good?"

I grinned. "Okay," I said. I was glad to see her. It was nice to have a reminder that this wasn't in my head.

The drive was treacherous, with actual zigzags of lightning touching down around the car. Thunderstorms were one of my favorite things, and I remembered as a kid going camping with Aunt Jo, the terrified elation of running to shelter to avoid getting hit by a flash. This morning I leaned my forehead against the window on the passenger side and watched the light streak across the sky. I tried to do what I had done with the clouds. It was like painting with my mind, as several bolts flashed and then swirled up, back into the clouds, before they ever hit the ground.

Ardith let out a low whistle. "Asher was right," she said.

"About what?" I asked. "What did he say?"

She glanced sideways at me. "He really believes you can do this. That you're stronger than all of us. He thinks you're going to change things. He's so happy you're on our side. Whatever comes." She smiled warmly. "We both are."

"He told you that?"

"We've known each other a long time. We don't always have to say things out loud to know what the other is thinking."

"Do you . . . ?" I started to say. "I mean, have you

ever . . . ?" I deflected a flash of lightning from hitting the car, sending it spiraling back into the sky.

"Do I love him? No." She laughed softly. Something in me relaxed a little. "My heart will always belong to another."

"Oh." I paused, trying to remember what I had overheard back at the cabin while I'd supposedly been unconscious. "Is it . . . Gideon?"

Glancing at me, she nodded slightly, then gazed back out the windshield.

"What happened?" I asked. I knew I shouldn't overstep my careful friendship with Ardith, but I had to know. "And why did we need him specifically for this mission?"

Ardith took a deep breath. The sky churned with phosphorescent light. "When your parents fell in love and were cast to Earth," she began, "it was the start of a great Truce. There was a tenuous peace for a long time, a balance between the Order and the Rebellion."

"Right," I said.

"But before that, we were at war. That's why we're so afraid of what is coming. Because we've seen the violence that can erupt between the sides when that balance shifts. And it's never shifted like this." She looked at me, then looked away. "The war was vicious and lasted for millennia. I was taken by the Order before I even knew what had happened. I was with Asher, and he—he only looked away for a second, but it was one second that counted. I can't say he's ever quite forgiven himself for it."

I didn't say anything. I didn't know what to say. I just continued to stare out the window, sending bolts of lightning back into the wild morning.

"Gideon came after me," Ardith continued. "We were young and in love. He thought he was invincible. But they caught him. They tortured him, used all kinds of mental tricks, manipulations. They wanted Asher. But Gideon wouldn't give in. He wouldn't sell out his friend."

"He must be so strong," I murmured.

"He was there for a long time." Ardith nodded to herself, and for a moment it seemed like she'd forgotten I was there, so completely was she brought back to the memory. "I don't know how long in human time, because that's not how things work for us. They kept us apart. Eventually he learned their ways—and taught himself to fight back. He beat them at their own game and escaped. He saved me. But it took such a toll on him."

We were pulling up toward school. The rain had slowed to a drizzle, the thunder and lightning more sporadic.

"It had been so long since we'd been together," Ardith continued. Kids were getting out of cars, slamming doors, calling to their friends. I felt a million miles away. "And he'd changed," she said. "He was distracted and moody. Sometimes he would vanish in the middle of a conversation, go somewhere far-off, as if his mind wasn't truly there." She paused. "Someday I am determined to make it up to him and prove that I am as devoted to him as he is to me." She took a deep breath. "But it's so hard, Skye. That's the kind of test you hope you never have to face. I could never love anyone else while Gideon is still alive."

We pulled into a parking space, and Ardith cut the engine. I didn't want to get out of the car.

"That's why we need him," I said quietly. "He's the only Rebel who knows how to fight their mental influence."

Ardith turned to me and nodded. "Not even Oriax could."

"You'll find a way to show you love him," I said, putting my hand on hers. "I know it."

She looked into my eyes, and her smiled was tinged with sadness. "You are going to save all of us," she said. "You're going to destroy the Order. You'll make them pay."

Ardith got out of the car, and I followed. I wanted to be the heroine that they thought I could be. But I felt so far from being ready to fight.

Ardith tossed me back my keys and started for the front archway.

"Asher thinks it's his fault, you know," she said, turning around. "That he let Devin hurt you. He let something like that happen once before. He can't believe he let it happen again."

"That's why he's so intense about protecting me." It made sense now. The worried looks. The fierce insistence that I join the Rebellion. The white feather, crumpled in his fist.

Ardith nodded. "Just so you know where he's coming from. How serious he is."

A lump formed in my throat. I needed to find a way to let him know it wasn't his fault. I was grateful for the Rebellion's protection. But I needed to protect myself.

Homeroom was tense. Devin didn't look at me, and Asher's arm around my shoulders was tighter than it had been the day before. Now I understood why. I couldn't help but look at him in a new way.

When the bell rang, Ms. Manning pulled me aside to let me know I could meet my new tutor after lunch in the library. I glanced over to where Devin had been sitting, but he was already gone. Rather than the twinge of sadness I might have felt the day before, I just felt anger. The Order were monsters if they were willing to use torture to win a war. And the Guardians were just their mindless, soulless puppets. That's all Devin was. If I hadn't understood it before, I did now.

When I walked into the library later that afternoon, another blond kid was sitting in his place. I'd seen him before, with the group of Guardians. My pulse sped up, but I had to remind myself what Asher had said: They'd never do anything out in the open. School is the safest place to be. No matter that Raven had implied otherwise.

I walked toward him.

"Hi," he said. "Skye? Ms. Manning said you needed someone to catch you up on your homework?"

"Yes," I said, sitting down. "Thanks." He opened his notebook, and we started with English. I glanced at him over my textbook. He didn't seem like a Guardian. He seemed normal. Nice, even. And he was *really* smart.

I was so confused.

It's only a matter of time, the notebook had said.

What were they planning?

My body ached to run. To get better, stronger. Protect myself. It was all I could think about.

After school, I was loading books into my locker, fantasizing about the run I was about to take, when Cassie hobbled over to me. Ian wasn't far behind, carrying her books.

"So," she said, "I'm thinking Bean. I'm thinking free chai lattes courtesy of everyone's favorite barista. I'm thinking disaster-movie marathon, your place. Thoughts? Comments? Questions?"

"Still grounded." I shrugged. "But Friday night, it's on. Okay?"

Cassie pouted. "Fine. Man, Aunt Jo is really taking this hard, isn't she?"

I thought about her coldness toward Asher and the general mood around the house.

"Yeah," I said. "She's not happy."

"Well, give it time," Cassie said. "She loves you. She's just glad you're back, that's all."

I hoped that was it.

As soon as I was home, it was school clothes off, running clothes on. I was itching to get out and pound through the trails. The morning's storm had cleared up with my mood, and the air was fresh and clean.

I raced up a different trail this time, feeling the earth crunch beneath my feet, the wind whip at my face. The remaining raindrops on the branches twinkled around me, scattering with each new breeze and falling into my eyes. I felt even more connected than the day before. As I snaked up the path, trees moved, their roots untangling from the earth and then retrenching again in my wake. Branches bowed to let me pass. I was a part of the natural world, working in tandem with it and yet controlling it, too. It was exhilarating and strange.

The end of the trail opened into a clearing at the base of the woods. The sky was beginning to grow too dark for me to continue back through the heavy brush, so instead of doubling back through the trees, I jogged out onto the road. As I ran along, I created a tiny bright ball of fire in my hands, setting it free to guide me in the darkness.

I was just rounding a curve when I heard a staccato noise behind me, growing louder. I sped up, and the noise behind me sped up, too. My body jolted into high alert.

I'm being followed.

Dusk had settled along the tree-lined road. With the orb of light to guide me, I was fine as long as the true darkness held off until I got home. But it also meant that my pursuer had an easy way to track me. Spring was nearing, but it wasn't here yet, and I knew that as soon as the sun set completely, the freezing cold night would fall over the mountains. On the silent road, something crunched on the gravel behind me. I whipped around, my hands raised to throw fire or wind or sleet or whatever I needed to protect myself. I was pretty sure my practice would pay off.

Between my outstretched fingertips, I could just make out a face. Devin's. Our eyes met in the dusk. My body went cold.

"Don't," he called. "Don't attack."

"What do you want?" A familiar voice cut in from behind me. I turned to see Gideon. There was a hollow toughness to his eyes, and anyone could tell from looking at him now that he'd been in some difficult battles before. "Get away from her," he growled. "Leave her alone. Haven't you done enough?"

"She doesn't need you to fight her battles," Devin said calmly, his absolute tranquility radiating to me from where he stood. I began to let my hands fall to my sides. The calming shift in mood seemed to have no effect on Gideon.

"Did you hear me?" Gideon barked. "Leave her *alone*. She doesn't want you anywhere near her. I can't stand to look at you."

Devin looked at me—as if he was asking a question of me with his eyes. As if he expected me to understand what he was thinking. The look in his eyes was almost pleading. *What?* I wanted to say. No, I wanted to scream it. *What do you want?* But I kept silent, tried to look stony even though I was torn up inside. He didn't get to ask me questions. He didn't deserve my sympathy.

When he realized I wasn't going to say another word, he glanced over my shoulder at Gideon. Then he set his jaw, turned, and in a flash of white feathers, he was gone.

"Are you okay?" Gideon asked. His face seemed flushed in the dusk, and his dark hair was wild, as if he'd been running—or flying. "What happened?"

"Nothing," I said. "He was following me. That's all." Even though it was the truth, I realized there was a defensive note in my voice—like I was trying to protect Devin. Gideon frowned. He'd seemed so sweet and laid-back at school—but there was no mercy in his eyes tonight.

"Probably trying to shake you up, make you feel vulnerable." He nodded to himself. "He wants to get back on your good side. So he doesn't attack just yet. He doesn't come off as a threat right away."

I shivered. "You really think that's what he's doing?"

"He's trying to make you think he's asking forgiveness. I've seen it happen before. You're too smart to fall for that."

Am I? I wondered. If Gideon hadn't come along, would I have caved and let Devin talk? Would I have been powerless to his calming presence? Devin and I had spent so much time together. He had helped me so much, believed I could be the warrior he knew I was deep down. He'd pushed me harder than anyone had ever pushed me before. I'd felt so close to him, and when we were both able to break down each other's walls, it came as just as much a shock to him as it did to me.

But when I had stared into his familiar blue eyes just now, he seemed like a stranger.

"I'm glad you were here," I said to Gideon. "Thank you."

"Don't mention it," he said. He stared down the darkening road where Devin had vanished, his gaze losing focus for a second. It was like he was here and, at the same time, so many miles away from where we stood. I shifted slightly, my feet crunching on the gravel. His eyes refocused on me as if suddenly remembering I was there. "Come on. I'll walk you home. It's dark."

I was grateful for his company. He was smaller than Asher but tough and wiry. The intense look in his eyes remained. An idea was already forming in my mind. I just hoped he'd agree to go along with it.

When we got to the front door, I turned to him.

"Ardith told me . . . about your past," I said, trying to think of a way to say what I was thinking.

"Yeah," said Gideon, adjusting his glasses nervously. "I thought she might."

"I'm sorry."

"It's okay. It's good that you know."

"I was hoping," I began. "Would you help me? Will you teach me the tricks you learned? How to fight them?"

The look in Gideon's eyes folded inward to some private place. Pain flashed across his face, like he was reliving something terrible.

"It isn't easy," he said finally. "It took me a long time to learn. And there are . . ." He paused. "Side effects."

"Please," I said plaintively. "I need your help. It's the only way I can take control of all of this." I spread my arms to encompass, well, everything. "I don't want to be vulnerable again, Gideon. What if next time you aren't there to fend him off?"

He looked at me as if trying to appraise whether or not I was worthy. After a couple of seconds, the look in his eyes softened, and he was once again the boy I'd met at school. Poor Gideon. My heart felt so heavy with the weight of his story, I almost wished Ardith hadn't told me.

"I—I want you to be as strong as you can be," he said. "But I don't know if I—if I'm ready. I have to think about it. I need some time."

My hopes fell.

"Okay," I said. "I understand. But when you're ready? I hope you'll find me."

"I will," he said. "I will."

There was a strange energy buzzing through me as I stalked around the house that night. It all felt finally within my grasp—so close I could reach out and touch it. I was taking steps to control my own destiny. Soon I wasn't going to be confused anymore.

Aunt Jo was still tense and standoffish. I didn't know why. She had been okay the night I'd come home—mad but happy I was safe and alive. Was it only just sinking in for her? Or was it something else? This new tension had started right around the night Asher had come over. Was it possible her anger had something to do with him? It didn't make any sense. Asher was charming—even the most difficult of teachers loved him. So why didn't Aunt Jo?

I locked myself in my room to try to tackle some of the mountains of catch-up work I'd been assigned, but my mind wandered and I couldn't focus. Eventually I gave up and got ready for bed early, wondering if Asher would come. I hadn't seen him since study hall, and I realized, laughing to myself, that I missed him. *So this is what it feels like*, I thought, a small private smile stealing across my lips.

I didn't want to spend my time away from him. Every minute that passed was one minute closer to the next time I'd see him again.

When I got back from the bathroom, freshly showered and with my hair knotted on top of my head, I paused. There was something dark resting on my pillow. As I drew closer, I noticed it was a small, delicate, purple flower—the kind that grew along the side of our house in the spring.

It was the same kind of flower that Devin had tried to get me to resurrect. My powers had failed me, and when I'd opened my hands, the flower was still cold and lifeless, a withered brown. The flowers around our house didn't appear to be in bloom yet, so they definitely wouldn't be as purple or alive as the flower that lay on my pillow now. This one had been brought back to life. By a Guardian.

Was it a threat? Or did it mean something else? My mind reeled as I wondered if it was Devin's way of asking for a chance to explain. Did I really want him to?

I placed the flower with the other artifacts I'd been collecting on my dresser: the white feather and the notebook. The confusing ephemera of my life.

I got under the covers and switched off my bedside lamp, but I couldn't quiet my mind. The energy from my run and the adrenaline from everything after pulsed in my ears. Where was Asher?

If Gideon wasn't sure he could teach me to fight the Order's mental manipulation, I needed to find another way. Running was one way to channel my powers. It was a start, but it wasn't intense enough. It was sloppy and freeing—it didn't require the precision I knew I needed in order to focus. Only one thing I knew could do that.

Skiing.

I'd quit the team because I'd been afraid of what my powers might do if I *lost* control in the heat of the moment. My teammates would get hurt. I'd been terrified that I might cause another avalanche, or worse.

But I knew that I had changed. In the woods the night I'd almost died, I'd caused the earth to shake and lightning to crack and trees to split and fall to the ground. And I couldn't control it, couldn't stop it. Now I could feel myself grow stronger with each run. I was learning control.

I'd been so afraid before that night when Devin had tried to kill me. But strangely, I wasn't afraid anymore.

This time I knew that skiing would help me to focus my powers—not threaten the balance within me. Through skiing, maybe I could find what I'd been searching for.

I made a decision right then. The next day, I would rejoin the ski team.

In the morning, Aunt Jo flitted about the kitchen like a trapped bird, not sure what she was doing or where she was going next, only concerned with keeping alight.

"I'll be home for dinner," she said. "What else?" She rested for a second by the counter. She looked tired, like she hadn't been sleeping very well.

"Are you okay?" I asked.

"Me? Fine, fine. You'll call me if you need anything, right?" She'd finished washing the dishes and was still holding an empty mug in her hand, turning it over and over. "Right?"

"Right . . ."

She absentmindedly put the mug in the sink, even

though she'd just washed it, and left the room. A few seconds later, I heard the front door slam and her car start. If it was possible to feel like an outsider in your own home, that's how I felt. Like she couldn't get away from me fast enough. Like she didn't want to talk to me or touch me or even be in the same room.

I finished my cereal and left a few minutes later. On the way to school, I tapped my fingers against the steering wheel in time to the music, giddy at the thought of being back on the ski team. I hadn't realized how much I'd missed it.

Even though it was only March, everything felt like it was coming alive—including me. It had been a long, cold winter, a dark winter, full of fear and an aching I'd never known before. But now the spring was coming and I could feel it at the tips of my fingers and on my cheeks. I could choose what I wanted to be.

The student lot was deserted, and I pulled into a spot close to the front doors. I had gotten to school especially early today. I had a feeling I would run into someone here. And I wanted to be alone with him when I did.

The halls were mostly empty. As I walked, the heavy soles of my boots echoing against the shiny floor, I caught sight of a dark figure retreating at the other end of the hallway. His solid frame was silhouetted against the window.

For a second I thought I'd fallen into one of my dreams, the ones that kept repeating until I could barely remember what the truth was anymore. But this wasn't a dream.

I stopped short.

"Hey," I called. "Hey! Devin!" My voice echoed down the empty corridor. The figure stopped walking and stayed still. His head was lowered as if he was looking at the ground.

I sucked in my breath. Suddenly I wasn't so sure I wanted to do this.

Slowly he turned around and lifted his eyes from the ground in front of him. They were cold, blue as a frozen lake. Memories of Devin came rushing back to me. I remembered the night I first saw him at Love the Bean; the day we met, outside of homeroom; our snowball fight; and the morning after when I woke up lying next to him. How could those eyes, that had looked so sleepy and innocent and surprised to find me in his bed that morning—how could *those eyes* be capable of such coldness? How could they look at me as if I meant nothing to him? As if emotion wasn't something that you felt but that you chose—cold and calculated just like the Order had taught him?

Hadn't he cared about me at all?

Hadn't he *loved* me?

"What do you want?" he asked.

"Did you want to talk to me? I thought . . ." I wasn't sure what I thought. "Didn't you leave me . . . a flower?"

He looked at me questioningly.

"Look, I have a lot of questions," I said. "And I think I deserve some answers."

He looked away. "What makes you think I have the answers?"

"Because you're the one who tried to kill me."

His attention snapped back to me. His eyes were hard.

"Go ahead, then."

But suddenly confronted with the idea of finding out the truth, my heart shrank. If he didn't love me, it would hurt. Even though I was devoted to Asher, had chosen him completely, there was something about the Guardian that I felt so sad about giving up. If he didn't love me—or if he did love me and had agreed to kill me anyway—well, then, the pain would be like the sword he'd stabbed me with, twisting sharply in my gut.

Suddenly I didn't want to be hurt again by him. By anyone, really. The Skye who had waffled back and forth for so long between the Order and the Rebellion—between

Devin and Asher—seemed like a person in a book who I had read about once. Someone remote and fictional. She wasn't me. She never would be again.

"Never mind," I said. "I don't want to know." I started to turn, to walk away back down the empty hall.

"I dreamed about you," he blurted out. His voice broke into the silent hallway, catching me off-guard. "Every night . . . after it happened. I still do."

I turned around in shock. "What?"

He looked just as shocked as I did at the words that had flown out of his mouth. But he kept talking. "I thought you were dead. When I drew the sword out and you fell, and . . . *he* . . . pulled you away, I thought you were dead. But then when none of the Gifted would tell me the status of the mission, I knew they didn't know. And I had to hope that if they didn't know, it meant you were still alive, blurring out your own destiny and that of the people whose lives you touch. Hiding from the Order. I had to hope that I had failed. And you were still alive."

"Why are you telling me this?" I felt shaky, my resolve cracking.

"If you're still able to do that—blur destiny—then soon there will be no such thing as destiny at all. And the Order will be pointless. They know that, Skye. It's not safe for you here." He paused, his voice level and even, as if he wasn't affected by what he was saying, as if he had no fear at all. *How could someone seem to be so full of so many different emotions and yet be incapable of feeling any of them?* "You're going to destroy us all," he said. The calm in his voice was maddening.

"Now you're warning me?"

"No," he said softly. "I'm just telling you the facts."

"Skye, Skye, Skye," a voice chimed like a crystal bell behind me.

Devin's head snapped up and his eyes focused over my shoulder. I didn't have to turn around to know that Raven was standing there, preventing me from asking what I had been about to.

"Raven," Devin said warningly under his breath.

"I'm *so* glad you're both here."

"What do you want?" My voice was cold, hard.

"Who, me? I was just looking for my fated one." She sauntered over and offered Devin a hand. He glanced at me before reaching out—and taking it. "We're bonded now, Skye, didn't he tell you?"

What? I looked at him, my eyes wide, but he stared at the ground.

"We underwent the ceremony just a couple of days ago,"

Raven continued, her fingers tightening around his bicep possessively. *As if I might still want him. As if I might still trust that the angel in front of me wanted me to succeed.* The idea was so horrible, it made my blood seethe. I could never want Devin. I hated him. *Hated him.* I heard the locker doors that lined the hallway begin to rattle as the floor beneath us shook. Raven raised an eyebrow. "Don't be mad, Skye. He thought he'd killed you, after all."

Involuntarily I found myself backing away.

Raven was soulless, dangerous, the perfect, obedient Guardian. I knew what she was capable of, and if she and Devin were now bonded, it meant the Gifted had another way to make sure Devin stayed in line.

It also meant that even though it had been crazy to think it, even for a second, there was no way I could ever trust him.

I was so upset that I had to jam my hands into the pockets of my jeans to keep from shaking. What was wrong with me? How could I be disappointed that an angel whose job had been to kill me was celestially bonded to another?

Maybe it was because my gut was telling me something else.

Deep down I *knew* that, while the Order had control over Devin's mind and body, they couldn't control his heart. They could force a sword into his hand and force Raven into his life, but they couldn't force him to be happy. And when I looked at him, I knew he wasn't. There were so many things he was holding back. His eyes told me all I needed to know.

There was someone good in there, someone who wanted desperately to escape. I knew it even if he didn't.

"Oh, Skye, don't go so soon," Raven said sweetly.

"I hope you two are happy together," I said. "But you both better stay far, far away from me."

"Skye, wait," Devin blurted.

"Devin," Raven said sharply, and he fell back.

I turned and walked away down the hall.

Asher was waiting for me at my locker, wearing his familiar beat-up army jacket and jeans. There was something so comforting about seeing him there waiting for me. He was my rock, my reality, and the weird encounter with Devin and Raven was just another bad dream. Asher was the one I woke up to. He broke into the slightly wicked grin that used to make me fight back a smile. But now I let myself get lost in it.

"I missed you last night," I said, inserting myself under

his arm and snuggling in. He kissed the top of my head.

"Gideon told me what happened on the road. Are you okay?"

Was I? I thought about all that had happened in the past twenty-four hours: focusing more of my powers, asking Gideon to help me, my decision to rejoin the ski team. Even my confrontation with Devin. All of it felt like it was leading me toward some kind of moment of clarity.

"I've never been better," I said, standing on my tiptoes to kiss him. His lips were soft and warm and sent tiny pinpricks of light through my nerve endings. He wove a hand up my neck and through my hair.

"Mmm," he murmured. "So I don't need to kick anyone's ass?"

"Not unless you want to." I grinned, pulling away.

"Oh, you have no idea." Asher's eyes clouded over.

"Get a room, you two," Cassie said, her locker door slamming shut next to us.

"You're one to talk!" I yelled, swatting her. *"Babes."*

"Babes?" said Asher. He turned to me. "Really?"

"Shut up." Cassie laughed. "Dan said it first."

The bell rang, and we headed for homeroom.

Devin was standing at the opposite end of the hall,

watching us. Alone. When our eyes met, he turned and walked through the doorway.

Cassie and I were the first ones at lunch. She sat across the table, sipping her Odwalla juice and eyeing me.

She glanced around to make sure the boys were out of earshot. "That was cute this morning," she said.

"What was cute?" I asked, playing absently with the crust of a slice of bread.

"*Almost* as cute as me and Dan. Are you trying to compete with us? Because it won't work. We've already won."

"Are you talking about Asher?"

"The very same." She grinned.

"Well," I said, "I hate to break it to you, but you guys don't stand a chance."

"No, but seriously, though," Cassie said, spearing a sprig of broccoli. "You seem really happy." She paused. "I've never seen you like this. So are you? Happy? Tell me for real. Because it's about time you were."

"I am," I said, unable to stop myself from smiling stupidly. Everything in my life was converging toward what I wanted. I was on a path, and the trees were bowing to reveal the way to me. "I really think I am."

"So . . . have you guys done it yet?"

"Cassie!"

"Well, you were staying with the guy in a cabin! In the woods! Cut off from the rest of humanity! Seems like plenty of opportunities might have arisen."

"We're not—" I started to say. "We haven't—" but stopped. Why *hadn't* we come closer? It's not like I hadn't wanted to. There were a few times at the cabin when we'd been alone, but I'd still been recovering. And now that Aunt Jo was home every night, we ran the risk of being interrupted—like the other night. "It just hasn't . . . felt right yet." I paused.

But that wasn't exactly it. The real reason was much more complicated. I was afraid. And not for the obvious reasons. When I was alone with Asher, our lips sparking in the night when they touched, I had so much trouble controlling my powers. He had that effect on me, the singular ability to turn my blood hot and make the room sweltering and cause the hems of my jeans to go up in flames. What if things got *really* intense and something way worse happened? In the cabin, we put the fire out in time. What if next time I hurt him?

No, I definitely wasn't ready yet.

"Why?" I said suddenly. "Have you and Dan?" Cassie gave me a smug look. "Really?" I gasped.

"Not yet," she said, grinning and raising her eyebrows. "Because of, you know, cement leg." She gestured to the blue cast. "But we've come *very* close. If you know what I mean."

"Wow, thank you for painting that mental picture."

"Oh, don't mention it. You'd be surprised, actually—"

"Okay, Cassie, I have to *keep* being friends with Dan. I'm drawing a line."

"Wuss," she said. She took a sip of juice and clapped her hands together. "I'm so glad you're home," she sang. "I didn't have anyone to talk to about boys! I can't exactly talk about Dan to, well, *Dan*. You know?"

"Ian said no way, huh?"

"Before I could even finish the question." She laughed. "So . . . Devin. That is definitely over, right?"

"*So* over," I said. *You have no idea.* I glanced up, and she was eyeing me. "Why? What did you hear?"

"Nothing," she said, going back to her lunch. "Not a thing." She crunched a carrot and muttered, just loud enough for me to hear, "Except for that *way* defensive answer . . ."

A group of the new transfers from River Springs High walked by our table, and I was pulled out of my thoughts as the air around us seemed to grow colder.

"Those new kids are so creepy," Cassie said, shivering dramatically. "I feel like they're going to kill us in our sleep or something."

"Yeah," I said. "Me too."

You have no idea, I thought for the second time in that conversation.

After school I marched to the gym, and into the office of the director of athletics.

"Skye," she said, surprised, looking up from some paperwork. "Looking for Coach Samuelson?"

"I am," I said. "Is he around?"

"You're in luck." She smiled. "They haven't left for the slopes yet. He should be in his office."

"Thanks," I replied, turning before she could ask me anything else. I walked into his office as he was stuffing some equipment into a duffel bag.

"Skye," he said. "Coming to watch the match?"

"Actually, I want to rejoin the team," I announced.

He paused and eyed me up and down.

"You miss it?"

"So much."

"You more committed this time?"

"You bet." I put my hands on my hips like I knew

what I was talking about.

He puckered his face in thought.

"Can you come today?" he asked. "Race against Brighton Academy?"

"Yes!" I cried, jumping up and down. "Thank you!"

"I'll just bump Ellie down to third."

"What?"

"Ellie," he said. "To third." He put his hands on my shoulders and looked me square in the eye. "You know," he said. "A little competition is healthy. Fuels the proverbial fire. You could be the team captain next year after Maggie graduates, you know."

"I could?" I asked, perplexed.

"Parker, you're my star skier! Of course you could. But you were gone, and you have some catching up to do. Ellie's really proven herself to have the grit I need in a team captain." He looked at me like he was looking straight into my soul. "Do you have that grit, Skye? Can I count on you?"

I swallowed. "Yes," I said, much more confidently than I suddenly felt.

He patted me on the shoulder. "Good," he said. "Then prove it. Beat Ellie's time today. Then we'll talk."

Great, I thought, as he slung the duffel bag over his

shoulder and walked out of the office. *Like Ellie needs another reason to hate me.*

Sucking in a deep breath, I followed.

The top of the mountain was cold and white. The clouds moved slowly, changing shapes, as if winking at me knowingly. *We know what you can do, Skye.*

Good, I thought. *Let me show you.*

I was racing against Claire Fincher, arguably the best skier on the Brighton team. I'd faced her before, last year. She was famous for being competitive and fierce, and the last time we'd raced against each other, she'd knocked into me, drawing blood. She was terrifying.

Coach Samuelson came up behind me and put his hand on my back. "You can do this, Parker," he said.

I let his words sink into my gut as I pulled my goggles down over my eyes. I could do this. Claire was fierce, but I had power. And I wasn't just trying to beat her— or even Ellie's time two spots after me. I had a purpose. The thought of finally controlling my powers sent a rush through me so heady that for a moment I saw stars.

At the signal, we both pushed off. The wind wrapped itself around me, and soon I was flying down the mountain. I could feel every bump, every slight turn in the course. I was moving so fast that I saw nothing but whiteness. I felt nothing but joy.

I crouched lower as I took a sharp bend, the wind smacking me hard in the face. I spat back at it—and then, as if by magic, it seemed to retreat. *Not magic*, I thought. *I'm doing this.* The clouds swooped in, surrounding me and then whipping away behind me—covering my trail. I could hear the swish of Claire's skis, keeping pace, and I glanced back to see if she was okay.

"Skye!" her voice rang out. "The weather changed! Can you see?"

"I'm fine!" I called. "Are you?"

"I think so!"

I trained my eyes on the clouds and dispersed them, letting the feel of the ground beneath my skis guide me the rest of the way down the mountain. I wanted control, but I didn't want to win by blocking her way. My goal was to beat her, fair and square.

Out of the corner of my eye, I saw Claire pull up alongside me. I crouched lower, leaning into the wind.

Focus your energy.

Find the switch.

Flip it.

I pulled ahead, pummeling toward the finish line.

Everything was within my grasp. The power rushed through me, and I no longer felt like I was skiing down the mountain. I felt like I was a *part* of it. I pushed myself forward, slicing across the finish line and swishing to a hard stop. I stared back up at the mountain, breathing hard, alive. I knew that I was right—this was what I needed.

Claire came tumbling over the finish line, screeching to a halt beside me.

"Amazing time, Parker!" Coach called. "You beat your own record!" But I didn't need him to tell me that. I already knew.

Claire drew up beside me. "Whoa," she said, pulling her goggles up. "That was crazy intense."

"I know." I panted. "Good race. You were incredible."

"Not as incredible as you, Skye, jeez. You going out for captain next year?"

"Yeah," I said, pulling my own goggles up. "Yeah, I think I am."

"Me too." She grinned. "Here's to more races in our future." She reached out to shake my hand but stopped cold. "Dude," she said. "Those are some wild contacts."

Contacts? "Oh, um, yeah." I pulled my goggles back down. "I'll see you later," I said abruptly, turning and racing for the equipment house. The sky was already fading into twilight and the first stars of evening were beginning to twinkle on. I locked myself in the bathroom, pulled up my goggles, and faced myself in the mirror, grabbing the sink with both hands.

Claire was right. I'd never before seen my eyes burn a brighter silver than they were right then.

I tried to keep my adrenaline in check as I trooped back to the bus with the rest of the team. I was one of the last girls to get on, and as I walked down the aisle, I got the weird feeling that the others were watching me. Had I been that fast? That powerful? Ellie in particular eyed me as I passed her. I swung into an empty seat behind the one she shared with Maggie.

"So you're going out for captain," Ellie said, leaning over the back of her seat. "You know I am, too."

"I know," I said.

She shook her head. "You think you can just waltz back in here after leaving the team like that?" She spat the words. "What makes you think we want you?"

"I don't care if you want me," I said, my temper rising. "I want to be back." I would have been lying if I'd said I'd never dreamed about being captain of the team my senior year. I looked her square in the eye. "And I want to be captain." Ellie had been so smug all winter when she thought she'd snaked Asher away from me. It must have been just killing her to see us together.

"You would," she said. "It's just so typical of you. You think everything you want should be yours. And you don't care who you hurt in the process." She smirked at Maggie. "Ian was right about you."

I felt my cheeks flush.

"What?" I said, suddenly feeling sick.

"When we hooked up last weekend, at Carmen Shane's party." She tossed her blond curls over her shoulder. "He said you only care about what you want. That you're too wrapped up in yourself to care about anybody else."

Could that possibly have been true? Would Ian say something like that?

But then it hit me: the change I'd seen in him the night I got home. Maybe Ellie had given him that confidence. On the one hand, I was happy for him. But my stomach dropped as I thought about him saying such cruel things. Is that how he really felt about me? That I was selfish and didn't care who I hurt as long as I got what I wanted?

"You're one to talk," I shot back without pausing to think. "You're always taking what's mine."

"Or what you think is yours," she snapped. "Ian's not your property. And you're not taking captain from me, either. I worked too hard for this. It clearly doesn't mean as much to you, seeing as you were ready to just throw it away."

My cheeks burned, but I couldn't think of any kind of retort that didn't make me sound like the worst person on the planet. I fell back in my seat.

When the bus pulled up at school, Ian was sitting on the front steps. I saw him smile as Ellie wrapped her arms around him and kissed him. He glanced up, and our eyes met through the bus window. His smiled faltered, but only for a second. Then he took her hand, and the two of them walked toward the parking lot.

By the time I got off the bus, most of the girls on the team had left.

"Awesome job today, Parker," Coach said, coming around the side of the bus. "You keep that up and you'll make captain for sure."

"Thanks," I said, watching Ellie and Ian getting smaller in the distance.

Gideon and Ardith were sitting on the hood of my car, and Asher stood, leaning against the driver's side with his arms crossed. The collar of his jacket was pulled up against the wind. When they saw me approaching, Asher got up quickly. "We were waiting for you," he said. "How did it go?"

I smiled. "Coach thinks I could make captain."

Asher looked at me intently. "And did you—feel, anything?"

I nodded, squeezing his hand. "It felt amazing," I said.

A smile lit up his face. Behind him, from the hood of the car, Gideon watched me intently. Was he still trying to make up his mind? Maybe this would prove to him that I was ready.

"I knew you could do this," Asher said. "Actually, it makes total sense. You don't let anyone boss you around. Your powers were never going to emerge with Devin and me yelling at you."

I was about to say that yes, it was true—I'd needed to do it on my own. But the parking lot began to fade around me. Still feeling strong from the race, I was ready this time for the vision. I closed my eyes and tried to stay standing.

When I opened them again, I was in the upstairs hallway

of my house. *Strange*, I thought. I glanced to my right, at the door to my bedroom, which was slightly ajar. Light spilled out into the dark hallway, and a pair of scuffed-up boots were just visible at the foot of the bed. Asher's? To my left was the bathroom. The door was open and the lights were off. I peeked over the railing, down the stairs. The whole house was dark and silent. Where was Aunt Jo?

Directly ahead of me was her bedroom. I walked toward it, almost like gravity was a force inside, pulling me along. I ran my hands along the walls to guide me in the semi-darkness. The door to Aunt Jo's bedroom wasn't closed all the way. I pushed it open and turned on the light.

Her room was empty. The bed was unmade. Clothes were draped over the chair in the corner. She wasn't home yet. I turned toward the closet, and slowly, slowly reached my hand out to open it.

What was I looking for?

Rows of Aunt Jo's familiar sweaters hung in a faded rainbow. Her jeans and work pants were folded haphazardly on a tower of shelves, poking out and flopping over the edge like she went to pull out several pairs each morning before deciding on the right one. I ran my hands over the soft fabric of her coats, lingered on the laces of a pair of hiking boots. These were familiar to me, comforting. The shapes and images, colors and fabrics that populated my childhood.

In the corner of the closet was a stepladder, and I climbed onto it, peering at the upper shelves. That's where I spotted it. A nondescript, plain, unmarked shoe box. As if time were moving in slow motion, I opened the lid. . . .

The parking lot came rushing back. Asher, Gideon, and Ardith were peering at me. I was still standing, but the ground pitched beneath me now, and I leaned against the side of the car for support.

"What did you see?" Asher asked, reaching out to help steady me.

"Aunt Jo's closet?" My hands were shaking. "I'm not sure."

"I wonder what it means," Ardith said.

Gideon stayed silent.

As Asher drove the four of us back to my house, I felt jittery and distracted. What *had* I seen? Part of me wondered if the shoe box was real. If something was in there that I was meant to find.

Aunt Jo wasn't home from work yet, so we went out onto the deck and pulled several of the Adirondack chairs into a circle. The early evening was clear and bright. The mountains loomed over us in the distance.

"I *love* Colorado," Ardith cooed. "The mountains are so passionate. They just make me want to run to the top and yell obscene things to the valleys below."

"Ardith," Gideon said. "Really." But he was smiling, and in the light his brown eyes looked softer than they had the night we'd encountered Devin. He put his hand on Ardith's, and she smiled adoringly at him.

"It's true! Don't you want to?"

Asher was leaning back in his chair, legs splayed out in front of him and a grin on his face. "I like Colorado, too," he said. I glanced at him, and he met my eye somewhat conspiratorially. Was he implying he could stay here? *Would* stay here? With me?

"There's something majestic about it," Gideon said, smiling. "Like there's some ancient magic in those mountains." He looked at me with interest. "When you're skiing, you're more connected to the forces around you. Skiers are very connected to the natural world. To the ebb and flow of life. I'm not surprised the Rebel powers are so strong in you."

Asher and I looked at each other, breaking into smiles at the same time. I knew that we were both remembering the avalanche I'd caused.

"Just like with skiing," Gideon said, "the key to

unlocking the true potential of your powers is control."

"Great." Asher laughed. "Skye needs more control issues."

"Hey!" I whipped at him with my scarf.

"I'm serious," Gideon continued. "If you want to learn how to fight the Order's mental manipulation, I will help you."

The group fell silent. Ardith looked uncomfortably between us.

"You'll teach me?" I asked. "Really?"

"Gid, are you sure?"

There was anguish in Ardith's eyes. I knew she felt torn. I needed this to get stronger, more powerful. But would it take a toll on Gideon's mind? Or my own?

"I'll try," he said, nodding absently to himself, as if confirming some question only he could hear. "Instead of relaxing your mind—which is what you want to do when you're trying to make it rain, or say, ignite a spark—when you're blocking your mind, what you're working on is building and deconstructing walls."

He paused, making sure I understood. I nodded and he continued. "Now close your eyes. What do you see?"

"Darkness. Nothingness."

"Good. Now I want you to picture a wall going up. Brick

by brick. A thick, impenetrable wall."

In my mind's eye, I pictured bricks stacking themselves one on top of another. Blocking out the darkness. Creating further darkness.

"Okay," I said, my eyes still closed. "I'm doing it."

"Now I'm going to try to do what a Guardian might do—try to subtly influence your mood and feelings, what you're thinking. And I want you to recognize it, and block it out."

I closed my eyes again. Within moments an unearthly calm began to creep over me. I felt secure, comfortable, happy. At peace. It reminded me of Devin's perpetual state of calm. This time, deep down, I knew that it wasn't real.

As soon as I realized it was mental manipulation, a fresh wave of calm washed over me. But I didn't want to block it out. I wanted to feel this calm and happy forever. If I joined the Order, would I feel this way all the time? I really could see what Devin had been saying about the Order this whole time. How wonderful would a place with no troubles be?

But something about it didn't feel right. Like when I was skiing and the ground beneath me shifted dangerously, I knew I couldn't trust this feeling.

Slowly and with great effort, I began to stack the bricks again, but they were so heavy. My mind was buckling under the weight of them. The calm persisted, forcing them down in my hands. I couldn't lift them anymore. They were too heavy . . . and the calm washed over me, obliterating all other feelings in the world. I was floating on a cloud, blissful, oblivious. . . .

Someone had taken hold of my arms, and I heard a voice. "Skye. Skye!" The peaceful tranquility washed away, and as I opened my eyes, I found Asher, Ardith, and Gideon staring at me. A cold, empty unease sat in my chest.

"Are you okay?" Gideon asked, still holding my arms. "Was that too much for a first try?" I blinked several times, trying to refocus my vision. The cold pit in my chest began to soften, breaking into fine pieces and scattering away with each breath I took. I continued to breathe deep, steadying myself.

"Skye," Asher said, looking concerned. "Answer us. Are you okay?"

"Yes," I said faintly. I felt violated, used, manipulated. I understood now how Gideon couldn't endure a constant stream of this and fully make it back. It took something from you. Maybe that was the way to recognize when the Order was influencing your mind. This—this was abuse.

"You did well for your first time," Gideon said. He looked like he was trying to focus his own eyes, too. I wondered if it was hard for him to see me go through it, if it brought back memories he'd rather bury. "You came very close."

"It's easier now than it will be when you're up against a real Guardian," Ardith said, coming up to me and putting her hand on my back. "He learned from the Order, but he's nowhere near as strong as they are."

My palms had begun to sweat and nausea was sweeping through me. I leaned back in the chair and closed my eyes. Somewhere, in the far reaches of my mind, I heard a car pull up in the driveway and cut the engine. There were footsteps on the gravel leading up to the house. I opened my eyes and sat up quickly.

"Aunt Jo's home." The footsteps were now walking through the house. Asher glanced uneasily at the door to the deck. Gideon and Ardith shifted as the door slid open and Aunt Jo walked out. Her eyes moved from Asher to the Rebels and then landed on me. Something was raging in her eyes, but I had no idea what.

"Skye," she said. "You're still grounded."

"I know," I said quickly. "But I figured—if we were at my house—"

"Everybody out," she interrupted. The quiet in her

voice was almost scarier than when she really got mad and was yelling all over the place. This was a side of Aunt Jo that I'd never seen, and I didn't like it.

"These are my friends," I said, my voice rising. "You can't—"

"It's my house," she said. "I can."

"It's okay, Skye," said Asher quietly, putting his hand on my back. "We'll leave."

"No!" I shouted, turning to Aunt Jo. "Why are you doing this? You would never kick out Cassie and Dan."

"I don't know these new friends of yours," she said. "Why have I never met them before?"

"They're . . . new in school," I said, glancing at Gideon and Ardith. "They're friends of Asher's." Aunt Jo met Asher's eyes. Something passed between them—so quickly I wondered if I'd imagined it.

"Leave," she said, her voice like cold steel.

Asher bent in to kiss my cheek. "I'll be here," he whispered. "Outside. Around. All night, okay? If you need me."

"Thank you," I whispered back. I wanted to squeeze his hand, but Aunt Jo was watching me in a seriously unsettling way.

Asher nodded once, politely, to Aunt Jo as he left the deck. Ardith and Gideon followed him.

I stood up, too, facing her and crossing my arms.

"I don't understand what I did," I said, totally aware of the fact that I sounded like a little kid. "Why do you hate me all of a sudden?"

"Hate you?" Her eyes softened, and she looked so tired suddenly. "I don't hate you."

"Then why are you being so mean to me? What did I do? I said I was sorry about leaving. But you can't stop me from leaving again, Aunt Jo. I'll be eighteen in less than a year, and I'm going to go to college soon, or . . ." I trailed off, wondering, for the first time, if college was still possible for me. What if my powers got stronger? What if war really was coming again?

What if I don't make it to eighteen?

I shook off the thought. "I'm not a kid anymore," I continued. "You can't keep treating me like I'm still that six-year-old you have to take care of. I can take care of myself. I basically did all winter while you were gone."

"I know you can," she said quietly. A breeze blew between us, and I noticed that there were more gray wisps in her blond hair than there used to be. "Can you blame me for wanting to protect you? For wanting to keep you safe?"

"I'm trying to protect myself, too!" The words flew out of my mouth before I could stop them. She looked at me curiously. "I mean, junior year is . . . really tough and . . ." I paused. "I have to look out for myself, because no one's going to do it for me."

"Your new friends," Aunt Jo said suddenly. "How well do you *really* know them?"

She looked at me pointedly, and I felt a fist clench around my heart. Did she know something that I didn't?

"Very well," I said. "I feel like . . . I can be myself around them." I eyed her.

"And do you feel like you can't—be yourself—around Dan and Cassie?" She paused. "Or Ian?"

Were we talking about the same thing? I hesitated for a moment, trying to think of how to explain it to her.

"I love my friends," I said, choosing my words carefully. "But sometimes I feel like . . . I'm growing into a different person. Someone they might not understand."

Aunt Jo sighed quietly and sat down on the arm of a chair. I sat down across from her. Something in me was stirring in a way it hadn't in a long time. I felt raw and vulnerable, after trying for so long to close myself off from everyone I loved, to protect them—and myself. Suddenly all I wanted was for someone to tell me what to do. I was so tired, so completely exhausted, from trying to figure it out all on my own. What if every decision I'd made so far had been the wrong one? All I wanted right then was for Aunt Jo to take me in her arms and tell me everything would be okay. And I wanted so desperately to believe her.

"We all grow up," Aunt Jo said, looking into my eyes. "It's a part of life. But it doesn't mean you have to grow into a different person. Just wiser and stronger."

I fought back the tears that were pricking behind my eyes.

"It's harder than I thought," I said.

"I know, Skye." She wrapped her arms around me. "I wish I could make it easier for you. You have no idea how much I wish . . ." She left her sentence hanging there in the cold night air.

We all grow up. But why did it have to feel like leaving everything and everyone I loved behind?

Later I crawled into bed with the little black notebook. I thumbed through the pages as if this time I might find another clue, something to connect me to this nameless person who, at one time, had been in the same place as me. I longed for some little tidbit—anything, really—to guide me. To help me stay sane in all this chaos.

I flipped over onto my stomach and stared at the handwriting on the first page. The letters looped together in a loose script, swooping across the page like they were flying. The way an angel might fly. The way I might fly, one day.

I sat up straight in bed, my heart pounding. I realized where I knew this handwriting from.

It was mine.

My heart was racing as if I'd just flown down a mountain. Was I delusional? How could I have written this? I'd been unconscious almost the whole time we'd been at the cabin, and I would have remembered writing it when I was awake. I briefly entertained the idea that I'd written it in my sleep, during a particularly vivid dream. Except all of my dreams had been about dying.

No. I was just exhausted—mentally, physically. Skiing again had taken a lot out of me. Fighting off Gideon's mental manipulation had messed with my mind. When I thought about the sheer weight of *everything*, I couldn't keep my eyes open.

I was looking for connections where there weren't any. That was all.

I got up and buried the notebook in my bottom drawer under a mountain of socks. If it was out of sight, I wouldn't have to think about it anymore. It didn't exist. I crawled back into bed and turned off the lamp. Soon I was drifting off, letting every thought, every fear, every hint about my past and clue to my future slip away into the night.

When I walked into the kitchen the next morning, the smell of chocolate and bananas beckoned.

"Wow," I said as Aunt Jo flipped pancakes at the stove. I walked over to the coffeemaker and poured myself a steaming mug. "Did I do something right today to deserve this? It's only seven thirty."

She placed a stack of banana chocolate-chip pancakes on a blue-and-white floral plate and set it hesitantly on the kitchen table. I put the milk back in the fridge and turned to face her, raising my eyebrows.

"I'm sorry I've been so hard on you," she said, fidgeting with her own mug of coffee as we sat down. "I was scared, too, okay? You *are* growing up and . . ." She stopped. "Oh god, this is so hard for me to admit, but you're not going to live here with me forever. And it'll just be a little lonely when you're gone, that's all." She sighed. "You've always been one to follow your own star, Skye. Just make sure to pick a good one to guide you."

I stared down at my pancakes and took a thoughtful bite. How was I supposed to know which star was the best one to follow?

"Do you want to have your friends over for dinner tonight?" Aunt Jo asked. "Cassie, Dan, Ian?" She took a deep breath. "Asher, if it means that much to you?"

"Really?" I said through a mouthful of pancake, perking up.

"Yeah, why not." She smiled back. "I need to properly meet Asher. He's your boyfriend, isn't he?" She kicked me under the table.

I grinned. "What gave it away?"

"He can't take his eyes off you. I don't know what you've done to that boy, but that's the kind of look that's hard to erase from someone's eyes, once it's there."

I felt something expand in my heart.

"Yeah, well, you know," I muttered, trying not to let my burning cheeks give too much away.

Aunt Jo smiled and cocked her head. "I know what that feels like," she said. "But just make sure you don't pick your star because it's the star he's chosen. Be your own person."

"Jeez, Aunt Jo. Seriously."

"I'm just saying!"

"Okay," I said, swallowing my last mouthful of banana chocolate-chip mushiness and standing up. "If you're done with the lecture, I have to get to school."

"Listen to me, Skye. I know what I'm talking about!"

I kissed the top of her head.

"Love you, crazy," I said.

"Yeah, yeah." She grinned. "Get to class."

I hesitated in the door to homeroom. Cassie sat in her usual seat by the window, her blue cast sticking out into the aisle so that people had to go out of their way to walk around her. I wished my old seat hadn't been given up when I'd been out. With a sigh, I turned to the back of the room—and stopped short. Asher was leaning over my empty seat, talking heatedly with Devin.

I couldn't suppress the creepy feeling that they were talking about me. Devin remained stiff in his seat. He said something in a low tone, and it seemed to enrage Asher, who leaned forward and gestured heatedly. The animosity between the two of them was so electric that I could feel it all the way across the room.

My presence must have been palpable, because Asher looked up right then and spotted me, guilt flashing across his face. Devin turned, too, and when he saw me, he dropped his gaze to his desk. I didn't want to get between them again, but I had no choice. Asher sat down, and slowly I walked down the aisle and slid into my seat, aware that Devin was watching me again out of the corner of his eye. I didn't look at him, but glanced over at Asher instead. He looked away. His foot was tapping loudly against the floor.

"Hey," I whispered, putting my hand on his arm. He was so angry that he was shaking under my touch. "Hey," I said again. "Calm down."

He muttered something I couldn't hear.

"Asher," I said. "What's wrong?"

"Nothing," he said, his voice a storm in the blackest night.

"Is now a bad time to ask if you want to come to dinner tonight?" I asked. "Special request from Aunt Jo."

His resolve faltered, and he looked at me questioningly. "Really?"

"Yeah." I gave him a small, persuasive smile. "Will you come?" His foot kept tapping a constant rhythm in the background.

"Yeah," he said. The worry line dissolved from his forehead. He took my hand tightly in his and lifted his dark eyes to meet mine. "I'd love to."

I felt a swell of happiness, had a brief vision of Asher and

Aunt Jo and all my friends getting along in one big wonderful, happy family. But Asher's foot tapping continued, and a dark, uneasy feeling edged out my joy. *What had they been talking about?*

At lunch, Cassie had that gleam in her eye.

"Uh-oh," I said, sliding in across from her. "I've seen that look before."

Cass glanced behind her, pretending I might have been talking to someone else with a gleam in her eye. She looked back at me and pointed at herself, mouthing, *"Who, me?"*

"Yes, you, Crazypants. What's going on?"

"I was just thinking I'm so effing *bored*," she said. "I hate this stupid cast. I can't do anything fun. I miss the Mysterious Ellipses. We haven't had a gig in weeks. Plus," she added, "it's been forever since we had a rager. The last one was the party at your house. I want some drama!"

I raised an eyebrow. I knew what was coming.

"No way," I said. "I can't host it this time. I'm on dangerous ground with Aunt Jo as it is."

"Fine." She sighed. "Well, at any rate, I'm going to talk to Ian today."

"Talk to me about what?" Ian asked, plopping down next to Cassie and ripping into a huge slice of pizza. "I can't give you guys any more free cupcakes," he said through a huge mouthful of cheese and sauce. "My boss said he's gonna fire me for real."

"If you haven't been fired yet, it's never going to happen," Cassie said, brushing him off. "Cupcakes are child's play. I have a real favor to ask you."

Ian rolled his eyes and glanced at me, but what Ellie had told me he'd said was still eating away at me. I couldn't make eye contact with him.

"Okay." He turned to Cassie. "What's the favor? I'm not agreeing to anything without hearing what it is first."

"Will you book the ME at the Bean?" she asked, fluttering her eyes.

"I'm sorry, the ME? Is that what you're calling yourself now?"

"The Mysterious Ellipses," she said with a pout.

"Can you really perform in that thing?" he asked, looking dubiously at her cast.

"Well, that's the favor. I was thinking maybe you could, like, ramp-ify the stage."

Ian laughed. "Oh my god, Cassie."

"Pleeeease?" More eyelash fluttering ensued.

He shook his head. "Okay, fine, I'll ask. But I can't make any promises."

"Well, I'm looking forward to a potentially legendary ME performance this weekend," I said as I got up. Ian opened his mouth to say something else, but I bused my tray and walked out into the hallway, eager to get away from him.

"Skye! Hey!" He came running up behind me. I stopped and looked at him, one hand on my hip. "What's your deal?" he asked.

"So you're hooking up with Ellie?" My voice came out angrier than I'd meant it to. Weirdly, I felt my face growing hot. I couldn't possibly have been jealous—it was *Ian*!—but still. She was my archnemesis. And he liked *me*!

"Um." He turned red. "Just once. Well, twice. But it didn't . . . I mean, I don't . . . *like* her or anything."

"Oh, that's great Ian. That's real mature."

"Wait, what's the problem? *You* turned *me* down, remember? We're not together, so what does it matter?"

"Well, it matters when you talk shit about me behind my back!"

"Oh," he said quietly. "She told you."

"Yeah. She *told* me."

Ian sighed. "Look, Skye," he said. "You know I love you. Okay? But I have forgiven you a lot of things. Too many things. I forgave you every day that you pretended not to notice how I felt about you. I forgave you when you started pulling away from me—from us—when those two new guys showed up, and I forgave you again when you ignored my warning that I didn't trust them, and when you decided you would rather be with either of them than with me."

"I—" I said, not sure what I thought I was going to say.

"But when you ran away with Asher, you have no idea what it did to me! I was mad, okay? I may let you hurt me, over and over again, and that's my own problem. But you don't get to tell me what to do anymore!" His eyes were blazing.

I stumbled backward. I'd never seen Ian get this angry in my entire life.

"I—I had no idea," I said quietly.

"So, yeah. I went to Carmen Shane's party and Ellie was flirting with me and I hooked up with her. And honestly it's none of your business."

"Wow," I said. "I'm . . . I'm so sorry."

"Yeah," he muttered. "Well, whatever. I gotta go. I'll see you or something." He turned around and took off down the hall in the opposite direction.

As I stood there, dumbfounded, the weight of his words crushed me, almost making it impossible to breathe. And the worst part about it was that he was right.

All day, frustration and rage cycled through me. I couldn't stop thinking about what Ian had said. If only I could tell him the truth about where I'd really been and why I'd left without a word. It wasn't my fault. None of this was.

I wanted to run away again, to hide. I pictured driving cross-country, my car kicking up dust as I crossed the flat middle of the map. In the rearview mirror, a flash of white feather. Everywhere I looked: a flash of sharp white feathers. Walking down city streets, between buildings, silhouetted against the glow of the sunset. Angels following me, a part of the skyline, for as long as I lived.

What kind of life would that be? I knew running away was impossible. I had to face this. I just wished I knew what "this" was. And, despite what Aunt Jo had said, there was still a part of me that felt deeply that wherever Asher was, that's where I needed to be, too.

I couldn't wait to get on the slopes that afternoon for our race against Holy Cross. I'd raced against them before. They weren't as fierce as the Brighton girls, but I still had to do my best if I ever wanted to be captain. I crouched low at each bend in the course and leaned into the wind, imagining huge, feathery wings extending from my back. In my mind, they guided me, directing the wind to make me more aerodynamic, my path easier. I was gliding, flying. But when I closed my eyes and tried to see if they were white or black, I couldn't.

The sun grew low in the sky, and the dusk was rolling in, cold and crisp and blue. As I flew down the slope, an idea struck me. I focused on the sun, squinting my eyes as it sank lower, so that just a luminous arc was peeking out above the mountains. What if I wasn't ready for it to set just yet? What if I needed more daylight to finish the race?

My eyes stung, but I forced myself to keep staring directly at the sun, the force of my mind pushing with all its might. *Come on*, I thought, taking a sharp turn in the course with exact precision. *Come onnn.*

And then the strangest thing happened. The sun stopped setting suddenly, and it began to float *upward*. I faltered slightly, then righted myself as my competitor drew up just behind my right elbow.

"What the—" I heard her say before her voice was swallowed by the wind. The sky began to lighten, the dusk withdrawing into itself, pulling back the darkness. I swished across the finish line and slid to a stop.

Coach clicked his stopwatch and looked up to catch my eye. He nodded. "You keep this up for our last big race next week against Southfield," he said, "and you'll be our next captain."

I fell back onto the snowy ground, breathing hard, staring up into the sky. I could feel my powers getting stronger, more controlled. I was exhausted but exhilarated at the same time. I closed my eyes and felt the sun begin to set again as the dusk settled in around me.

I sat by myself again on the bus. Ellie was talking loudly about me a couple of seats away.

"Freak," I heard her mutter. "I bet she's on steroids or something."

I sighed and leaned into the seat. The trees blurred past my window. Only a month or so ago, Ellie and I had kind of been friends. I closed my eyes again, willing the bus ride to be over.

Aunt Jo had cooked a feast. She let me shower off from the race, and then the two of us set the table while we danced around to romantic comedy soundtracks. At eight, the doorbell rang, and I opened it to see Cassie and Dan standing on my doorstep. Cass was dressed up in her favorite vintage dress, the yellow one with the little flowers. One leg was cut off a pair of tights to fit over her cast. Her red hair was piled into a purposefully messy bun. The fact that Dan was wearing a jacket instead of his navy-blue hoodie meant that he had dressed up, too.

"Yay!" Cassie said, clapping her hands. "Dinner party!"

I hugged them both. "Come in!" I said with a flourish.

"Hi, guys!" Aunt Jo called from the dining room. As we walked in, Cassie presented her with a bottle of red wine.

"From my mom." She winked. "She made Dan promise not to drink any so he can drive me home."

"That's responsible," Aunt Jo said, patting Dan on the back.

Dan mumbled something under his breath.

Aunt Jo brought heaping plates of food to the table while Cassie and Dan sat down. The doorbell rang again, and I got nervous, like Asher was here to pick me up for a date or something. I hoped he was in a better mood than he had been in this morning. Later I'd confront him about his conversation with Devin.

Asher was standing on the porch, and when I opened the front door, he smiled down at me. There was a shyness in his eyes, a vulnerability that I still wasn't used to. He was wearing a deep green sweater and brown corduroys, and held out a bouquet of flowers.

"Don't get your hopes up." He smirked. "They're for Aunt Jo."

"Did you dress up for me?" I asked, smiling widely as he walked in.

"No." He shook his head.

"You did," I said. "You totally dressed up." With a glance over his shoulder to make sure no one was watching, he turned on me, taking my waist and drawing me close to him. I shivered. He leaned in as if to kiss me but instead moved his head to the side and whispered in my ear.

"I should probably say hi to everyone else."

I knew for a fact that I was turning red, and the room was growing warmer. Asher laughed. It seemed like no matter how good I was becoming at controlling my powers, he could still swoop in and ruin all of my progress with a single touch.

"Guys?" Aunt Jo called. "Dinner!"

It was the best dinner I'd ever had. Aunt Jo had prepared heaping family-style bowls of pasta, lamb tenderloin just the way I loved it—smothered in her ancho chile rub—and her special string beans. We'd opened the bottle of wine, and Cassie, Asher, and I were all flushed and happy. Dan was good-natured about it, but I couldn't help but think how sweet it was that he was listening so intently to Cassie's mom's instructions. Cassie and Dan were like my couple role models. Maybe one day, when all of this was over—*if* it ever could be—Asher and I could be together in a normal way, living in some normal house, just being . . . *normal.*

Sometimes, as I looked around the table at my old friends—Cassie, beaming at Dan as he passed her the pasta—I almost forgot what was happening to me, that I was trying to turn myself into a fighter. I felt strange, like I was keeping something from almost every single person at the table. And I was. But a houseful of people determined to keep me safe was better than a lonely, empty house. It was a feeling I'd never really had before. This was my family.

Aunt Jo was laughing and smiling, but I noticed that the smile never fully reached her eyes. She looked far away, and every time she glanced at Asher, she began to fidget nervously, an uncomfortable look washing over her face. What was going *on* with her? I'd never seen her act like this. I started to wonder: had she been so upset because I had run away—or because I'd been spending so much time with *Asher*?

After dinner, we nibbled on some lemon bars. I got up to bring a stack of plates into the kitchen, and Cassie followed me. The bruises on her face were looking a lot less purple now, but her eyes were still ringed with a muddy yellow. "Do those hurt still?" I asked tentatively. I put a large ceramic bowl in the sink.

"Getting better," she said, flinging a stray hair over her shoulder with a dramatic sigh. "I hate this effing cast, though. Do you see how stupid this looks?" She motioned to her one-legged tights.

"Maybe it could be a new look?" I asked. "Like cutoff shorts?"

"Not likely." She snorted.

I patted her head. "I'm glad the accident hasn't affected your adventurous fashion sense."

Cassie giggled. "I like Asher," she said, glancing over her shoulder to make sure no one could hear.

"You do?" I beamed. "I just want . . . I want us all to, you know, get along."

"No, he's really great." We peeked into the dining room, where Asher and Dan were apparently having some heated music debate. "I'm glad you don't hang out with Devin anymore," she said suddenly. "He's really such a creep, Skye. He gives you the weirdest looks in homeroom."

I hesitated. All I wanted was to come clean about everything. "I know," I told her. "You don't know the half of it."

"I mean, he didn't treat you very well at all, even as a friend. And he wasn't very nice to any of us."

I busied myself arranging the remaining string beans on a platter into a haphazard flower pattern.

"Yeah," I said. "I know."

"And his new girlfriend's the worst. I mean, seriously. What a bitch."

"Cassie, come on. I know all this." I turned around, and

we looked each other straight in the eye.

She gasped. "Oh my god. Skye, no way."

"No way, what?"

"You still have feelings for him!"

"What? That's crazy. I so do not."

"Do we really have to go through this again? You absolutely do. I can tell these things."

"You're losing your touch," I said.

Her hand flew to her mouth.

"Skye Parker, you can abandon me in the hospital to spend time with your disgustingly gorgeous boyfriend and you can invite me to dinner and get me tipsy, but you wound me on the very deepest level when you insult my ability to detect matters of the heart—especially when it comes to you. Did I or did I not call Asher from Day One?"

I smiled, despite myself. "You did," I admitted.

"So what is happening with Devin?"

I wanted to tell her. I wanted to stay up late after everybody left, gushing about everything that had happened to me since her accident. But what if the Order was watching? Lurking in the woods, just like the notebook said? Was that a risk I could take? What if this time, they actually took her life? I couldn't be responsible for that. I *wouldn't*.

And then there was that other troubling thought. What could she see in me that I couldn't? Did I still have feelings for Devin? Even after everything I'd been through, was it possible I still cared about him?

"You're wrong this one time," I said. "There's nothing happening." And I wasn't lying about that, at least.

She stared at me, and I could tell she thought I was holding back.

"You know, we used to tell each other everything," she said. Then she turned and walked into the dining room.

I sighed and threw the rest of the string beans into the composter. I had a feeling that Cassie would never truly forgive me for leaving until I could finally tell her the truth. But I knew that if I told her, she could get even more hurt than she would if I didn't.

Aunt Jo went upstairs to go to bed, and the four of us spilled out onto the deck. The night was so balmy that we didn't need jackets—or maybe we were all just flushed and a little giddy from the wine. Cassie kept ribbing Dan for being her Designated Driver. "No, no," she kept saying. "It's cute! You're my knight in shining armor!"

"All right," Dan said. "That's it! You better run!"

Cassie shrieked and slowly made her way down the steps of the deck, and Dan pretended to chase after her, into the field behind our house. We could hear them laughing, and then suddenly we couldn't hear them at all—which meant their fighting had devolved into making out.

Would I ever find something like that? All I wanted was to feel safe and stable, like my life wasn't going to suddenly change in the middle of the night. I loved Asher so much, but he was part of a scary and unpredictable world. And now, for better or for worse, I was, too.

As if reading my thoughts, he came up behind me and wrapped me in his arms. I leaned back against him, letting my cheek graze against the soft wool of his sweater. Above us, a shooting star streaked across the night.

"Make a wish," Asher whispered.

"I think I already have."

"You know," he said, "if I didn't know any better, I'd say you caused that shooting star yourself."

I laughed and nodded. He pulled me even tighter against him, and I could feel his breath rise and fall more rapidly against my back—and the marked lack of a heartbeat.

"We're so close," he whispered into my ear. "Every day, you're getting stronger. The universe is shifting. Can you feel it?"

"Yes," I said, gazing out at the stars. "I can."

I had no idea what the future held, but for now I'd just have to be happy resting in the arms of my dark angel.

That night, after everyone had left, I lay in bed, staring up at the cracks and water marks on my ceiling. I was still warm from being with Asher, still felt his arms wrapped tightly around me. I tried to let the memory comfort me, lull me to sleep. But my brain kept working, and I knew sleep was impossible.

The notebook called to me from the bottom drawer of my dresser, under all those socks. I tried not to think about it, rolled over, and stared at the blank wall—but something pulled me back. Finally I couldn't hold out any longer. I jumped out of bed and thrust my hands into the bottom drawer, digging around until I found what I was looking for. The little notebook stared up at me, taunting. Whose was it? Could I have really written this? It seemed so unbelievable.

It had to have been a relic from a different time. Another hand had held the pen that formed those words. Another set of Guardians had stalked those woods. In a time before I was born. A time—I realized, staring harder at the date—*right* before I was born. Then a strange, new thought lit up my mind, and I sat down hard on the floor where I had been kneeling. What if it wasn't *my* handwriting that I was staring at? I stared at the page as the words came to life in my mind, and a whole story for the cabin and the little notebook wrote itself in my head. What if it was someone whose handwriting I had recognized?

What if it was my mother's?

Jan came through, after all. The Mysterious
Ellipses had a gig at the Bean on Saturday
night. Cassie sent me a thousand and one texts
informing me of this.

I had an early-morning ski practice with the team. Asher
was right: each day I felt myself growing stronger, learning to control the power that surged through me in the
most mind-blowing ways. My times were getting better,
too. I knew my chances of making team captain were looking good. I'd always had a great relationship with Coach
Samuelson, and even though I'd left the team, he didn't
seem to be holding it against me.

When I got home, the energy still crackling off my skin,
Asher was leaning against the front porch with his arms
crossed.

"Hey," I called. "What are you doing here?"

"I miss the old days." Asher grinned, some of the familiar playfulness returning to his voice. "I thought we could go out back and practice together." He laughed. "I miss you getting all huffy and yelling at me."

"Aunt Jo's home," I said. "We can't go out back."

"Then let's go for a hike or something." He winked at me. "Where no one will see us."

I felt my cheeks redden. "Let me just run in and drop my stuff." It took me a few minutes to convince Aunt Jo I was responsible enough to go on a hike with Asher, but I finally met him out back, and we hiked out to a trail I rarely used. It was a warm morning in early March, and the sun crept through the heavy evergreen trees, throwing beams of light across our path. We hiked single file, not speaking much. Every now and then, Asher would grab my hand and spin me around for a kiss. When he did, the sun burned brighter, making the trees shimmer with thousands of tiny evergreen flames. So much snow had melted and the purple alpine flowers were blossoming once again. I tried not to think about what they meant to me, but the purple flowers, like seeing Devin in the halls at school, reminded me that I wasn't *just* a Rebel. There was Guardian blood in me, too—my mother's. No matter what the Order stood for or what they had tried to do to me, the more I thought about the notebook—that small piece of her, the only piece I had left—I felt I couldn't just abandon the part of me that she was responsible for.

Just because that part was harder to see didn't mean it wasn't there.

I was now sure that my visions were my mother's powers flowing through me in some way. Those were powers of the mind, vaguely precognitive in some sense, even though I wasn't manipulating anyone else. It was my own mind I was controlling. My own thoughts. I just had no idea how, or what they meant.

"Have you had any word from the Rebellion?" I asked Asher as we neared a clearing in the trail. "Do they know what the Order is planning?"

He avoided my gaze.

"Asher?"

"No, nothing yet. They're biding their time, waiting for you to get stronger. Killing Oriax was sort of the first shot fired—the official end of the truce. But the Rebellion will come back with something fierce, don't worry."

"How will we know when they do? Aren't the Guardians nervous?"

"We'll know," said Asher. "And yes, I imagine the Guardians are just as concerned about the coming war as we are. They know we'll retaliate, but they don't know how—because of you. Don't forget, Skye, your powers are making it impossible for them to foresee the outcome of this war. Thanks to you, they don't know what we're planning. That's one of the reasons why the Rebellion needs you."

An uneasy feeling made the hair on my arms prickle. I'd known this in the clearing in the woods the night that the Order had tried to kill me. Whichever side I chose to align myself with would have untold power. I didn't want to believe that was the reason Asher wanted to be so close to me, but a small part of me couldn't help but feel it was awfully convenient that we were suddenly inseparable right when the Rebellion was trying to hide plans for a retaliation.

I shook my head. No, that couldn't be it. Asher loved me. He just wanted to be with me as often as I wanted to be with him. I couldn't believe that he would use me for the Rebellion's purposes just to win a war. Wouldn't that make the Rebels—my friends—just as bad as the Guardians?

This was a dangerous train of thought. I had to wipe it from my mind.

"Asher," I said suddenly.

"Yeah?" His eyes were focused on the edge of the woods at the far end of the field.

"Think fast." He whipped around just in time to dodge the fireball I lobbed at him. He grinned and threw it back at me with lightning-fast speed. Rather than ducking, I closed my eyes and raised my arms high in the air, calling an enormous gust of wind that carried the fireball into the sky. It dissipated into the thinnest wisps of smoke.

"Not bad!" Asher called. He walked toward me slowly, an evil grin tugging on the side of his mouth.

"What?" I said, backing away. My voice was shaking slightly, but not because I was afraid. "What is that smile for?"

He reached me, running his hands up my waist and pulling me close. The sun burned bright through the trees, too bright, blinding, until the thousands of tiny evergreen needles erupted with real flames.

"Oh," I said under my breath.

"I think," Asher said, the evil smile widening, "that we need to work on your control when this happens." He trailed his hand up my neck until it was cupping the back of my head. I drew in a shallow breath. The fire consuming the pine needles began to crackle inward, trickling along the branches toward the trunk of the tree. Asher leaned in slowly. He touched his forehead to mine and tilted my neck up so I was gazing into his startling black eyes. Dizzying eyes. "Focus," he said, his voice no louder than a whisper.

"On what?" I asked, my voice shaking.

"Your emotions." His lips grazed my earlobe. "Use them to fuel your power. Put that fire out."

I closed my eyes, trying to block him out. I could feel the tickle of his breath on my neck, his eyelashes flutter against my cheek. I swallowed.

I could do this. *Focus.*

The crackle of the fire was growing into a roar. I opened my eyes, and the tree was ablaze. Panicking, I broke away from Asher.

"Come on, Skye," he said, pulling me back to him. "I believe in you."

Okay, I had this. All I had to do was conjure up a storm—something big enough to put out the beginnings of a forest fire. I'd done it before, right? In the car with Ardith, I'd controlled the streaks of lightning. I'd kept our small car from getting struck by the blinding flashes that touched down all around us. Flashes that my own volatile mood had caused.

As I turned in a slow circle, taking in the fire that was

now raging through the trees, Asher wrapped his arms around me and whispered into my ear. "Focus, Skye. Make the fire stop." It was almost impossible to focus on anything with Asher's hands running up my back, but I closed my eyes again and I thought of rolling black clouds, thunder rumbling so hard it shook the mountains, cracks of lightning that lit up the night. When I opened my eyes, darkness had fallen like a blanket across the Colorado sky, and I knew that they were glowing liquid silver.

Lightning flashed across the black, starless sky. It touched down a few feet away from us.

"Come on, Skye!" Asher's voice grew louder.

I tilted my head back and closed my eyes, letting every ounce of energy that I had flow through me.

That's when the rain came. A freezing, fast rain that drove down in heavy sheets, soaking us. I started to laugh as the thunder rumbled beneath us.

Asher took my hand, and we stood there, watching the rain wash away the fire. It soaked my clothes and plastered my hair against the sides of my face; made Asher's hair look even wilder and matted his eyelashes together like he was crying. I gripped his hand tighter, and he turned to face me. I wasn't laughing anymore.

The look in his eyes was so strange. A fierce mix of love,

fear, pride—and something else. Something that made me shiver in the icy rain.

Possession.

And that's when I dropped to my knees.

The rain swirled around me, so densely that soon it blocked everything out, and suddenly it was daytime and the rain had stopped and I was sitting on a rock overlooking the field on my favorite trail. I'd sat there so many times before. The last time I'd sat there had been with . . .

I looked up, and Devin was sitting next to me.

"Try it," he said softly. His voice was gentle, so calming. As always. "You have this. Just focus." I looked down at my hands. I was holding a small withered flower. Just a tiny, dead thing.

"I *am* focusing," I said.

"Focus harder." I closed my eyes. And when I opened them again, the flower that I held in my hands was purple, vibrant, and alive.

"You did it," he said, his voice quiet with awe. "I knew you could."

"Skye?"

I opened my eyes. I was lying on the soaking wet ground, completely drenched. My teeth were chattering, and I coughed up a lungful of water.

"Hey," Asher said, kneeling next to me. He brushed his hand against my cheek. "What happened? Another vision?"

I nodded.

"Can you sit up?" he asked.

"I think so." He put his strong hand on my back and helped me to a sitting position.

"Maybe things got a little intense," he said. "I'm sorry. It's my fault. I really thought you could handle it."

"I—I *can* handle it," I said, blinking slowly.

"I just thought . . ." He swallowed, and suddenly he looked nervous, vulnerable. Such a departure from his usual mask of confidence that, for a moment, I worried that something was really wrong. I reached my hand out and touched his cheek lightly.

"What?" I asked.

"I . . . hate that I can't be close to you without something bursting into flames. I feel responsible, like it's my fault." He looked at the ground. "I thought if we worked on controlling it, we could . . ." He took a breath, and I realized his hands were trembling slightly. "I wanted us to be able . . . I mean, one day, you know, I was hoping . . ." He coughed, and a shadow of the old cocky smile returned.

"Be together, you know?"

"Asher," I said, taking his face in both my hands and drawing his eyes up to mine. There were no witty retorts left in me. All I wanted was to be honest with him. "Me too. We'll get there. It will happen." I kissed him, a soft, tender kiss. "I promise."

"I love you," he whispered.

And all the snappy comebacks in the world couldn't compare to that.

Asher put my arm around his neck and helped me back down the trail. About ten yards from the house, I heard something snap behind us. When I whirled around, there was nothing there.

"What was that?" I asked, trying not to let my voice give way to fear.

"It was nothing," he said, but his eyes grew dark. "Nothing."

Cassie had outdone herself. Love the Bean was decked out for the ME show—but not in her signature fairy-tale twinkle lights. It felt darker somehow. Everything had a kind of edge to it. There was a lot of black. "She's still working through the accident," Dan said as Asher and I walked up. "It's some pretty dark stuff."

Ian had rigged a ramp to the stage, and Cassie hobbled to the microphone on her crutches. The Bean was filling up, and the Mysterious Ellipses began to warm up with an instrumental version of the theme song from Super Mario Brothers. It was secretly a little fun to see how Cassie worked her outfits around her cast. Tonight she wore a black, stretchy knit miniskirt with one cobalt-blue tight and her signature ankle bootie on one leg, the darker blue cast on the other. A few long drapey tank tops finished the look.

Behind her, the band paused.

Cassie grabbed the mic, and we cheered loudly.

"Go, Cass!" I shouted.

"Oh, thank you, thanks, guys," she said with the fakest modesty I'd ever seen. Dan and I shared a look and laughed. "No, please, stop. Thank you for coming out tonight. We've been working on some new stuff, and it's a little different than usual. I hope you like it."

"We already love it!" Dan shouted.

"I hope those of you who aren't my *boyfriend* like it." Cassie grinned at the crowd. Trey, the ME drummer, counted off on his drumsticks, and then the band burst into their first song. The crowd fell to a hush. Cassie was mesmerizing to watch.

Dan was right—the music was way darker than it ever had been before. A thumping bass line kept the rhythm, and Cassie's voice was a low growl.

Then the rhythm picked up, and she started singing faster, wilder. We were all hooked, moving in time to the music. Her voice rose to a high, sharp clarity. She sounded like wind chimes on speed. Whatever dark issues Cassie was still working through, it was doing wonders for her music.

It was the best the Mysterious Ellipses had ever played. We danced crazily, like the end of the world was coming and we had to let loose one last time before it did. What only Asher and I knew, though, was that it might. Soon. And that I was the one who might have to bring it.

Ardith and Gideon walked in, their faces serious. Ardith wore another long skirt that swept the floor, heavy boots, and an armful of gold bangles. Gideon wore jeans and a faded Rolling Stones T-shirt under a corduroy blazer. They looked so unassuming, like kids I might go to school with—but I couldn't help feeling nervous as they scanned the Bean, as if looking for trouble. When they spotted Asher, he stopped dancing and stood straighter. "Be right back," he muttered.

My heart beat fast as I turned around to face the stage. Was something happening? I tried to listen to the music but kept sneaking glances at the back of the room, where the three of them had their heads bent in serious conversation. Not one of them looked up at me. I turned my attention back to the stage.

"Man, I missed her," I said to Dan.

"She missed you, too," he said. "You know, she was

really torn up about it."

"I just want things to go back to normal between us."

"Then you may have to tell her the real reason why you left," he said, turning to me.

"I—I didn't—there's nothing—" I sputtered. Of all the people in my life, somehow, in that moment I remembered why Dan was my oldest friend. He didn't talk much, but when he did, he meant every word.

"Skye," he said. "You were acting strange long before you left. You don't think we know something's going on with you? All she wants is for you to tell her the truth."

"I did tell her the truth," I lied. Dan looked at me pointedly.

"Give me some credit."

I swallowed. "You don't want to know the truth, too?"

"I know you'll tell me when you're ready. I don't need everything right this minute like Cassie does. You've been my friend since kindergarten. I'm not afraid of you abandoning us. But Cassie—you know her, everything is drama, drama, drama." He rolled his eyes, but he said it with love. "She needs to be reminded sometimes that you're her best friend."

I looked around. The Bean was packed. People were dancing, music was playing—and there were, I was sure,

Guardians everywhere. Across the room, where he was busy ringing up someone's coffee, Ian glanced up and met my eye, frowning slightly. I turned to Dan. "Will you believe me when I say that I want to tell you, I just can't right now?"

"Look, are you in trouble?" he asked. "Because telling me will help. We'll get you help, Skye, whatever you need."

"No," I said. "But I may need your help later. Will you promise to help me?" I knew I was asking a lot of him. Dan couldn't possibly know that "help" might mean slashing at celestial beings with angelic swords or standing back as I lobbed a fireball at someone who was trying to kill me. But I knew that I would one day—soon—need his help. And Cassie's and Ian's. Even if it was just understanding when I needed to make a choice once and for all about what my future held.

"Of course I promise," he said. "I've got your back, Skye. Worry not." And somehow, just these words helped to ease some of my constant fear.

I glanced back at the bar, where Ian was counting change for someone. He looked up at me again, and this time he cocked his head to one side. He didn't look angry, more like he was lost in thought. It struck me that he was always watching. Always tentatively observing me when he thought no one else was looking. I'd always thought, somewhat sheepishly, that he'd just been checking me out. But there was something else going on right now that made me wonder. . . .

Dan slapped his hand on my back and set off to maneuver his way to the front of the stage. *My friends aren't mad at me*, I realized. *They're worried about me.* I decided to go apologize to Ian. He didn't deserve the way I'd treated him. I didn't think I'd ever led him on, but somehow he'd never stopped believing that we might end up together. *He should go out with Ellie*, I thought. *He should give someone else a real chance.*

I made my way through the crowd. Ian was wiping off the counter and bouncing along to the music. When he noticed me coming, he tried to back away into the supply closet, but he knocked into a broom and it clattered to the floor. He rushed to pick it up.

"Hey," I said, hopping up onto the counter.

"Hmm? Oh, hi." He averted his eyes.

"Look," I said. "I think you should date Ellie. She's a really good skier. And . . ." I tried to think of more compliments. "She's pretty, in kind of, like, an obvious sort of way, and—"

"Skye," Ian interrupted. "You suck at this."

"I mean it," I insisted. "I think you should date her. I'm not mad. I'm happy for you."

He stopped nervously wiping down the counter and looked up at me. "This is it, huh?" he said. "There really is no chance you secretly love me, is there?"

"I'm so sorry, Ian."

"It's cool," he said. "Ellie's a good kisser."

"I'm not really asking for details here, okay?"

"Yeah," he said, grinning shyly. "Okay."

As I started to jump off the counter, Asher sauntered up. "Hey," Asher said, nodding. "Two lattes." He slapped a ten-dollar bill on the counter. Ian gave Asher a look that could kill. I knew the two of them didn't exactly love each other, but I'd never seen Ian look at him like this. He started turning toward the steamer, then stopped and doubled back. A smirk played on Asher's lips as he waited to see what kind of new amusing challenge Ian would bring.

"Skye may be into you or whatever," Ian said coldly, the ten slowly crumpling in his fist. "But it doesn't mean I'll ever stop hating you." He glanced at me, his eyebrows knotting. Then he went to get us the lattes.

"Why do you do that to him?" I asked, turning on Asher.

"Stop smiling like that. It's so mean."

"I don't like the way he looks at you," Asher said. "Like he thinks he's got you all figured out or something." But something in my gut told me that wasn't what was going on here. Ian *hated* Asher—and not in a jealous way, the way I felt about Ellie. It had nothing to do with the fact that I loved Asher instead of him. He would have disliked anyone I dated, but his hatred of Asher was *specific*.

Strange, I thought. Asher was so charming. He came across as a little cocky sometimes, but underneath it all, when we were alone together, no one I knew had a better or a stronger heart. I didn't know why Ian couldn't trust my judgment more. Or Aunt Jo—who seemed to seethe with dislike for Asher, too. Dislike—or maybe even distrust. Ian and Aunt Jo were two of the people I cared about most in this world. How could they both hate Asher so much? What was the connection there? What was I missing?

What had he done to make them turn against him?

"Thanks for the latte," I said.

"Don't mention it." He handed it to me and didn't remove his hand right away. I tried to take it from him, but he held on tight. When I looked up, I realized he wasn't looking at me. He was staring over my shoulder. I followed his gaze.

Guardians. A whole group of them had just walked in

from the cold, their glossy blond hair glinting menacingly in the light of the coffee shop. Across the room, Gideon and Ardith looked up, too, their gazes steely and cold. An invisible fist clenched my throat. Asher had said they would never do anything out in the open—but did that mean Love the Bean was safe, too? I wasn't so sure. They moved as a group, fluid, seamless, and calm.

The bell on the door rattled, and Raven walked in behind them—followed, seconds later, by Devin. She looked around appraisingly, and slipped her arm into his, as if everyone in the room wanted him.

Not everyone.

His eyes met mine—piercing, blue, and impossible to read. I looked back at Asher. Pure, unadulterated hatred burned across his face.

"They wouldn't do anything," I said. "Right? Not here, in the open like this?"

"Not if I can help it." He strode across the room, Ardith and Gideon falling into formation behind him. The Guardians tensed and strengthened their stance. Onstage, Cassie was still singing. Her voice cut across the room, an eerie soundtrack to what was starting to take place. I stood by the counter, watching, wondering how, or when, I would need to act.

Before Asher and the Rebels reached the group of Guardians, Ian swooped in.

"Hey," he said, holding out both hands like a traffic cop. "Hey, hey. Be cool."

"We're fine," Lucas, who was at the head of the Guardian group, said. He raised his hands in protest. "These guys look like they want to start something." He gestured at Asher. "Not us."

"I don't care," Ian said. Onstage, the band had stopped playing. Cassie was gaping at the scene in front of her. "But you need to stop. Okay?"

Asher took a step backward. "We're fine, too," he said. His black eyes were searing. "Forget it."

Feedback split from the amp behind Cassie, cutting into the hushed crowd as she took the mic. "Is this a bad time to let you all know about the party?" she asked sweetly.

But I didn't hear how people responded. I was falling, fast and hard, hitting the floor as the room faded away to someplace else.

The mist cleared away on the wind, and I was standing on the beach again. The waves crashed stormily against the rocks, breaking with a vengeance and slipping away with the tide. I was trudging through the surf. The hem of my beautiful dress was soaked and dirty. In places, I noticed now with a sinking sense of dread, it was streaked with red.

Blood.

Ahead of me, I could make out a crumpled shape on the shore, dark and still. As I drew closer, I saw that it was a body.

Which one of them did I hit?

I opened my eyes, gasping.

*L*ove the Bean was strangely quiet, and something feathery and light tickled my forehead. As my vision came into focus, I realized it was wisps of reddish blond hair. Cassie's green eyes were staring into mine. When I tried to sit up, she pulled back.

"You're awake!" she said breathlessly. "Are you okay? You fell hard."

"Who says you have to look before you leap?" I said in a weak attempt at a joke.

Cassie smirked. "I made them all leave." She helped me up and guided me over to the faded velvet couch. "I told them to go on ahead to Foster's Woods. Are you sure you're okay?" She held my hand in hers and brushed the hair back from my face. The gesture was so maternal, so caring, that I leaned into her, and she put her arm around me.

"I missed you so much, Cass," I said. "You have no idea."

"Aw," she said. "I missed you, too, buddy. You're my bestest. You always will be, no matter how many guys you run away with."

I felt a pang in my heart at her words. I had to tell her.

"Cass, I—"

"Shh. I'm only kidding. Come on. Want some water?"

I shook my head. "I think I just want to go to the party."

"Sure," she said. "Let's go."

Foster's Woods was up past Cassie's place. There was an empty field a few miles back from the road, and everybody parked their cars there, trekking out to the woods beyond.

It was the perfect place for covert partying. Someone had built a roaring campfire in the fire pit. Its orange glow flickered between the trees.

We found Dan and Ian stoking the fire.

"You feeling okay?" Ian asked, that inquisitive look in his eyes again. "Has that been happening a lot?"

"Maybe you should go to a doctor, Skye," offered Cassie. "Get it checked out. I'll go with you if you want."

I wished I could tell them it wasn't something that a doctor could fix.

"I'm fine," I said. "I've just been eating differently lately. I think it's affecting my blood sugar or something."

"Okay," said Cassie dubiously. "But for real, though, the minute you want to go to a doctor, just say the word."

I smiled at her. "I will. You'll be the first person I call." I scanned the dark woods around us. "Have you seen Asher?"

"I think he went off that way," Cassie said. "With Ardith and Gideon." She grinned mischievously and whispered, "If I wasn't, like, in love with Dan or whatever, I would so go for Gid. He is *cute*. Very my type, don't you think?"

"You can put the girl in a relationship . . . ," I began, putting my arm around her.

"But you can't take the boy-crazy out of the girl," Cassie finished.

"Would you kill me if I looked for Asher?" I asked.

"Nah, go ahead. I'll hang with the boys. Boys!" she called.

I walked off in the other direction, through the low tangle of trees. I was partly looking for Asher, but the truth was that I needed some time by myself, to think. My mind was racing.

The vision I'd just had haunted me. What had I meant when I thought, *Which one of them did I hit*? Whose body was it? Why was I having such strange and violent visions? They swirled into one another in my head, and I couldn't figure out how they fit together. The visions of Devin, of opening the shoe box in Aunt Jo's closet, of trudging down the beach in a bloodstained dress—what did they all mean? Were they connected somehow? If they were, it was in ways I couldn't fathom.

"You look lost in thought," Ardith said gently, her gold bangles jangling softly as she came up behind me. "Can I help?"

"Not unless you can make sure nothing will happen to Cassie if I tell her the truth," I replied.

"I wish I could. I can see how badly you want to. But you know it's too dangerous, right?"

"Yeah," I said. "I just miss talking to her. She's shockingly clear-headed sometimes. She always helps me put things in perspective."

"You can talk to me, you know," Ardith said warmly. "Anytime you need a friend."

I turned to her, unable to stop the swell of gratefulness from bubbling up within me. The orange light flickered across her face.

"You have no idea how much I needed to hear that," I said, breathing a sigh of relief.

"You know you don't need to worry about Asher or his feelings for you." I lifted my eyes. "Asher's a difficult creature," Ardith continued. He has been living for much longer than you have. But I've never seen him look at anyone the way he looks at you."

"You haven't?"

"Never." She smiled. "I don't know how, but you tamed him. I think he'd spend another thousand years by your side if he could."

I let the words sink in as the firelight cast strange shadows on the trees and across our faces.

"I'll let you get back to your thoughts," she said, and before I could say anything more, she hugged me and left.

I was so grateful to have at least one person in my life who knew exactly what I was going through.

I wound my way back through the trees, searching for Asher, wondering if what Ardith had said was true. The flames cast shadows of branches and leaves across the people appearing and disappearing among the trees. It was hard to see who anyone was in the uneven light. As I stumbled over roots and stones back toward the bonfire, I heard two voices speaking in hushed tones on the other side of a tree. I was about to walk in the other direction when I realized one of the voices belonged to Gideon— and I stopped.

I heard my name.

I drew closer to the tree, making sure to stay hidden behind it.

"I've just talked to her." Ardith's voice slipped out of the darkness. "She really does love him. I've told her he feels the same."

"I don't know," said Gideon. "I still think she's a liability. You've seen the way she and that Guardian look at each other."

"They can hardly stand to be in the same room."

"Asher says they still talk in secret. He says she used to have feelings for him, that if she knew what we were planning, she'd never let us go through with it."

What?

"Skye feels betrayed," Gideon continued, lowering his voice. "Don't you think he's playing to that weakness? Killing her obviously didn't work, and now they're realizing you trap more flies with honey than you do by stabbing them."

I heard Ardith sigh. "Do you think he's manipulating her mind?"

"It's possible," said Gideon. "We need her to get those powers under control, fast. The Guardians are getting restless. They want a fight."

Was it possible they didn't care about my safety at all? That they just wanted to use me?

"Asher says to give it a little more time. He hasn't decided what to do just yet. He's afraid that if he goes through with it . . . she'll never forgive him."

I stifled a sharp breath and stayed hidden in the shadows.

"But how could she still even consider aligning herself with the Order?" Ardith sounded shocked.

"Asher's convinced Devin's influencing how she feels. She's not strong enough to fight him yet."

"You have to train her harder. Prevent that from happening. We need her on our side, Gid, and you're the only one who can help her to prevent Devin from getting in. If the Order claims her, they'll destroy us."

"I know. And if we keep her—"

"We destroy the Order."

"She's the ultimate weapon."

My mind was racing. I hadn't told Asher I'd talked to Devin—but either he was more aware of my feelings than I'd thought or someone had told him.

Suddenly I felt racked with guilt. What was I doing?

Of course the Rebellion could trust me—I would never fight against them. But I knew I could never let them hurt Devin. I just couldn't.

He was so much more helpless than I was—he had no free will.

I thought I'd known where I truly belonged, but now, suddenly, I wasn't sure of anything anymore.

My back stiffened. Nobody was going to use me in this war. I needed to understand my Guardian powers as well as my Rebel ones. I was beginning to think that the clue to everything lay in my visions. The gift from my mother.

"Hey," said a familiar voice. I whipped around, startled, to find Asher. Had he been behind me this whole time? I hadn't heard him approach. "I've been looking everywhere for you. Are you okay?"

In the flickering light, his face looked menacing, strange. Not like the Asher I knew at all. I thought about what I'd just heard.

How well did I really know him?

"These woods remind me of home," Asher said softly, almost to himself. He stepped out of the shadows and took my hand. It wasn't the first time I found myself wondering if his home could be my home, too. Except now I was more confused than ever about where my home should be.

A tiny spark ignited between our fingertips.

"Asher," I said. "What's our next move?"

He leaned in closer to me and raised an eyebrow. "Well, I'm glad you asked."

"No, stop." I pushed him away. "I mean the Rebellion. The Order fired the first shot, right? They killed Oriax. So what's our move? Shouldn't we retaliate?" I was fishing for information, but all it did was make him take a step backward. He let my hand fall to my side, and his eyes grew stormy and even darker than usual.

"We don't know that yet," he said. "We're waiting for you to get full control of your powers. Then we'll strike. The Rebels don't feel that we have to rush this. They're biding their time."

"But I *am* stronger. You said so yourself. I'm getting stronger every day."

"Look, it's not time yet. All I know is that I have to protect you until you're ready. I have to make sure there are no threats to you." The unspoken subtext was clear: *Or to your allegiance to the Rebellion.* "Is it so much to ask"—he ran his fingers through his hair in frustration—"for you to trust me?"

"Maybe I should be saying the same thing to you," I said quietly.

He met my gaze for a full beat, fire with fire. Then he turned abruptly. I watched him wind through the trees and disappear among the shadows.

I started to make my way back to where I'd left my friends when the hairs on the back of my neck prickled. I looked up—and saw Devin standing several feet away, in a dark cluster of trees. Even in the darkness, I could see his blue eyes flashing. I met his gaze head-on, but he seemed to hesitate.

I wouldn't look away. Even from where I stood, I could tell he wanted to ask me something. And curiosity got the better of me. I had to know if what Ardith and Gideon had said was true—if he did still care about me. Or if everything he'd ever made me believe was a lie.

Everything seemed to move in slow motion as we walked toward each other.

"Skye," he said, his voice hushed, muffled by the trees and the sounds of the party.

"Hey," I said softly.

"Are you all right? I saw you fall and—"

"I'm fine," I said. He eyed me with cautious interest.

"When you blacked out," he said carefully, "did you . . . see anything?" In the distance, I could hear the fire crackle and snap, the occasional laughter. If I said too much, it could be dangerous. But if I didn't say anything at all, Devin wouldn't be able to help me.

"I had this strange sort of dream." I was afraid to meet his eyes, but when I did, he looked almost excited, though it was hard to tell with his face half obscured by shadows.

He leaned in closer, dropping his voice. "You had a vision, didn't you?" My heart was racing. How did he know? *What* did he know? I nodded as if in a trance. "What did you see?"

Could I trust him? *Of course not.* I answered my own stupid question. *But the thing is, can you really trust Asher now, either?*

And the truth was that I had to tell someone about the visions. I needed help figuring out what they meant. And right now Devin was the only one who might give me that help.

"I was on a beach," I said slowly, gauging his reaction. His eyes widened, but he let me continue. "And I was walking through the mist. I wore a beautiful dress, the most beautiful dress I've ever seen—but it was soaked and dirty from the sand. It was stained with blood."

"Is that it?" he asked quietly.

"No. Ahead of me, I could see a shape on the ground. And in the vision, I knew it was a body. Someone was lying there, and I couldn't see who."

I wondered if I should tell him about what I'd thought to myself in the vision. *Which one of them did I hit?* But I didn't want to tell Devin *all* of my secrets. I had to hold a couple of them close to my chest.

"Skye," he asked. "Have you ever had visions of things that have happened?"

I thought about it.

"I—I think so. Before that night in the woods, I passed out in the parking lot at the mall, and I saw Asher telling me everything was going to be okay. And he was going to find someone to save me." I wondered how I hadn't realized this before. Though it wasn't exactly like I'd had a lot of free time to sit and puzzle it out. "That night, Asher flew me off into the clouds. And he said the same words to me. 'I can't save you, Skye. I'll find someone who can.'"

Devin's eyes remained impassive as he studied me. I felt the need to keep talking.

"But there were other things, too, that were total fiction. Like the moment on the beach. I couldn't live farther from a beach, so that one seems unlikely. And one time, I saw myself opening a shoe box in Aunt Jo's closet. There was also one . . ." I blushed violently. I couldn't finish the sentence.

"What?" he asked.

Could I?

"One time I saw us dancing." I wanted to look away, but I willed myself not to back down. If Ardith and Gideon were right, I couldn't let him think I was weaker than him.

"You and me?" His eyes flickered with uncertainty.

"Yeah," I said. "You and me." I held my ground.

"You're sure?"

"Yes, Devin, I'm sure. I—" I cut myself off abruptly,

realizing that I'd fallen too easily back into the teacher-student rhythm we'd become so practiced at. Devin pushing me to my limit and me pushing it right back in his face. I crossed my arms and looked him square in the eye. A challenge. "What about it?"

"You had a vision that we were dancing." He repeated it not as a question but as some long-sought-after fact he'd suddenly stumbled upon while looking for something else; he could hardly believe the words. I nodded. My voice was lost somewhere in my throat.

Before I knew what was happening, Devin wove his fingers through mine. They were slightly cool, and smooth—so unlike Asher's, which were always the opposite: wind chapped and warm from the elements. When Asher touched me with those hands, I couldn't think straight; my mind went blank. Devin's touch brought a kind of clarity with it.

It wasn't his fault.

I closed my eyes and my fingers wove through his.

The Order forced him.

"Skye," he said, his voice coming out so strangled. "I didn't want to do it."

I opened my eyes again and found myself lost in his. So many different feelings trapped beneath a hard layer of ice.

"I know," I murmured. "I mean, I think I knew that all along."

His grip on my hands tightened, and his eyes flicked over my shoulder, scanning the woods for anyone who might be listening in. "It wasn't me that night," he said urgently. If a Guardian heard what Devin was telling me now, I could only imagine how dangerous the consequences might be for him. *And possibly*—I realized with a twist of my gut—*for me*. "It was the Order. They gave me a command. I had no choice. I've never had a choice. Not when it comes to you. Controlling your life—or ending it. It's all the same. Something they tell me to do, and I have to obey."

"But why?" I asked, the trembling in my voice threatening to take over. "Why do you have to?"

"It's who I am. It's who I've always been and who I'm fated to be. The Order will make sure of that."

"And Raven?"

"We've been destined for each other since we first grew wings. The Order saw it, and so it was." He swallowed hard. "Everything they can foresee will happen. They'll make sure it does, even if their ability to see is now more difficult." He looked at me pointedly. "They'll only find fiercer and more determined ways to manipulate fate. There is nothing we can do about it."

It was shocking—scary, almost—to hear him talk like this. Devin had always been so quick to defend the Order and their ways. Now that their path encompassed something so personal to him, was he faltering in his beliefs?

"The purple flower," I said. "You left that for me. I know you did. Why?"

"At first, I had to stay as far away from you as possible. I was sure that your Rebel"—a fresh layer of ice seemed to crystalize in his eyes—"was planning revenge for what I did. Or worse—that *you* were."

"Tutoring. Homeroom."

He nodded, closing his eyes as if in pain. "I was sick with what I almost did to you. But then, after that morning in the hall, I thought that maybe I could make you understand. You know what it's like to feel as if you have no say in the course of your life. I left you the flower. I hoped you would understand what it meant."

"I did, but—"

He took a small, tentative step forward. "But what?"

"But there's a difference between you and me. You let them control you, and you do nothing to change that. I never could! I have to figure out what's happening to me—control it—*fight*. I've been fighting since you first showed me your wings and made me understand that the same thing awaited *me*."

"You have a choice, Skye. I don't!"

"You do," I said, my voice rising. "All Guardians do!" I paused, breathing deep to steady myself. I knew that the second I said the words that were on my lips, I could never take them back. And who knew what kind of chain of events they would set into motion. "You can jump."

"What?" His fingers unlaced themselves from mine. His hands fell to his sides.

"Jump," I said again. "Leave the Order if you hate it so much. Pledge yourself to chaos, fight against their commands—do *some*thing to change your fate. Become a Rebel." I grabbed his hands again. "You could be *happy*, Devin. Have you ever been happy?"

"No," Devin said, backing away. "That's impossible. No, I could never. I couldn't just turn my back—"

"But think about it—"

"What you're asking of me is enormous—"

"You wouldn't have to adhere to their rules anymore." I wanted to grab him by the shoulders and shake him. "You'd be free!"

"Rules are all I know." He said it fiercely, and for a second, I swore that the fine layer of ice in his eyes shattered with the effort it took to control himself. His hands were curled tightly into fists, shaking by his sides. "I wouldn't know how to live without them."

"But you'd figure it out!" I gasped. "That's all we can ever do, Devin!"

His fists shook harder and then his arms—as if it took more effort than he could exert to hold them down—and before I knew it they had flown up to grab me by the shoulders and pull me to him tightly.

"Why?" he growled. The anger that boiled below the surface of his voice was terrifying. I had seen him yell at me plenty of times, but this—the depth of this—was something new. "Why do you care about this so much? Why do you care about *me*? I failed you. I could do it again. You shouldn't trust me." His voice broke on the word *trust*, and our bodies were so close that I could feel a shudder wrench through him. "You deserve so much better!"

"You believed in me," I said. "When I didn't believe in myself, when I didn't think I could make wind or rain or bring a flower back to life, you knew I had it in me." His grasp on my shoulders tightened, just barely—but something new was stirring in his eyes. "Well, I believe in you, too. I know you could live a far better life as a Rebel than you ever could as a Guardian. And—I miss you." I'd said it. The words I'd been denying to myself since I woke up in the cabin. They were words I'd been longing to say for so long, and they'd come flying out of my mouth before I had a chance to stop them.

Devin looked like he hadn't heard me right. "What did you say?"

"What?" I tried hard not to laugh. "No one's ever missed you before?"

"No," he said simply. "No one."

And then it was like the force of the world was at his wings, pulling him toward me. And his lips neared mine, and his hands were running through my hair, and his body was pushing me up against a tree that was hidden in shadows. And he kissed me. For the first time, he kissed me.

And I remembered something.

In a flash, Devin's body was pressed against mine, backing me into the row of lockers. But it wasn't cool, smooth metal that I felt behind me. The floor had prickled up into frosted grass, and I was leaning against a tree under a canopy of night.

"Skye," he murmured, bringing me back to the present. He ran his fingers slowly down my arms, leaving trails of tiny goose bumps.

Wait.

His kiss was passionate, angry, sad. It was so full of

longing, full of everything that a Guardian wasn't and couldn't ever be.

This happened before.

I felt dizzy.

No—it didn't happen. I saw it.

Fear ripped through me. This didn't feel right. I started to struggle against him.

"Stop," I said. "Stop. Stop!"

"What?" he asked, breaking away. I pushed my hands against him, sending him stumbling back. "What's wrong? Are you okay? Did you see something?"

"No," I said, struggling to catch my breath. "It's this. You! This isn't right. There's Asher, and you—you tried to kill me!" I felt myself growing angry again, felt the heat begin to rise in my chest. At any second, the ground should have rumbled beneath us. But this time, I focused on Devin and held my wild emotions at bay. "You did what they told you to because they told you and for no other reason. You didn't even believe that you should. You just *did it!*" I yelled that last part, and I could feel my face turning red. But there was no fire, no thunder rippling through the clouds. I was just angry; that was all.

My training with Asher was working.

Devin looked at me sadly.

"You're right," he said. "It isn't meant to be. I don't deserve you."

The shadows seemed to come between us then, or maybe it was just my heart playing tricks on me. But I couldn't bear to look at him anymore. I turned and walked away.

Dan drove us home.

He and Cassie murmured softly to each other in the front seat. In the back, I curled myself up against the window, beating back the memories of Devin's lips and ignoring Ian's concerned glances in my direction.

In bed, as I was falling asleep, I clutched the notebook to my chest, trying to hold on to my mom's words, hoping that somehow, in some small way, this tiny book would guide me in the right direction.

I fought against the wind and leaned over the edge of the slope.

Coach stood behind me, timer in hand. "Ready, girls?"

"Ready," I said, pulling my goggles down.

"Ready," said Ellie, doing the same.

It was our final Sunday practice before the last race of the season. The final race was the upcoming Friday afternoon, and the claws were out. Ellie had spent all morning staring me down and talking about me loudly with her friends. Girls who I used to be friends with, too. Whatever.

"On your marks," Coach said. We crouched low at the same time. "Get set." We leaned forward. "Go!"

I pulled ahead, but Ellie was on my tail. Out of the corner

of my eye I could see her pulling up alongside me, trying to edge me out. I pushed forward, let the wind swish past my face. *This isn't about the best time*, I repeated over and over in my head. *It's about keeping control. You're not trying to beat Ellie. You're trying to make yourself strong.*

That was what mattered, right? Not getting named captain. I had huge and important decisions to make, outrageous powers to learn how to use effectively. Becoming captain of the ski team seemed so frivolous.

So why was this so important?

It just is. There was some part of me that wasn't ready to let go of my normal teenage life. I'd wanted to be captain since Aunt Jo had taken me skiing for the first time, when I was eight. You don't forget about the things you've always wanted just because your boyfriend is a Rebel angel, a Guardian angel kissed you in the woods—oh, and you're preparing for a battle between the forces that control destiny and those that fight against it.

I tried to channel that energy into my race. I closed my eyes and tried to feel the course, remembering how Asher had tried to help me control my powers when my emotions ran high. His lips had been so close to mine, our foreheads nearly touching—and yet I had focused all of the energy between us into summoning a storm large enough to wash the fire from the trees. I tried to recapture the moment. But something wasn't working. Instead of Asher's face, I saw Devin, kissing me hard, running his fingers down my arms. . . .

"Eat my powder, Skye," Ellie called, sailing ahead of me.

"Not likely!" I shouted. But it was too late. I'd never be able to catch up to her. I saw clouds rolling in, dark and ominous. Reminding me that if I lost focus for one fraction of a second, I could lose everything.

And when it was a matter of life or death, losing everything wasn't how you wanted things to end.

At the finish, Ellie whooped, pulling up her goggles and throwing her fists in the air.

"Good job, El!" my teammates called from where they were watching. God, why were they so obvious about picking sides? I swished over the finish and scrunched to a stop on the hard snow, panting.

"Nice job, Skye," Ellie said, skiing up to me. "Looks like you may have some competition after all."

"Really?" I asked, looking behind me. "Where?"

She huffed and skied off to rejoin the team.

I threw my head back and tried to get a grip on the rolling clouds, but they kept churning above me, closing in. It started to snow. *Great*, I thought.

The last race of the season was five days away. And I was

determined to win it. Not only that, I was going to control my dark powers once and for all.

After practice, Aunt Jo sat with me while I ate lunch and griped about the team. "I don't know why they hate me now," I mumbled through bites of leftover pasta.

"People hate what they think is a threat," Aunt Jo said in an annoyingly rational voice.

"Do you have a masters in I'm Always Right or something?"

She laughed. "No, Skye, but you left the team—that was something you chose to do. You left them. Then you swoop back in and expect that everything is going to go back to normal. But it takes time for that to happen." The subtext of her little speech was crystal clear. My life wasn't just waiting for me with open arms. I had to work at regaining everyone's trust. She leaned across the table and took my hand, fork and all. "Give them time," she said. "They won't hate you forever." I sank back into my chair and polished off the rest of the pasta.

"Whatever happened to Devin, Skye?" she asked, catching me off-guard. "He was one of the two new guys you were spending time with, wasn't he?"

"He was," I said. *He still is*, I wanted to add. But I kept that to myself. Cassie would yell at me. Dan would take Cassie's side. And Asher—

Asher would never look at me again.

What had happened in the woods the night before—that could never happen again. Whatever I had once wondered about between me and Devin was in the past. If I tried to revive it now, it would only lead to trouble. And trouble was what I was trying so hard to avoid.

"Which one was he again? Snowball Fight?"

"Yes." I twirled my fork along my empty plate, not offering any more information.

"Got it," Aunt Jo said, taking the hint. "Shutting up now." We sat in silence for a few seconds. "That Asher's pretty cute, though." She frowned to herself. "He's charming, and he knows it. The flowers . . . and the sweater . . ."

"He just wanted to impress you," I said. "And can you blame him? You glared at him all night and barely gave him a chance!"

"He's your boyfriend! Of course I'm going to be judgmental. I'm not going to tell you what to do, but I want what's best for you."

"And you don't think he is?"

"He's just so charming, Skye. Don't let him pull you along with whatever he has planned."

"Who said I am?" I felt my temper rising, and tried to calm my mind, focus my emotions. *Keep control*, I told myself. *Don't let go.*

"No one, but I see the way you are with him. You'd do anything for him. Just make sure it's the right thing." She stood up.

"You have no idea what you're talking about," I said hotly.

"Then why are you getting so defensive?" Aunt Jo crossed her arms and gave me a pointed look. "Why would you care if there wasn't a kernel of truth to it?"

I took a few deep breaths and tried to keep my voice as calm as possible as I said, "I'd rather be in love and make the wrong choice once in a while than always be right and be alone." I pushed my chair back and walked out onto the deck. I felt the slight tug of guilt at what I'd said, but I didn't dare turn around and admit defeat. How could she possibly give me advice like that about Asher? She didn't know him at all! She thought she had him pegged, but there was so much more to him than what she saw.

I looked up, and Asher was standing by the railing. His foot was tapping.

"I thought I'd surprise you after practice," he said, shrugging.

"How much did you hear?" I asked.

"Oh, everything."

"I'm sorry," I said. "I have no idea why she's being that way."

"Don't be. She's just being protective. I'm the same way." He looked a little sheepish. "Do you forgive me?" he asked. "For the other night? I don't like keeping things from you, but honestly there's not a lot I know."

I looked down. I felt so, so terrible. Asher would never betray me the way Devin had. Why was I suddenly acting this way all over again?

"I know," I said. "And I do. Forgive you. I'm sorry, too."

"Come here." He sat down and pulled me into his lap in the Adirondack chair, wrapping his arms around me. We stared out at the mountains as the peaks began to turn pink with the sunset. I leaned my cheek against his chest and sighed.

"I think this is my favorite place," I said. "Here, with you. It may be my favorite place in the whole world."

"Yeah," Asher said. "Mine, too. And I've been a lot of places." He squeezed me. "But only as long as we're together. Otherwise it's just a sunset."

"I don't want to watch any more sunsets without you," I said quietly. I felt him kiss the top of my head.

"Me either, Skye," he whispered into my hair.

I tried so hard to keep my focus the rest of the week. It was difficult, and there were a lot of rainstorms because of it.

Asher loved creating fire—it was his signature move. But my favorite element to control was the weather—the storms in particular. I could feel the lightning aching in my fingertips and surging across the sky. For once, my name didn't feel like such a coincidence. It felt like something massive, so much larger than me or my problems. When I could think a simple thought and cause rain to fall from the sky, I felt so connected to the earth and to the forces of nature surrounding me.

Standing in the middle of the field, soaking wet and beaming, I would look at Asher and see his eyes flashing. With the lightning crashing around me, the sheer force of everything I felt for him would threaten to topple me, and I drew from it. I knew my feelings for Asher made my powers stronger, and he knew it, too. We fed off each other.

"You're killing it," he'd whisper into my ear as he helped me draw the strength I needed to inspire a clap of thunder so loud it knocked my teeth together. "You'll be the strongest Rebel yet."

"Tell me what we're preparing for," I asked over and

over again. "Tell me what's coming."

"I don't know," he kept repeating. "I don't know what's coming, yet."

I knew he was hiding the truth from me. And my annoyance would cause the sky to crack, and Asher would grasp my hands tightly in his, and the power surged between us, so that there was no difference between love and anger, frustration and joy. It was all the same when we were together. It was exactly what he'd said that day back at the cabin. It was a partnership.

I hadn't yet told him about what, exactly, I'd seen in my visions. I wasn't sure he'd understand. I hadn't had one in a few days, and I was thinking about this one day in the field as we worked silently, side by side, at manipulating the size and shape of raindrops. If I concentrated hard enough, could I force myself to have a vision? And if I could, what would that mean? Did any other Guardians have the same kinds of visions? I knew I shouldn't, but I needed to talk to a Guardian about what I was seeing. I still needed to talk to Devin.

When the house was dark and quiet that night, I opened the door to my room just a crack. No light shone under the door of Aunt Jo's room, which meant she wasn't up late reading. Here was my chance. I needed a way to talk to Devin outside of school, where Guardians and Rebels might be watching us. I'd blurred his destiny—the Gifted wouldn't be able to track where he was. As long as we met outside of school, we were fine.

At least that's what I told myself.

I waited ten minutes to make sure Aunt Jo really was asleep before tiptoeing through the front door. Summoning my dark powers, I caused a massive clap of thunder to mask the sound of the car starting. Then I drove.

I hadn't driven to the apartment complex on the edge of town since that one time I'd gone home with Devin, but it wasn't hard to find. The light was on in his window when I pulled up. I hesitated. What if Raven was there? Or the other Guardians? What if they were all staying with Devin now? My heart pounded audibly as I got out of the car and walked to his door as quietly as possible.

In my hand was a small purple flower I'd picked outside my house. I tied it to the doorknob with a length of string. He would know what it meant.

I drove away as quickly as I'd come. I knew he would find me. I would just have to wait.

I woke up before the sun rose the next morning and got ready for school in a fit of nervous excitement.

Instead of going right to my car, I veered left and found the entrance to my favorite trail in the woods that ran beyond our house. It was still early. I had time. I began to climb, inhaling the fresh, morning scent of the evergreen trees that lined the path.

Soon I reached the spot, halfway up the mountain, where the trail curved and the trees gave way to a sweeping view of the valley below. In that spot, in the dead of winter, Devin had saved me from slipping on the ice and falling over the side of the cliff. That day felt like a lifetime ago.

I knew he would know to meet me here this morning, and I couldn't believe I was walking into this on purpose. But something in me propelled me forward. Something I felt like I couldn't refuse.

The sun was peeking over the gap in the mountains when I reached the clearing, casting the trail in an orange-pink glow. Devin was sitting on the same rock we'd sat on together that winter day, staring out over the vast fields below. He turned when I stepped on a twig, the brittle crack startling both of us.

"I knew you'd come," I said. "Thank you."

His face was stoic and reserved. He'd probably been telling himself the same thing I had. *Behave this time. Don't you dare lose control.*

"I probably shouldn't have," he said.

I stepped closer to the rock, but stayed standing, kicking lightly at the undergrowth that covered the trail. He was looking at me with that calm that I found so unnerving. *What is he thinking?*

"I—I have some questions." I paused and took one step closer, but he drew back. "I know. Part of me knows I should stay away from you, for all the reasons you said. But another part of me doesn't want to. And I don't know what to do about it."

"I understand," he said. "I came here, didn't I?" It struck me that the more time he spent here, on Earth, in River Springs, with me—the less stiff he sounded.

"I need your help. There's so much more I have to learn, and you're the only one who can teach me."

He sighed heavily. "I know," he said. "I've been thinking about your visions. That's why I came to meet you. Your light powers are an undeniable part of who you are, and the sooner you can accept that, the sooner you can master them."

"Even if I'm a Rebel now?" I asked. "I chose. I made a promise. I can't leave them. And I won't leave Asher."

"You can deny it, but those are just words. You can't convince yourself that what you're experiencing aren't Guardian powers." His voice was impatient. "You can't ignore them."

"So what do they mean?"

"Skye," he said insistently, leaning in close to me. "Did it ever occur to you that your visions might be telling you something important? What if they're not just dreams? What if what you're seeing is the *future*? Things that haven't happened yet."

I started. "Like prophecies?" I asked, not quite sure where he was going with this.

"Not prophecies," he said, standing up and looking at me. "The Sight."

"The Sight?" I tried to process what he was saying, but the words felt like another language on my tongue. "You're telling me I can see the fate of other people?"

Devin paused for a moment, lost in thought. "Maybe not of other people," he said. "Maybe—just your own."

"You're saying I can see things that are going to happen in my future?" I balked. "Is that normal?"

"No," he said, breaking out into a small grin. "Not for a Guardian. But nothing about you is normal."

"I can't believe it," I said in bewilderment. "The beautiful dress. The beach, the sand, the blood. The shoe box. Those are all things that are waiting for me in my future?" I looked at him. He seemed to know what was coming next. "You and me, dancing."

Devin stood up abruptly. "I wondered that," he said. "But it can't happen. It's more than just dangerous—it's not right. You and Asher, and me and . . . Raven."

"I know."

He shook his head. "I don't want you to think—"

"Think what?" I spoke too quickly. I could tell from the look of concentration on his face that he was trying to come up with the best and most diplomatic way to phrase whatever he needed to say.

"I guess I didn't want you to get the wrong idea." Diplomatic, maybe, but it still stung. I tried to keep a blank expression.

"Well, give me the right one." I sat down next to him on the rock. My arm brushed against his, and we both moved away quickly.

"I thought you were dead," he said.

"I know."

"Asher took you away, and Astaroth forced me back to River Springs. He left me here with no word of the outcome, no indication of the status of the mission. He simply told me that my fate was sealed and I had to await the consequences. And so I waited."

I pictured Devin waiting in his tiny, clean apartment. No word from his people. Nobody to wake up next to. How lonely he must have felt.

"Okay," I said.

"And Raven came. She told me I couldn't just waste my life waiting for you to come back. Even if you hadn't died, you were with the Rebellion now. There was no way you would ever choose to join the Order knowing that they tried to kill you." He took a breath. "Deep down I knew she was right. Even though our destinies were impossible to discern anymore, thanks to you, we always had been fated to be together. And so we were bonded."

"Well," I said, "now I get it." I looked away. He was watching me closely.

"I thought you were dead," he said again. "I didn't think you would ever come back."

"Look." We were veering onto dangerous territory. "I came here because I wanted to talk to you about my visions. That was it."

He stood up, rigid. As if one step out of line would cause his whole world to come crashing down around him. "I want to help you. But you can't trust me with this information. I'm still under the Order's control. I still have to report to the Gifted. I could turn on you at any second. Skye, I don't trust them, and I definitely don't trust myself."

"But—"

"They made me a murderer, and I'll have to live with that for eternity. Can you imagine what that feels like? Knowing I could have killed you and then continuing to live for centuries?" He turned to leave, then looked back at me. "If they find out about your visions . . ."

"I'm not going to tell them," I said. "Are you?"

A long pause stretched out between us.

Without a word, his wings unfurled from his back, huge and white as the clouds above. And he took off through the trees.

I sat down on the rock and stared out at the field below me.

The Sight. It was the very strongest of the powers of the light. Something only the Gifted possessed. So what did that mean?

School that day was a waste.

I didn't absorb anything, which was bad, because I'd just finished all of my catch-up work and was starting to feel on top of things again. I wanted to throw myself anew into the college process, but my brain was everywhere all at once. To force myself to focus, I swung by the guidance counselor's office between classes and signed up for an appointment later that week.

At lunch, Cassie, Dan, and Ian laughed about something hilarious that I was too spaced out to hear. They recapped events from the party in the woods that I'd been too wrapped up in my own issues to have seen. I nibbled absently on my turkey sandwich, and nobody seemed to notice. During class, I practiced building up walls and breaking them down. So far, though, I was convinced that what Gideon had said was a lie. Devin wasn't influencing me. I was sure of it.

After school, I lost myself in ski practice, blocking out the taunts and jeers of the other girls. I focused instead on channeling the wind, making my descent to the finish smoother, sleeker. I held the clouds at bay.

But I couldn't push from my mind what Devin had said. The Sight. There wasn't anything in my mother's notebook about that. I'd read the lines so many times that I had the entire entry memorized:

> *Guardians haunt these woods, watching us. I know they know. It's only a matter of time.*
> *We have to act quickly. There are too many of them. We need more recruits.*

So maybe Devin was wrong. Maybe my visions were something else entirely. A result of my mental and physical exertion lately: skiing, controlling the elements, being with Asher. Or maybe, practicing to fight the Order's mental manipulation was taking a toll on my mind, as it had done to Gideon's.

But I didn't want to face the thing I knew deep down, which was that these visions had been going on much longer than I'd known Gideon. They'd started right around the time I'd met Asher and Devin. My seventeenth birthday, when everything strange began happening to me in the first place.

Asher wouldn't leave my side that week. We practiced sometimes at night, after Aunt Jo had gone to bed. When we were too tired to continue, he'd follow me upstairs in the dark, holding my hand to guide him, and we'd curl up in my bed and sleep. "You need to rest," Asher whispered to me in the darkness. "You need to be strong."

On Wednesday night, we followed our routine, and both of us were sleeping when I woke with a start. If my visions were glimpses into the future, then finding the shoe box in Aunt Jo's closet was going to happen at some point. She was in there, sleeping now, but in the vision, the room was empty, and the last light of day peeked through the curtains.

Not tonight, I thought. *Tomorrow night. Before Aunt Jo gets home from work.*

There was something in that box I needed. Something that was going to help me. I let Asher curl himself around me. *What if it's something that has to do with my parents?* I wondered. *What if it's one more thing that will bring me closer to my mom?*

I fell asleep not knowing the answers.

The next day was the day before the race, and practice after school was tense. Rather than racing freestyle, we

ran drills. Coach watched Ellie and me with close attention, his ever-present stopwatch starting and stopping
with an obnoxious little beep. Once or twice, Ellie and I
glanced at each other and tried not to laugh. Maybe things
weren't going to end up so bad between us after all.

On the last drill, Ellie and I went head to head.

"Step it up, girls," Coach said. "Captain's on the line
here."

"Like we could forget," Ellie muttered under her breath.
He blew his whistle, and we took off, weaving between a
series of slaloms that were set up for the drill. We started
off smiling at each other tentatively, but the more we got
into it, the fiercer the competition became. At first, I was
winning, making my turns with much more precision,
feeling out the snow and the bumps in the ground beneath
me. Then Ellie picked up speed, pulling ahead. I leaned in,
focusing every ounce of my being. I couldn't let her beat
me. Suddenly my anger at her raged.

Who did she think she was? She had flirted with Asher
when she had clearly seen something brewing between the
two of us, even if it hadn't been official. And when she
didn't win that round, she decided to hook up with Ian.
And now she wanted to be captain.

Aunt Jo was right. People hate things that they think are

a threat to them. And Ellie somehow found me threatening. It wasn't that she particularly cared about Asher, or Ian, or even making captain of the ski team. It was just about beating *me*. But what had I ever done to her? How had I threatened her in any way? Annoyance and frustration burned through me.

For the briefest of moments, I forgot to focus.

I seemed to feel the rumble of the mountain before anyone else, and so I had a few seconds to try to stop whatever was about to happen from happening. But I was still too late. I may have prevented a full-on avalanche, but a large chunk of ice dislodged from a rock face and came rolling down the mountain. It gathered more and more snow the faster it rolled.

"Skye!" Coach called. "Look out!"

I swerved to my right, but I couldn't get out of the way fast enough. The icy snowball clipped the side of my ski, sending me careening backward. I tried to grab on to something to steady myself, but I couldn't find a hold. Panicking, I felt myself falling, rolling head over foot down the mountain. I dug my nails and heels into the snow to gain traction and felt myself slowing.

"Skye!" Ellie called from far below. "Are you okay?"

"Skye?" Coach Samuelson yelled. "Say something!"

"I'm okay!" I called, my voice shaky as I came to a rest. But when the shock of the impact wore off, a stabbing pain ricocheted through my left ankle.

I was close enough to the bottom so that I could ski gingerly down the rest of the way. My team crowded around me, suddenly—finally—showing support.

"Skye, this doesn't look good," Coach said, kneeling and examining my ankle.

"It'll be better by tomorrow," I insisted. "I promise. I just twisted it, that's all. It'll be fine after I ice it. Really." I needed to race tomorrow—so much depended on it.

"Kiddo, I don't know if promising is going to do you any good at this point. You may just have to sit this one out."

I'd come this close. I was almost there. *No*, I thought as the bus drove us back to school. I couldn't let that happen.

The race was too important to miss. I'd sprained my ankle skiing before—and it had healed quickly, miraculously, even. But this time, I couldn't go to Devin, or anyone else, for help.

Maybe this was supposed to happen. Maybe I needed to figure it out on my own.

·23·

I drove home from practice slowly. There was no way I could sit out the race tomorrow. Not only would it mean forfeiting the title of captain to Ellie—something I was determined not to let happen—but the race was an important milestone. It was all supposed to come together for me tomorrow on the slopes, and the thought of being forced out by injury brought angry tears to my eyes. I wiped them away with the back of one hand, gripping the steering wheel in the other.

When I pulled into the driveway, I cut the engine and began to hobble toward the house. But halfway there, I stopped. I couldn't let anyone see how badly I'd hurt my ankle. Aunt Jo would be concerned and fuss around me.

Asher would be worried—but for different reasons.

If he saw me limping tonight, he would inevitably want to know how my ankle had suddenly healed come tomorrow. And then I was going to have to explain just how strong my powers of the light really were. I knew he wanted me to be as powerful as possible, but still, if he was looking for reasons not to trust me, that was as clear a sign as any.

Because that's what I was planning to do. Harness my ability to heal. I was determined to do it, and yet the idea of doing something so powerful terrified me. I'd only ever tried and failed. What if I messed up and ruined my ankle forever?

I pushed open the front door with my shoulder and tried to keep the weight off my ankle. Low voices carried from the kitchen, and I immediately got a strange premonition of the scene I was about to walk in on. When I threw my bag down in the hall, the voices stopped talking abruptly. "I'm home!" I called.

"In the kitchen!" Aunt Jo shouted.

The scene did not disappoint. She and Asher sat across the kitchen table from each other, in uncomfortable silence. Asher's foot was tapping wildly against the floor, and he was squinting at her with a weird, uneasy look on his face.

She was staring into a mug of coffee.

"You two having quality bonding time?" I asked, raising an eyebrow at the awkwardness.

Asher jumped up when he saw me come in.

"Oh, no, please sit," I said, smiling obliviously on purpose. "Don't let me interrupt." Careful not to limp or wince, I walked stiffly to the table and fell into a chair between them. "So," I said, "what are we talking about?"

"Aunt Jo was about to show me baby pictures of you."

"Wait," I said, sitting bolt upright. "What? Is this what happens when you guys hang out without me?"

"He's kidding, Skye," Aunt Jo said, cracking a careful smile. "We were talking about your race tomorrow. We'll both be there."

I gulped. "Yay," I said halfheartedly.

"How are you feeling about it?" Asher asked. The look in his eyes implied he wasn't just talking about my time to beat.

"Good," I said, giving him a meaningful look. "I'm ready."

"Great!" Aunt Jo said, much too enthusiastically.

"I think," I added.

"You're strong, Skye." Asher's voice was low and serious. "You're ready. You know you can do this."

I looked at him gratefully. It felt so good to know he believed in me that much. I reached out and grasped his hand. He grinned.

Aunt Jo cleared her throat. "You must be famished, hon," she said. "I'll heat up some leftovers."

I turned to Asher. "Want to go out back while we're waiting?"

He nodded, squeezing my hand in his.

"It'll be ready in just a few minutes," Aunt Jo warned.

"Can Asher stay for dinner?" I asked.

"Yeah?" he said eagerly. "Can I stay? I've been dreaming about your lemon bars every night."

She looked like she might be about to give in. Then Asher smiled his charming smile at her, and her face hardened.

"Oh, not tonight. Skye needs her rest! Besides, Asher, you're over here so often, I bet your parents are wondering if we kidnapped you." Asher's smile faded into a scowl, and his eyebrows knocked together.

"No," he said. "I doubt they're thinking that."

"Well, either way, I think we'll all call it a night early tonight—okay?" She looked at me pointedly.

"Fine," I muttered. I took Asher's hand, and we walked out onto the deck. It was excruciating to put all of my weight on my ankle, but I couldn't let him know anything was wrong. I tried to smile through the pain.

Once we were alone outside, Asher laced his fingers through mine and kissed me. "You sure you're okay?" he asked. I nodded. And even if I wasn't, I wouldn't have told him just then.

The sky had faded from dusk to darkness, and it looked like someone had flung up a handful of stars like confetti. I breathed deep and closed my eyes. Asher stepped closer to me, squeezing my hands softly in his and bringing my arms around his waist. I nestled into him and felt him shiver under my touch.

"You don't feel any warmer," he said. "Not like you usually do. You okay with this?" His voice was low and scratchy and familiar and thrilling all at once. Though my eyes were closed, I could feel my energy focusing, the stars move above me, forming constellations, rearranging themselves.

"Fine," I said.

He moved closer still, and my breath grew shallow as I struggled to maintain control of my powers.

"And this?" he whispered, lowering his face until his lips were barely grazing mine. My skin grew warm, and I could feel the pain flare up in my ankle, shooting through the rest of me. I let out a sharp gasp, and Asher stepped away quickly.

"Too much?" he asked.

"Skye!" Aunt Jo called, too loudly, from the doorway. "Dinner!"

"Crap," I muttered.

"Come *on*," I heard Asher groan under his breath, running a hand through his hair.

I looked up at him and ran my thumb along his chin. "See you tomorrow?" I asked.

"Count on it." He jogged down the stairs of the deck to the field below, and before my eyes could adjust, I'd lost him in the darkness.

As I turned around to go inside, I glanced upward. The stars had arranged themselves into a tiny heart. I smiled to myself, suppressing the pain in my ankle, and went inside for dinner.

While Aunt Jo was clearing the dishes, I hobbled frantically to the downstairs bathroom. There was no way I could climb the stairs to my room just yet. I locked the door behind me, sat down on the lid of the toilet, and brought my foot up onto my knee.

Okay, I thought. *You can do this.* I tried to remember

what Devin had done to me when I was in the infirmary after the avalanche. He'd wrapped both hands around my ankle, and the pain had flared up, fantastically intense before subsiding into nothingness.

I wrapped my own hands around my ankle. I closed my eyes and tried to let the energy flow through my fingertips. What had Asher told me that very first night we'd kissed in my room?

Just pretend that everything inside you is lots of unfiltered electricity. Imagine what you want to do with it. And then imagine flipping a switch—and turning it on.

With my eyes still closed, I focused on the energy, curling it up into a ball of light in my hands. *Flip the switch*, I thought.

The ball of light grew brighter and more vibrant as I held it steady. I brought it toward my ankle and spread it over the pain, like a salve. I directed every ounce of energy I had, flowing through the tips of my fingers, and suddenly I felt an intense pain flair up in my leg, blinding, overwhelming. A white-hot flash burned through me. "Ow," I gasped, hoping Aunt Jo couldn't hear me.

And then, just like that, the pain faded away. A cooling relief tingled up from my ankle, flooding through the rest of my body. I tried to catch my breath.

I had done it! My ankle felt fine—*better* than fine. Amazing.

"Skye?" Aunt Jo called. "You feel okay, hon?"

"Fine!" I called. I danced around silently. It had worked! I'd healed *myself*. I looked up into the bathroom mirror, and my eyes flashed silver and intense. For once, I didn't look away or feel uncomfortable. I didn't wish that they were just a normal gray like anyone else's. I was proud of what my silver eyes meant. My light and dark powers had woven together, to help me when I needed them. I'd drawn on them both to fix what was broken. And now I was ready. Ready to fight, to win, to take utter control of who I was. I wasn't afraid of my powers anymore.

I went to turn the doorknob when my mind suddenly went blank, and I found myself, once again, walking down the darkened upstairs hallway. I managed to stay upright, to let the wisp of a vision flow through me. The door to Aunt Jo's bedroom loomed at the end of the hall. Empty.

And then I was back in the downstairs bathroom again, my hand still gripping the doorknob. Devin's last words to me echoed in my mind.

Did it ever occur to you that your visions might be telling you something important? What if they're not just dreams? What if what you're seeing is the future?

My hand gripped the doorknob tighter, so tight that my knuckles were turning white. The blood drained from my face.

"Not prophecies," he'd said. *"The Sight."*

My mind spun and my heart raced. As I turned the knob and slipped out into the hall, the sound of water and dishes clattering echoed from the kitchen. Now was my chance. The upstairs hallway would be dark. Aunt Jo's bedroom, empty.

With the noise from the kitchen as my cover, I tip-toed up the stairs. If I strained my ears, I could just hear her humming softly as she worked. I'd seen this happen before. When she started singing, it meant she was lost in thought, her mind shut off from the rest of the world.

I had only a couple of minutes, if I was lucky.

I moved quickly and silently up the stairs and down the hall, the memory of my vision blurring with reality.

I glanced to my right, at the door to my bedroom, which was slightly ajar. Light spilled out into the dark hallway, illuminating my path. To my left was the bathroom. The door was open and the lights were off. I peeked over the railing of the stairs. The whole house was dark and silent. Directly ahead of me was her bedroom.

I walked toward it, as if pulled by an invisible string.

The walls on either side of me were smooth under my hands as I let them guide me in the semidarkness.

The door to Aunt Jo's bedroom wasn't closed all the way.

I pushed it open, carefully, silently, and turned on the light.

Her room was empty.

As I knew it would be.

The bed was unmade. Clothes were draped over the chair in the corner. I turned toward the closet.

Slowly, slowly, I reached my hand out to open it.

I knew what I was looking for.

In the corner of the closet, I spotted the stepladder. Downstairs, I heard the rush of water from the faucet in the kitchen sink. I didn't have much time.

I climbed onto it, peering over the shelves above my head. That's where I spotted it.

The shoe box. The same one from my vision. The one I'd been looking for.

As if time was moving in slow motion, I opened the lid. . . .

I sat down on the floor of the closet and peered inside. With hands that trembled slightly, I picked up a small velvet box, and opened it to find a glittery diamond ring. I snapped the lid shut and moved on to the next artifact—an old photograph, yellowing slightly at the edges from weathering years inside a shoe box in a closet. In the photo, a couple leaned against a tree, oblivious to the camera. His hair was dark and wild, and his head was tilted down toward hers, as if they were sharing a secret—or were about to kiss. The woman smiled up at him, the corners of her eyes crinkled in laughter. Blond wisps of hair had come loose from her ponytail and were blowing in the wind.

Wait a minute.

I looked closer. The woman was Aunt Jo!

I squinted to inspect the guy. He was gorgeous in a dangerous sort of way, that was undeniable. But there was also something familiar about him. I couldn't quite put my finger on it.

I put the photograph back and moved on to the next item in the box. A stack of papers were tied together with a piece of fishing twine. I lifted them out of the shoe box and carefully undid the knot. The pages all had jagged edges, as if someone had ripped them hastily from a notebook. *The missing pages.* My throat was dry, and as the twine fell away, I realized what I felt was more than just the thrill of discovery. I was nervous—nervous that what I was about to read contained some valuable clue to a past that had forever seemed so hidden from me.

Sitting cross-legged on the floor of the quiet little closet, I could hear my heart beating. Its rhythm grew faster as I stared down at the first page. It was filled with the same looping handwriting I'd been staring at every night, in the notebook that was now hiding underneath my pillow. My handwriting. My mother's.

My eyes welled with years of grief. The words sprawled across the page as if speaking directly to me.

The Order knows about our new faction. They're coming to stop it.

I flipped to the next page, my heart in my throat.

We've moved into the cabin, are hiding here. Mer thinks it will happen any day now, but she and Sam continue to plan the uprising. There's no way we can know, with the Order, how it will happen. Mer has lost that gift. But she says we have to live our lives and what they see will come to pass. The two of them always knew that no place would be safe for a union of the Order and the Rebellion. They would have no real home. Neither would Skye, a mix of both worlds but truly from neither. Neither would the other Rogues. Neither would I. It's what bonds us together. It's what drives the uprising.

We're all nomads. Wandering, searching for peace. But the Order will never let us find it. They will never leave us alone, not until we've either been extinguished— or become one of them. They'll come for us, but it will never stop us from trying.

Mer and Sam—my mom and dad. But why would she be writing about herself in the third person? And the part about the Rogues made no sense. I flipped the page.

Mer and Sam gave me a home, something I've never had before. In return, they asked me one favor, one small favor in all of this. When the Order comes, when they crush our fledgling mission and destroy its founders, take Skye. Keep her away from them. Raise her so she'll never know. Protect her from her lineage. And from herself.

Wait. What was I reading? Whose notebook was this? I definitely hadn't written these words. And the more I read, the more I realized, with a heavy sinking in my chest, that neither had my mom. Even as I turned the last page, my hands trembling, I had a feeling I knew whose handwriting I was staring at.

Because when she finds out, she'll never stop fighting for their cause. She'll have the powers of Light and Dark combined—her mother and her father. No one knows what her powers will be. Both sides will try to claim her, but they'll be wrong. What the Rogues understand— what Skye will, too, one day—is that to choose one over the other is to deny the very root of who she is: a balance of both. They're watching, waiting—they'll come for her, too, when the terms of the pact have come to pass. And then she'll either fight to change the course of the universe—or they'll try to kill her. Just like they're trying to kill her parents.

My breath caught in my throat as I turned the last page.

We've left the cabin. It's no longer safe here. I'll spend the rest of my life protecting her from herself. I swear it.

And that could only mean one thing.

The book had never belonged to my mom. The loopy handwriting looked familiar because I'd seen it on Post-it notes on the fridge, on parental permission forms for school, on every report card and every doctor's note I'd gotten for the past eleven years. I knew it well, because it was my handwriting, too. I'd spent my whole life copying it.

"Oh my god," I said out loud. "It's Aunt Jo's."

She knew. She'd known all along.

And more important than that—she was a Rogue.

"Skye?"

I looked up, and Aunt Jo was standing there. The sadness in her eyes made her wrinkles even more defined. Like she'd aged immeasurably over the course of just a few days.

I had a handful of pages from her notebook and no excuse. I'd discovered her secret—and by virtue of that fact, she'd discovered mine. I was caught. We both were.

"I guess it's time we talked," she said quietly. She rolled up the sleeves of her shirt and sat down on the floor of the closet next to me.

"How could you not tell me?" I asked, my voice coming out choked. "You let me go through all this alone."

"I know," she said.

"If I had known, I could have at least been prepared! I could have known what to expect, or tried to run away, or—"

"Skye," Aunt Jo said calmly. "You couldn't have run away. And you wouldn't have known what to expect. The Order would have found you no matter what you did or where you went. If they'd marked you, they would have tracked you down—just like they tracked your parents."

"But—"

She reached over and took my hands in hers.

"I made a promise to them that I would protect you. And I was going to keep that promise if it killed me, too. They knew what they were up against when they took on the Order. They knew they were going to die. Protecting you was their only wish."

"I still don't understand why they didn't want me to know. They could have warned me. They could have let you tell me. Why keep it a secret? Why let me find out for myself, the hard way?"

"Because you wouldn't have been able to change anything." I'd never before heard such urgency in her voice. "You would have grown up with dread and fear in your heart, that every step you took, every choice you made, was being watched. It would have driven you insane."

"So it's better to turn seventeen and find out I've been stalked my whole life by angels? To find out I have powers that could sway the course of destiny?"

"No, better that you got to have a normal childhood, make amazing friends, and get to make your own choices—not based on what you think would keep the Order at bay for one more day."

"I still don't . . . ," I began, a huge sob racking my lungs. "This whole time. I kept it from you to protect *you*, when you were protecting *me*. You could have helped me!"

"If I had helped you, you would have done exactly what your mother was afraid of—something drastic and probably foolish—"

"Thanks," I said. "You're making this much better—"

"I mean that in running away from your life—or facing it before your powers began to emerge and you were ready—you would have done something to change the course of the universe. Or the Order would have killed you and you'd have died trying to change something you never could. Even then, your parents knew how special you were going to be. They wanted to protect you for as long as possible."

The torn edges of the notebook blurred in my hands. I blinked, fighting back the tears.

"But I *can* change things," I said. "I can change them now."

Aunt Jo looked uncertain. "I don't know, Skye. Others have been trying. For years. For millennia. Nothing has worked."

"I'm different." I stood up quickly, and the papers fluttered to the closet floor. "They're all telling me I'm special. That I'll be more powerful than any Rebel or any Guardian. I can do it, Aunt Jo. Aren't you the one who told me to follow my own star? Don't you want me to take your advice?"

"You should do what you feel is right," she said. "I'll always protect you. I will always, always be thinking of how to keep you safe."

She stood up, too. I didn't feel anymore like the little kid she'd taken in. I felt like I'd lived a hundred different lifetimes since then. But when she held out her arms to hug me, I rushed into them like I was six years old and she was the only person in the world who really cared.

I was lucky enough to know that it wasn't the case anymore.

When we pulled away, I bit my lip. "Aunt Jo," I admitted, "I love you and all. But I was kind of hoping that the notebook had belonged to my mom. I just don't have anything that belonged to her. I wish I did. It was nice to feel close to her for a little while."

Aunt Jo frowned, seemingly lost in thought. "You know," she said slowly, as if still thinking it through. "I do have something of your mom's, actually."

"You do?"

"I always forget that it belonged to her. I associate it with something else completely."

"What is it?" I asked breathlessly.

"It's right in here," she said, disappearing for a minute under a rack of sweaters. When she emerged, she was holding a large box, the kind you get from a dry cleaner for storing wedding dresses.

I gasped. "Is it her wedding dress?" I asked, reaching out for it. Aunt Jo batted my hand away.

"No," she said simply. "It wasn't her wedding dress. She gave it to me for mine."

"What!" I gaped. "I thought you said you never married."

Aunt Jo looked sad for a moment, then seemed to snap out of it and shook her head. "I didn't."

"Then what . . . ?"

She just pushed the box toward me. "Here," she said. "Open it."

I lifted the lid off the box with the edges of my fingers as if it was a photo I didn't want to smudge. Inside, tufts of tissue paper were layered on top of one another like a sugary, sweet cake. I gently moved each layer aside, and eventually my fingers touched fabric. But it didn't feel like any fabric I had ever worn. It didn't feel quite like fabric at all. I pulled out a long, flowing dress.

My jaw dropped.

It was the dress from my visions. But instead of streaked with salt and blood, it was ethereal, perfect.

The only word for it was *diaphanous*. The dress was a sweeping floor-length with layers of white melting into the sheerest blue silk and chiffon. I held it up to myself and grinned, suppressing images of the sand, the sword, the body crumpled on the ground. "What do you think?" I asked, twirling around. "Do I look like an angel?"

"I think you look just like your mom when it was hers," said Aunt Jo. She was beaming. "I never got to wear it, but you should save that. You know, for prom."

I pictured myself at prom in a couple of months, the beautiful gown sweeping the floor like a boat trailing stardust through a moonlit lake. It wasn't the kind of thing I would usually wear, but when I pictured myself in it, something clicked inside me and it felt right. Who would I be with at prom? My friends, of course. Cassie, in something fabulous with sequins and feathers. Dan and Ian, in tuxes. Would I go with Asher? Would we slow-dance together like a normal couple in front of the entire school, like we were the only two people in the world?

I closed my eyes and let myself imagine it. The soft material of the dress fell over my skin in drapes and folds, grazing the floor as I walked across it in dangerously high heels. There was a beautiful boy in a tuxedo standing on the other side of the dance floor. And as I walked to him, I knew in my heart that this was the person I was supposed to be with. This was my destiny, my one epic love. I reached out my hands to take his, and he pulled me into his arms. The music whirled and lilted as if being distorted.

But no matter how many times we twirled, I couldn't see his face.

"Babe," Aunt Jo said. "You okay? Do you like it?"

"Oh," I said. "I *love* it." She smiled, pleased, proud.

"Your mom would have wanted you to have it. And I certainly got no use out of it. It's angelic silk, sheer as clouds."

It was the only thing I had that belonged to my mom. I held the dress to my chest, and pretended she was the one who had given it to me.

"I'll wear it to prom," I said, leaning in to give Aunt Jo

a kiss. "It's perfect. Thank you."

"She'd be proud of you, Skye," she said. "They both would."

I lay in bed that night and tried not to think about the connection between the beautiful dress and my violent vision. Instead, as I hovered somewhere between dreaming and waking, I wondered if Aunt Jo had left the notebook in the cabin by accident—or if she'd left it there on purpose.

The morning of the race dawned, bright and clear. Coach was skeptical about my miraculous recovery, but I managed to prove to him that I was fine.

After my discoveries from the night before, I felt more ready than I ever had to hold my power in the palm of my hand, like fire, like snow, like freezing rain. Aunt Jo was there, with Cassie, Dan, and Ian. The four of them had scrawled a different letter of my name in puffy paint on T-shirts that they wore over sweatshirts. Cassie was S, Dan was K, Ian was Y, and Aunt Jo held up the rear with E.

A little ways off, Asher stood with Gideon and Ardith. The two Rebels talked to each other, smiling as they watched me prepare. But Asher looked so serious, so wholly focused on what was going on in his head. What was he thinking?

Probably he was just praying for me not to royally screw up. My pulse quickened as I thought of how embarrassing it would be to accidentally reveal my powers in front of everybody. The key, of course, was control.

As I scanned the crowd, I noticed Devin was there, too. Watching me. A spasm clenched my heart. The memory of our kiss still haunted me, but it wasn't that I longed to feel his lips on mine again or his fingers graze down my arms. Aunt Jo had reminded me how unrelenting the Order was—and how very little stood in their way. They would not have let that kind of transgression occur. Even if I was causing static in the frequency of destiny—they would have known, somehow. They always knew. They were always ready. There was no fooling them.

The morning was cold, but I shivered from fear. Had my kiss with Devin been genuine? Or, like everything else, had it only been some trick? The Order's attempt to shake me up, keep me vulnerable?

I tried to wipe everything clean and make my mind calm and focused. At the top of the mountain, I took a few deep breaths and stretched. I could do this. I was ready.

Ellie was racing first, and she crouched against her opponent at the starting line. The team cheered behind her. "Come on, El! You got this!" She frowned and leaned forward. Poles back. The whistle blew, and she and her competition from Holy Cross were off, a blur of school colors against the white snow. I found myself cheering along with the team. Soon I couldn't see them anymore, but when I heard the crowd cheer just minutes later, I knew without a doubt that Ellie had won. Her time would be hard to beat.

My number was up. I pulled my goggles down and glided forward to the starting point.

I was hovering on the edge.

I am hovering on the edge.

In the clear, cold light of day, the dreams that I'd had while unconscious came rushing back.

The dead of winter. Snow covering the slopes like it was trying to bury us all with it. I can hear the sound of my classmates' voices echoing off the mountains as they laugh and horse around.

No, not horse around. Cheer. Cheer for me. As I readied at the start, I could hear them cheering my name.

I looked down over the edge, into the chasm below.

Just like in the dream, I was torn. I was always torn. But now I felt like I was beginning to figure out an answer.

"Make a choice, Skye," I said to myself. *"You can't stare off the edge of this cliff forever."*

The whistle blew at the start, and we were off down

the slope. I felt the tension of opposites rush through me, keeping me in control. I passed through patches of sunlight and then shadows cast by the trees. Light. And then dark. Control and chaos.

I knew then as well as I ever would that Aunt Jo was right: I couldn't have one without the other. Destroy the Rebellion and life would be governed by an impossible set of rules for eternity. Destroy the Order and no place on Earth would be safe from the never-ending cycle of destruction and renewal.

I was the only thing keeping them in balance.

The powers of light and dark were twining themselves together inside me, into a power that only I possessed. Me—and no one else.

I couldn't make a choice between chaos and control. Not because it had been made for me. But because there was no choice to make. It wasn't one or the other. They were both inside me. They were both a part of me. I was nothing without both sides.

Take one away and I would fall.

I'd had the dream every night. And I never woke up to the relief that it was only a dream. Because for days, I hadn't woken up at all.

But I was awake now. I was out of the darkness, and

suddenly my world was flooded with light.

And as I sliced across the finish line, I knew that I had done it.

Coach Samuelson stood in front of the crowd with his stopwatch. He nodded at me imperceptibly, but his eyes remained distant. Ellie's time had been better than mine. She had beat me out for captain.

But as I saw Asher break through the crowd and rush to swoop me up in his arms, I knew it didn't matter.

She could be captain—that was what *she* wanted. I had found clarity at last.

And that was what *I* needed.

After the race, the whole gang of us went out for pizza.

I sat with Cassie, Dan, Ian, Asher, Gideon, and Ardith—and Aunt Jo, who beamed with happiness. A few tables away, Ellie and Maggie were sitting with a few of their friends and a couple of girls from the team.

"Be right back, guys," I said, sliding out of the booth. I walked over to them. Ellie looked up at me nervously.

"Hey, Skye," Ellie said. "Look, I'm sorry—"

"That was a great race." I cut her off. "You were amazing. You definitely deserve captain more than I do."

"I do?" She looked perplexed. "But I thought you wanted it."

"I did," I said. "I do. But . . . I can't just waltz back in here and expect everything to go back to normal." I shrugged. "Maybe it's good that it didn't go back to normal. Maybe things needed to change."

"Ooookay, Skye," Ellie said hesitantly, glancing at Maggie for support. "I guess? Thanks?"

"Good," I said. "You're welcome." I leaned my elbows on the table. Ellie and Maggie looked at each other. "El," I said. "Ian's into you. You should ask him out or something. He's kind of shy about it."

"Yeah," she said, her eyes glazing over as if she'd used too much brain power for one day. "Sure. Maybe. Okay."

"What was *that* about?" Ian looked nervous as I rejoined our table.

"Nothing. You may get a phone call soon or something. Just saying."

"Skye . . . " He looked livid. His face was red beneath his freckles, and even his ears had tinged pink. "What did you say to her!" Dan snorted next to him, trying to hold back laughter. Cassie elbowed him in the ribs.

"I just said you had the biggest—"

"Skye!" Ian was turning purple. "You didn't!"

"—heart of anybody I knew," I said. "If you'd let me finish. Thank you."

Everyone laughed. Aunt Jo ordered another round of pizzas, and Asher threw his arm around me.

"You were amazing up there," he whispered into my ear, squeezing me.

I smiled at him. It was the happiest I'd felt in a long time.

"I have an idea," I said suddenly. Everyone continued talking. "Guys. *GUYS!*" All eyes turned to me. "I was thinking. Spring break is coming up. Aunt Jo, would you let us hike out to the cabin for a few days?"

"You have got to be kidding me," she said, shaking her head.

"Come onnn," I pleaded. "I think we get cell reception out there, and we'd promise to call if anything happened. We're super responsible."

"You're also terrible actors," she said, looking around at Cass and Ian, Dan and Asher. She sighed. "But I'll think about it."

The group began talking excitedly about plans, with Aunt Jo interjecting, "I haven't said yes yet!" at regular intervals. I leaned back in my seat, fitting snugly into the crook of Asher's arm. It would be fun to spend a few care-free days in the woods with my friends. But I had another reason for wanting to go back there. The cabin was where my parents had lived once. It was where the uprising had started. It was where a new faction of angels and half-angels had begun to form. Rebellions happen when your will to fight is strong enough. My parents and Aunt Jo weren't able to succeed. But my will was strong. And I had the power to back it up, now.

Aunt Jo and I had taken separate cars to the race that morning, and I drove home alone in the twilight, the tiny car whipping tightly around the bends in the mountain roads. I felt giddy and alive.

I pulled into the driveway, realizing I was used to seeing Asher waiting for me on the porch or just inside. But today the porch was empty. Aunt Jo's car wasn't in the driveway, either, which meant that she'd taken a detour past the store to check in. I felt a little relieved to have the chance to be alone for a while.

I glanced around, instinctively, for Guardians, even though it was stupid. If there were any Guardians nearby, they would be hiding, making themselves scarce. *Haunting the woods*. Thinking of the Guardians made me wonder how Devin felt about my coup on the mountain. Of course, my friends didn't know about that part—they just thought I'd gotten the second best time of the day. Asher knew the real reason for my elation. I could only imagine that Devin had seen it, too—watched as I took control of both sides of my powers. I wondered if he was lurking somewhere now. Waiting for the right moment to say something—if he was planning to say anything at all. It always made me a little sad to think of Devin. In those marathon training sessions behind my house, he'd pushed me so hard, you'd never have thought he was capable of moments of great tenderness. But he could surprise you. He'd surprised me.

He'd hurt me, too.

But how could I forget the good times? I couldn't just throw those to the wind and let them blow away forever. I held on to those moments between us like a special secret. Maybe one I didn't want to share with anyone. Not even Devin himself, if it came down to it. I'd rather let those moments live inside me, where no one could tell me that I was wrong or naive for wanting to see the best in people. Even killers.

I got to the front door and stopped short.

A tiny purple alpine flower from the field out back was tied around the doorknob with the same string I'd used to tie it to Devin's door. Was it an extended olive branch? Some acknowledgment? Of what? I remembered the Devin who'd been my teacher, who'd first told me about my parents. Who'd hugged me awkwardly in the parking lot at school when it had all seemed too overwhelming.

Was it too much to hope that he was proud of me for figuring it all out? What a long way I'd come from the parking lot that night.

What if that was all this flower was: not a threat or a message but a simple, thoughtful gesture? Even though he was controlled by higher powers, Devin had found a secret way to let me know the truth.

I untied the flower and took the stairs two at a time to my room.

Happiness, compounded by the race and the pizza and the afternoon with friends made me lightheaded. Where was Asher? I wanted to share my excitement. Maybe I wasn't scared to be with him anymore. I could control my powers. I could keep it together around him now. Maybe I was ready.

No, I thought. *I am ready. I know I am.*

In a fit of joy, I opened the window wide and summoned the air with all my strength. With my hands, I controlled the flow of a gust of wind as it picked up the flower, floating it high in the air. Without losing concentration, I summoned a stronger gust of wind from out in the field. It blew through my open window, and with it, carried hundreds of tiny purple flowers like the one borne above my head. They caught the light in their translucent petals and cast a purple glow across my room.

Behind me, I heard a gentle knock, and before I could stop the flowers from fluttering above me like a hundred purple butterflies, the door swung open.

"Oh my god, Skye," Cassie's voice echoed loudly throughout every square inch of the house. "What are you *doing*?"

I let the gust of wind die, and all the flowers fell to the floor simultaneously. Cassie stared at me open-mouthed.

"God, Cassie, don't you knock?" I said sharply.

"Uh, yeah, Skye, actually I did. Maybe if you hadn't been too busy playing the Sorcerer's Apprentice with flying purple flowers, you might have heard me." She held up my shoulder bag. "You left this at the pizza place."

"Uh, first of all, you didn't knock that loud, and second of all—"

"*First* of all," she said, throwing her purse down and charging toward me, "did you forget that we were supposed to go out tonight? Or were you planning to ditch me for your *boy*friend again?" She snorted and paused for breath. "And *second* of all"—she pointed down at the heap of flowers—"what was *that*?"

"I can explain," I said again. But then I didn't. I just stood there, my arms at my sides, completely at a loss for any lie that could explain away what had just happened. And I was so tired of trying to think of one. I had been lying to Cassie from the very moment I turned seventeen. It had been months. I couldn't do it anymore. She was my best friend, and she didn't deserve it. I'd find a way to protect her. I was stronger now. But if I kept it up, the mental and physical exertion of lying to my best friend would drain me of all my powers, light and dark.

"Good explanation," Cassie said. "Very thorough. I totally get it now."

"Okay." I exhaled slowly. "Here goes. Cassie, I—"

"Stop, I can't take it," she blurted. "Whatever the reason you're mad at me, I'm sorry! Is it—"

"Cass," I interrupted. "I'm not mad at you."

"Just tell me why," she said. "Why aren't we best friends anymore? You've totally changed, Skye. You never used to keep things from me. What did I do to make you go away?"

"Oh, Cassie," I said, the guilt finally overcoming me. "You didn't make me go away." I grabbed her hand and pulled her over to sit with me on my bed. "I just felt so guilty. Because it was my fault. Your whole accident was my fault."

"How could it have been your fault?" she asked, perplexed. "Did *you* cut the brakes?"

"No," I said, my heart beginning to pound. "But I know who did. And it was because I almost told you what I'm about to tell you now. The truth. About everything."

"Skye, you're not making sense." Cassie shook her head. "The truth about what?"

"Hold on." I moved to the window and peered down at the yard. A shadow moved in the bushes. I'd recognize Asher's tall, lanky frame anywhere, and I smiled to myself, safe in the knowledge that he was out there, keeping watch. I trusted that he'd never let a Guardian hurt me again—not after what Ardith had said about his lingering guilt. And Cassie was an extension of me, so he'd never let anything happen to Cassie again. I'd just have to keep an extra close watch on her. And in the event that she did get hurt—I could heal her this time.

"This is going to sound a little crazy," I said. "But it will explain everything."

"You're kind of freaking me out." She adjusted her messy bun. "But okay. Go ahead."

And so I took a deep breath and told her. "I'm an angel,"

I said. "My mother was a Guardian, and my father was a Rebel. Just like in the campfire story Asher and Devin told us a few months ago on the ski trip."

"What?" Cassie said flatly, staring at me in disbelief. "Am I supposed to believe—?"

"Devin is a Guardian, and Asher, he's a Rebel. They were sent here to guide and protect me while I figured out what kind of powers I had, because of who my parents were and everything. They were each trying to get me to join them on their side of this . . . this big cosmic battle. They . . . well, I know it sounds weird, but they wanted me."

"I'll bet they did," Cassie said with a smirk.

"No, I mean they wanted my powers. Because whichever side could control them would almost certainly destroy the other."

Cassie's eyes were growing round. "Wow!" She didn't say it so much as breathed the word. "Are you sure you aren't making this up? Because it's a pretty elaborate lie, and—"

"I'm not," I jumped in quickly, eager to get to the part about her. "It turned out that Devin wasn't actually sent here to protect me or guide me. The Order—they're the faction of angels that control destiny—commanded him to kill me."

"No!"

"Yeah. He spent all winter trying to get me alone in order to do it. He made Aunt Jo have to lead all those trips out to the mountains, and when he saw that I was getting ready to tell you what was going on—"

"He cut my brakes?"

"No, Raven did. She's also a Guardian."

"So . . ." Cassie's voice grew strangely subdued. "Am I in danger now? I mean you just told me, right?"

"I think we're safe," I said. "We're prepared for it this time. Asher is standing outside my window right now. He won't let anything happen to you, I promise. We know what we're up against now."

We went to the window. Sure enough, Asher was skulking around the foot of the deck. "Hey Asher!" Cassie called. He glanced up, vigilant and intense.

"Cassie, stop!" I cried, pulling her back. "This is really, really serious."

"Oh, come on, lighten up," she said. "I know it's serious, but god, you almost have to laugh about it to keep sane, don't you?"

"And that is why I desperately needed to tell you. Cassie, no one in the world can beat your advice."

"So," she mulled, "all this time, the whole reason you didn't tell me was to *protect* me?"

"Yup." I smiled.

"Skye, I feel so *honored* to be your friend." She paused thoughtfully. "But what about Devin?" she whispered. "What happened to him after he—you know—*tried to kill you*?"

"He and Raven were bonded by destiny, and now he avoids me—but I know he's waiting for something. I just don't know what."

"I'm sorry," Cassie said. "I know that this is your life and all, but it's even better than that campfire story that they told on the ski trip. This is the most epic thing to happen to any of us!" She paused, then said, "Oh, poor Ian. He never stood a chance with you. Look what he was up against."

"It's true," I said.

"Wow, Skye, this is *huge*! I have to say, though, I don't envy you right now. How can you fight with the Order—they tried to kill you! But how can you fight with the Rebellion? They only want to use you."

"I know," I said, loving Cassie more and more by the minute. "You can't tell Dan, though. Promise?"

"Oh, no." Cassie shook her head violently. "No. No. Dan and I don't keep secrets from each other."

"Cassie, please? We can't tell him just yet."

"Skye, I'm such a bad liar. He knows. He knows every

time." Her voice dropped to a whisper. "He *knows*."

"Cass," I said, crossing my arms. "No means no."

"Fine," she grumbled. Then paused. "What about Asher? Don't you want to be where he is?"

Don't pick your star just because it's the star he's chosen, Aunt Jo had said. It seemed logical enough, but I really had no idea what the answer to Cassie's question was. I sauntered over to the window and peered out. Asher was patrolling outside, a Rebel angel and a soldier. What had Ardith said? *He'd spend another thousand years by your side if he could.* Yes, of course I wanted to be wherever he was.

But what if my powers told a different story? My story was about love, but what if the blood in my veins wanted it to be about war?

"I don't know," I said quietly. Behind me, I heard the bed squeak as Cassie got up. She put her arm around me gently.

"You'll figure it out, Skye," she said. "You always do."

Later that night, after many hours of talking, Cassie finally left me alone in the quiet of my room. I should have felt catharsis, relief, but talking it all over with Cassie only solidified the tension I was feeling. Of course I wanted to be with Asher—and not just now, here, or at the Rebellion, but forever. When I tried to picture a life without him in it, my mind grew as white and empty as the beach in my visions.

But I had to stay true to myself in this, too. And the powers that ran through me were greater than both the Order and the Rebellion combined. Both sides knew it.

I was just getting into bed when I heard a tap at the window. Seconds later it swung open, and Asher hopped inside.

"Close the window," I said. "Please. It's cold." He closed

it and came over to me.

"Are you okay?" he asked gently and sat next to me. He looked like he wanted to reach his arm around my shoulders, but he held back. "You're too quiet," he said. "You're worrying me, Skye."

I sighed and let myself fall back on the bed. "I hate this."

"Well, I can leave. . . ."

"No, I mean *this*!" I flung my arms wide. "What if my heart is telling me one thing and my blood is making me do the opposite?"

"*What?*" he asked so vehemently that it came out as two syllables. "Where is that coming from?"

"What if we can't stay together forever? What if the Rebellion isn't the place for me, after all?"

Asher tensed. "Why would you say that?"

"I'm a balance of both the dark *and* the light. It's who I am. You know that. You've seen it."

"That's okay," he said, finally reaching over to take my hand. "We want you. It's that blend of powers that makes you so strong."

"You want me as a weapon, you mean," I said darkly. "I won't be responsible for that kind of destruction—no matter what the Order's done to me."

Asher ran a hand through his hair, agitated. "What do

you want, Skye? Tell me. Do you want me to leave the Rebellion for you? Cut off my wings and become mortal? I'd do it. But I don't think that would make you happy, and I don't know what would." His eyes were wild, pleading. "Tell me what you want!"

I thought about his offer. It reminded me, hopelessly, of my parents being cast to Earth. Their great, romantic love story.

"I want you!" I cried, my voice breaking. "And when I try to picture my life without you, I—" Tears spilled fast and hot on my cheeks, and I couldn't finish.

"Skye," he murmured, leaning down to kiss me.

But I pulled away.

My parents had died. Despite the epic love story. Despite all they risked for each other. Even running away couldn't stop what was coming for me and Asher. Whether or not I let the Rebellion use my powers, I couldn't stop the universe from conspiring to destroy itself.

I looked up at him. His pitch-black eyes looked so vulnerable. I wanted so badly to take his face in my hands and promise him I would never leave him. But we'd both know I'd be lying.

"What if what I want isn't what has to happen?" I asked, my voice coming out so small.

Asher looked stricken. "I will always love you," he said to me. He ran his fingers through my hair softly, and let his hand rest under my chin. "Always. Do you even know how long that is?"

"A long time," I said, laughing through my tears. "Forever."

"Forever," he repeated. "No matter what happens, I'll *always* love you. Okay? No matter what threatens to tear us apart."

But what tore us apart—whether the universe was plunged into chaos or meticulously controlled for the rest of eternity, or if something new took over and overthrew the system, forever changing the course of fate—that was up to me.

The next couple of days ran together like rain.

In a moment of weakness, everyone's parents and Aunt Jo huddled together, and Aunt Jo finally agreed to chaperone a trip to the cabin because she had wilderness training. "But only in case someone gets hurt," she said. "I don't want to have to hang out with all of you around a campfire at night."

We agreed. We would have agreed to anything. We all needed a vacation. Or maybe I was speaking only for me.

Everyone was excited as we planned our trip to the cabin. Asher and I didn't leave each other's side. It made Aunt Jo uncomfortable, but now I understood that she was afraid it meant losing me to the Rebellion rather than college. It also explained her weird animosity toward

Asher—Rogues resented Rebels, even if they didn't quite know why or who was a Rebel in the first place. She was especially nice to me, baking me my favorite cookies and making all my favorite meals like she did when she'd get back from long trips in the backcountry. Whatever happened, I was grateful that she knew what I was going through.

As for me, I couldn't shake the feeling that my days with Asher were dwindling along with the frost. I was terrified that every second we spent together was one second closer I came to losing him.

One day, the two of us were sitting on the floor by my locker between classes. Gideon ambled over and sat down with us.

"I had an idea," he said. "About the trip."

"Oh?" Asher's eyes slipped from Gideon's to mine, but he didn't say a word.

"You're not going to like it," Gideon said.

"Work on your salesmanship a little, Gid," said Asher.

"Right. Well." He paused. "We have to ask Devin to come."

"*What?*" I cried. "No way."

"Think about it. If he's with us, then he's not helping them plan an attack. And they won't strike."

"I guess . . . ," I said.

"Plus, I want to work with you more, on blocking your mind to the Guardians. If he's with us, Asher and I can see how his presence affects you. We can tell if he's manipulating you."

"Whoa," said Asher, holding up his hands. "Leave me out of it." When he looked at me, his eyes were strangely subdued. I wondered where all his usual fiery hatred for the Guardian had gone. Was there an ulterior motive here? Were they testing me?

"He isn't manipulating me," I said. "I can feel it."

"Or maybe that's just what he wants you to think." Gideon's features drew in on themselves, and I knew he was remembering. "Either way, we'll know. Don't you want to be sure?"

Did I, at this point? I almost wondered if I'd rather never know the truth.

"You would be the bait here," Gideon prodded. "He'd come if you asked him."

I wasn't so sure he would, but I could never tell Gideon that. Beside me, I could feel waves of tension radiating off Asher. *But why isn't Asher fighting him on this?* I wondered. The Asher I knew wouldn't even be able to sit through the suggestion.

"Fine," I relented. "I'll ask him."

"Good." Gideon smiled ruefully. "'Keep your friends close and your enemies closer.'"

Great, I thought. I wasn't sure how much closer I could handle getting.

Still, as long as I was working with Gideon on my cognitive and precognitive abilities, it might be useful to have Devin there. In the woods, there were opportunities to be alone, to slip away from the cabin. I could ask him more about the Sight. He could help me figure out, once and for all, if what I was seeing could, in any way, be the future.

In the end, that's what I told Devin. "We don't have to tell anyone what we're working on," I pleaded. "It can be our secret."

And he agreed.

I packed for the changing seasons. Winter was thawing—we could all feel it—and there was a shift in the air. The breeze brought the smell of budding earth, and with it, a sense of renewal and upheaval. Spring wasn't quite here yet. But it was coming.

Layers were key. Things you could easily take off and put back on again. Moisture-wicking tanks and light-weight sweaters, waterproof rain pants and wool socks, an under-layer. At the top of my pack, I carefully folded in the fisherman's sweater I'd found the last time I was at the cabin. Now that I knew my parents had lived there, I wondered if it had belonged to my dad.

On the morning of our trip, I zipped myself into an all-black ensemble: black tank, black long-sleeved tee, black zip-up fleece, and black insulated pants. I pulled on thick wool socks and laced my hiking boots tightly. Halfway through getting dressed, I realized that I was dressing with a purpose: I was preparing myself for something. In my ensemble, I felt lithe and stealthy, ready to face anything. But was it something specific? Was it a premonition of things to come?

Dan drove Cassie and Ian to our place, where Aunt Jo had a fresh pot of coffee waiting and granola bars for everyone. Cassie's cast still hadn't come off, but the hike itself wasn't hard, and I pitied whoever would have gotten stuck with the task of telling her she couldn't come. The doorbell rang. I opened the door to find Asher and Devin standing there next to each other, still as statues. They wouldn't make eye contact and kept their eyes trained on me.

"Hi," said Devin. "Thank you for inviting me."

"Don't get used to it," Asher muttered under his breath

as he swept past him into the hall. Devin hesitated on the doorstep for a second, meeting my gaze.

So much passed between us. We were thinking the same thing. We were thinking a million different things. The truth of the matter is that I would never know entirely what Devin was thinking. Though if Gideon was right, I might be able to find out whether he was influencing what *I* was thinking.

I stepped back and let him pass.

Our three cars formed a caravan through the winding mountain back roads. Aunt Jo took the lead in her SUV. Cassie, Dan, Ian, and Ardith followed close behind— I could see them dancing along to some music on Dan's stereo. And my car was last. Asher sat in the passenger seat beside me, drumming his fingers along the base of the window and every so often glancing in the rearview mirror to keep an eye on Devin, who sat perfectly still in the back. It reminded me of the last time the three of us had shared a tense drive to a mountain. Except this time, the tension was worse. Gideon sat next to Devin, his arms crossed tightly over his chest. There was something odd about it, like Devin was a prisoner, and we were transporting him from one containment facility to another. I didn't like it, and I couldn't put my finger on why.

We parked at the trailhead, then set off on the winding path. The morning was overcast and the clouds hung low above us. The air was damp, and just walking through it made me feel clammy and wet.

I hiked a good part of the trail next to Ian. He was quieter than usual, lost in his own thoughts. I understood: the solitude of hiking had that effect on me, too.

"Okay," I said eventually. "That's like the fifth time you've sighed. What's wrong?"

"Hmm?" he murmured. "Oh, nothing."

"Do you want to talk about it?"

He turned to me. "Do you ever feel sometimes like you don't belong?" he asked. "Like everyone else is swimming downstream and you're the only one trying to make it against the current?" I was about to say, *"Do I ever!"* when he laughed, short and bitter. "Of course you don't. What a stupid question. Everything is easy for you."

I gaped at him. "Are we talking about the same me?" I asked.

"Yeah," he said. "Everyone loves you, Cassie and Dan would do anything for you, you get amazing grades, and Aunt Jo is, like, the coolest mom in the world." He sighed. "And you have, you know." He jutted his chin up ahead of us, where Asher was cutting something edible off a tree branch with a pocket knife. "Someone like that."

"And you think all that is easy? I mean, I'm flattered, Ian, really—but Cassie and Dan were, up until recently, still mad at me for disappearing, my grades are plummeting, Aunt Jo wouldn't speak to me, and Asher . . ." I paused, wondering what to say about that. "Things aren't ever as perfect as they look."

"I guess."

"Why the sudden melancholy?" I asked.

"I don't know," he responded morosely. "Things didn't really work out so much with Ellie. She never called. And there's you, and—sometimes I just wonder if I'm destined to be alone."

"Ian." I smiled, putting my arm around his neck. "You don't have to resign yourself to destiny."

It took only a few hours for us to make it to the cabin. We threw our packs down, and Cassie collapsed on the couch and promptly passed out. The rest of us made a late lunch and gathered kindling to build a fire that night. Devin was the first to volunteer as a kindling collector, disappearing into the woods before anyone else could even raise a hand. As I watched him speed off, I could have almost sworn I caught a glimpse of cascading blond hair, the arc of pale white wings flashing through the trees. But I attributed that to my paranoid mind. Raven wasn't here.

And yet, I wondered just how safe we really were with Devin among us.

Asher built a roaring fire in the fireplace, and it crackled as we sat around it, swapping stories. Even Aunt Jo's initial reluctance disappeared, and soon she was laughing along with the rest of us. Devin watched the fire, his eyes far away and intense.

And Gideon watched Devin. I couldn't tell what he was thinking, but he looked serious, disturbed. Every so often, he and Asher would exchange looks. But nothing was said. And nobody else seemed to detect a thing but me.

When it was dark enough to notice a fire glowing through the windows, we covered them with the dark curtains we'd used when it had just been me, Asher, and Ardith. We told Dan and Ian it was just to keep the heat in at night. Cassie bit her lip and, to her credit, didn't say a word. Her lying skills, apparently, weren't as terrible as advertised.

Cass needed to keep her leg stretched out at night, so she claimed sleeping on the couch right away. Dan spread his sleeping bag somewhat territorially next to the couch, and Ian found a cozy patch of rug near the fire. Gideon and

Ardith decided to go for a walk, but I knew that they were really just patrolling the area for Guardians. They held hands as they left.

"You know"—Aunt Jo yawned in the direction of me and Asher on her way to the bedroom—"there's a whole other attic room. It may not be the most comfortable, but you can check it out and see for yourselves." She closed the door to the bedroom, and we stood still in the darkened hallway.

The attic. I nodded at Asher. "Let's go up there," I murmured. Even in the dark, I could see him flash a mischievous grin my way.

"A dark attic? Alone with you? You don't have to twist my arm."

The staircase was pitch-black as we fumbled our way to the top. Asher and I both grabbed at each other for support more than once. After the final stair, I tripped, expecting one more, and felt the room open out before me.

"We're here," I whispered. "Watch the last step."

"I—" said Asher, but before he could finish his thought, he'd knocked into something, a cardboard box from the sound of it, that fell from its perch and spilled its contents across the wooden planks of the floor.

"Shh!" I whispered, but we were both laughing. My foot

hit something that had fallen from the box, inadvertently kicking it farther away from me in the darkness. The object made a light tinkling noise as it rolled away. "What was that?" I asked. I heard the pop and hiss of fire igniting, behind me, and soon the attic room was filled with a soft warm glow. Asher brought the ball of fire toward me. He held it out in front of him.

"Where is it?" he asked.

"There!" The fire floated alongside me, as I bent to retrieve the object. I held it toward the light. It was a baby's rattle. It was tiny, a burnished silver that looked antique. Shaking it produced a muffled jangle that echoed across the room. I turned it over in my hands, running my fingers over the tarnished metal. Something was engraved along the side, and I could just make out the letters *Sk* and a date—my birthday.

It was my baby rattle. It had been left behind.

I shook it again, and the sound was clearer now, like a little silver bell chiming out the hour.

Little silver bells.

"Skye?" Asher asked. "What is it? What did you find?"

It was the lullaby my parents used to sing to me. The melody came flooding back, like it had only been yesterday that the two of them were singing softly.

Little silver bells. When they ring, we'll know.

We'll know *what*? I'd always wondered. But now I knew.

We'll know *it's time*. They had been trying to warn me, even then.

When my eyes flashed silver, when my powers kindled within me, when I turned seventeen, when I learned the truth. When I found the cabin and heard the little silver bells of the rattle I was meant to find.

I could feel my eyes burning bright in the dark room.

That's how we'll know it's time to fight.

"Nothing," I replied. "Just something somebody left behind."

Birds chirped as I opened my eyes the next morning, a sure sign that spring was on its way. I looked around, forgetting for a moment where I was. Light filtered in through a small window near the ceiling, illuminating the attic room.

I remembered last night. The lullaby. The rattle. The clue my parents had been trying to tell me. I sat up—but a pair of warm arms wrapped themselves around me, pulling me back into the folds of the sleeping bag. A sleepy voice said, "Don't go yet. Letting all the cold air in."

I let Asher pull me back down, and snuggled into his body heat. He'd held me all night—just held me, as if he was afraid of what would happen if he let go. It was the first time we'd ever woken up together.

"Mmm," he murmured, kissing my neck. "Much better."

A sharp knock on the door at the foot of the stairs nearly made me sit bolt upright again. "Skye!" Aunt Jo called. "Asher! Breakfast!"

"I don't think," Asher muttered as he sat up and rubbed his eyes, "that you and I will ever have five minutes alone together as long as she's around."

"She's very good at her job," I agreed.

I tried to keep the memory of Asher's warmth wrapped around me all morning, but my thoughts were still trapped in the chilly attic room from the night before. My parents had wanted me to figure it out—they knew I would when I was ready. They wanted me to fight. But how would I start? And what, exactly, was I fighting?

I was grateful that we were going on a long hike after breakfast. I needed the time to walk and think.

We stopped near a clearing for lunch. A small brook was thawing, the ice melting away into the earliest trickles of a babbling stream. I was just unpacking a bag of trail mix when the evergreen trees swirled around me into mist and the trickle of the stream became gulls cawing gently, the lapping of waves on a shore. I knew where I was. I'd been here before. *The mist cleared and I was on a gray, empty beach. The hem of my diaphanous dress floated like sea foam in the shallow surf, but I kept moving forward along the shore. A figure moved toward me in the mist, growing closer, looming. But I couldn't see who it was.*

Someone came up beside me, his sword raised high over his head. I turned and saw that I was standing next to Ian. He nodded at me, looking into the mist. I said a prayer for luck, and threw my own sword at the approaching figure.

The mist swirled and faded, and I was suddenly back on the trail, sitting on a rock by the thawing brook. Nobody had noticed a thing. I was getting better at controlling my visions, just like the rest of my powers. Even if I still had no clue what they meant.

I bit into my sandwich. Ian had been in this vision. He hadn't been there before, but now he was standing next to me, fighting by my side.

I looked up from my sandwich to find Devin staring. *He saw it happen.* He gave me a meaningful look and walked off into the trees. Devin would know. He'd have the answers. He knew he could help me.

I counted to ten, and then I followed him into the woods.

He was waiting for me. "You had a vision," he said.

I nodded. "Another one. On the beach. I was wearing this beautiful dress, and—I recognized it."

His eyes grew brighter, wider.

"You did? From where?"

"Aunt Jo gave it to me the night before my race. It used to be my mom's."

"And the vision," Devin said. "What happened in it?"

"I had a sword," I said. "And . . . this is the weird part. Ian was right there next to me."

"You had a sword?" Devin asked, drawing his eyebrows together. "An angelic sword?" I nodded. "Was it yours?"

"Yes," I said. "I'm pretty sure it was."

"Skye, you're seeing visions of the future."

"How do you know for sure?" I asked.

"Because you were wearing the dress that Aunt Jo gave you."

"I could have just been dreaming about it."

"And Ian was with you."

"It could have been for anything. We could have been hanging out. It might have been pro—"

"You had a sword," Devin said, his voice urgent. "Angelic swords are made from the single feather of an angel's wing. You don't have your wings yet, Skye. You saw a vision of the future—*after your wings have grown in.*"

"But how?" I asked. "How is that even possible?"

"There's only one explanation," Devin said, awe filling his eyes. "Only one way you could possess the sight. Your mother wasn't a Guardian. She had to have been a Gifted One."

"But," I stammered, "that—that doesn't seem right. That would mean my blood is so much stronger in favor of the light. And my powers—"

"Your powers are a blend of both. But visions of the future—that's the strongest power of the light that there is. It may outweigh any other power you have." His face softened. Suddenly he looked so much like the Devin from before. "Skye," he murmured.

"What?"

"It's amazing."

Something—a sixth sense—was prickling up the back of my neck.

"I'm sorry," he said. "I can't do this anymore. I can't take it. Why don't you see it? Why can't you see what I see?"

"What do you see?" I asked, not sure I wanted to know the answer, but positive I needed to.

"You belong with the Order. We can teach you how to refine your visions. We can show you how to see what will happen to you—to everyone you know! You can hold the future in the palm of your hand."

"The Order tried to kill me," I said. "I could never join them."

"Then do it for me," he begged.

"Why?"

"Because I love you! Do I really have to say it? Don't

321

you believe me by now?"

My heart almost stopped beating—because the last time he'd said something like that was only seconds before I felt the cold steel of his blade spear through me. I tensed, getting ready to fight if I had to.

"You don't love me," I said. "You couldn't possibly. It's not real love. You've never made it possible for me to love you back. You push me away every chance you get." His eyes were so sad, helpless, but I had to keep going. "You hold yourself at arm's length, bottle everything up inside. You think it's love, Devin, but it's not. Not really. You admire my strength. You want to help me. But you're not even my friend."

"How do you know?" he asked, his voice perfectly controlled. "How could you know what I'm feeling? I wear a mask to keep it from you. From everyone. I would do anything for you. All I've ever wanted is to get you to the Order, where you'd be safe from any more Guardians trying to kill you."

He moved toward me, and I saw that Raven had been standing behind him the whole time. My heart pounded wildly. Had she followed us to the woods? Was she alone—or were there others?

"Well, that was sweet," said Raven. Devin spun around. "We all knew it, of course, but I didn't think you were stupid enough to say it out loud. You broke the biggest rule. Do you know what the Order is going to do to you? Do you understand what has to happen now?" For maybe the first time, I could detect real anger, real emotion in Raven's voice. What had happened to make her so close to losing it?

"No," Devin said. "There's still a chance—if she comes over, if she joins the Order, then nothing has to change."

"What about us?"

"There *is* no us." Devin was shaking, his hands balled into fists by his sides. "It's all just a big lie. The Order can't see my destiny, thanks to Skye. She changed everything, blurred our fate so much that it doesn't matter anymore. She changed the course of time! She's one of us, Raven. Don't you see it? She was supposed to die, and she *healed herself.*"

I had? That would explain how quickly I'd gotten better, the lack of scar anywhere on my body. But it would also be—

"You poor, sad fool," Raven sang, her voice fierce. "You really believe she healed herself? She could barely control her own dark powers. What makes you think she was so skilled with her light ones?"

"Then who did?" Devin yelled. The intensity of his voice surprised me, echoing through the trees. "It wasn't me! It couldn't have been any Guardian!"

"I did!" Raven's eyes brimmed with tears. It was shock-ing to see someone so strong, so terrible, on the verge of breaking down. "I did, for you! Because I couldn't stand the thought of you having to live the rest of your days knowing that you killed the one person in this world you love."

Devin stopped cold. He tilted his head and stared at her.

My jaw dropped as I realized she looked almost human. She did have a heart. She had a soul. All of the Guardians did. No wonder their eyes always looked so full of emotion but their faces remained stoic. They couldn't—weren't allowed to—express any of it. It made so much sense.

"You did?" he said quietly.

"Yes, Devin, I did. I would keep my archnemesis from dying, just to keep you from pain. I would defy every order I've ever been given just so you wouldn't have to live the rest of your life with the guilt of killing someone you love. But it's too bad," she said, her voice taking on a terrifying edge, "that I won't be so lucky."

"What?" Devin said.

"No!" I yelled. "Stop!"

But it was too late. Raven's wings had unfurled in the blink of an eye, and before anyone could stop her, she'd plucked a single white feather from them. As she held it in her hands, I watched in awe as it grew longer, shinier, sleeker, and before I knew it she was holding a sword. *An angelic sword.*

She rushed at him as Devin produced his own sword.

"Raven, don't do it!" I screamed. "Don't kill him!"

But she swung violently. I heard the sickening slice of metal against skin, and suddenly all I could see was blood. I fell to my knees, sobbing. "No," I choked. "No!"

"Oh, stop it," Raven said, her voice heaving in ragged gasps. "Don't waste your tears."

I looked up. And that's when I knew something had changed; something strange had shifted around us. It had only just been early afternoon, but now, under the darkening evening, the first stars were beginning to blink on through the canopy of trees, casting menacing shadows over everything. I noticed Raven first, crumpled on the ground. The twilight and shadows were playing tricks on my eyes, and at first I thought they had cast an awkward angle on her wings, making them look broken, oddly twisted. Then, with horror, it dawned on me. Raven's gorgeous white wings were no longer attached to her body. They'd been cut from her back. Now they lay next to her, ragged, mangled, and streaked with red.

As my eyes adjusted to the image, Devin's hulking figure came into focus. He stood above her, looking down, breathing hard. His sword was raised above his head, where it glinted in the starlight. Blood ran down the blade, dripping onto the ground.

Raven shuddered. "Well, who could have predicted that?" She smirked ruefully, wincing a little and holding her hand to her side. "You've cast me out! Cut off my wings, banished me to Earth forever. Don't you see what you did? The Order won't take me back like this."

"He sees," Ardith said from the edge of the clearing. "He's never going to stop, Skye. It's how he was programmed. He's a machine. He's just a pawn."

Ardith marched over to me and picked me up off the ground. I shook my head, sobbing. "He'll never change," she said. "He'll always do their bidding. *Always*. He'll keep feeling bad about it and keep the pain hidden away deep inside where no one can see it. But he'll keep doing it all the same."

"I don't believe you!" I cried. "We can save him!"

"No, we can't," Asher said. His voice was colder, sharper than I'd ever heard it before. I hadn't even seen him approach.

He extended his blade, the edge of it dangerously close to Devin's throat. "But we can stop it from happening again."

"Asher!" I yelled. "What are you doing?"

"It's better this way," he said. "Trust me. I swore I would protect you. I made a promise to them that I would. With Devin gone, you'll be happier. Safer. You won't have to worry about him any- more."

"You made a promise to them?" I repeated, and it took a full second for the meaning of his words to sink in. "To the Rebellion? This was just another mission to you? Protect me—and kill Devin? And you kept it from me?"

"You know it's always been more than that for me." I remembered what he and Ardith had said that day in the cabin, when I'd first woken up. *Passion is our way, but love can drive an angel mad, Asher. It can disrupt the heavens, change the outcome of a war.* Ardith had been warning him not to let love interfere with his mission. This mission.

"How can you ever separate duty and love?" Asher asked now. "How can you ever make that distinction? How can you choose? I protect you for both of those reasons and more." I opened my mouth to say something, but he said, "Don't call me a traitor. Don't say that I betrayed you. Everything I do is for you. Killing Devin will be, too."

I noticed Cassie, Dan, and Ian standing just behind him. Their mouths were hanging open in shock, and they looked terrified.

"Stop," I said, faltering. "You should have told me."

"I couldn't, Skye. You'd never have let it happen."

"Of course not!" I yelled. "But I deserved to know!"

"If you'd stopped it, it would have been fighting against us—against yourself. He was trying to win you over to his side! He didn't care about you! He never did. You think if he loved you, he would have stabbed you in cold blood? I'm trying to *protect you.* It's all for you!"

"He doesn't know what he's talking about." Devin spoke suddenly, and I whipped around. "It's so much more complicated than that. I never had a choice. Not about any of this—but especially not when it came to you."

I no longer knew what to think or who to believe. But

instead of the confusion I'd felt all winter, I was suddenly seeing things with an aching clarity. The time had come for me to stop listening to all the noise around me and focus on what my own blood was telling me to do.

Devin turned to me. "Skye," he said quietly, simply, "I'm sorry for everything. They made me do it. They keep making me hurt the people I—" He stopped abruptly. Then he turned to Asher and fell to his knees. "Forgive me," he whispered. He lowered his head. "Just do it. Get it over with."

"What?" I gasped. "No, stop!"

Asher didn't look at me as he stepped back. Then, he took two running steps forward and brought his sword down in a swooping arc. "*No!*" I yelled. "He just needs to be free of the Order! If he can make his own choices, you'll see he isn't bad." But I couldn't watch. I looked away, covering my face in my hands.

I didn't hear anything. I opened my eyes.

Asher's sword was just inches from Devin's neck. He was looking right at me. "Okay," he said, his voice low and even. "Jump."

Devin looked up. "What?"

"Jump," Asher said again. "Become a Rebel. Or I'll kill you."

Slowly Devin stood. Asher backed up a step, but he kept his blade level with Devin the whole time.

"If I join the Rebellion," Devin said, "you'll let me live?"

"If you join and fight with us, if you pledge to help us destroy the Order and restore freedom to the world, then yes, I'll let you live."

"Jump, Devin," I pleaded.

His massive white wings folded in on themselves, withdrawing into his back. He closed his eyes and placed a hand on the flat blade of Asher's sword. "I pledge myself to chaos," he said. "To passion, disorder, and renewal. I pledge myself to love. To the freedom to love." As he said his last words, he raised his eyes and met mine.

And when his wings unfurled again, they were a deep, rolling black. Feathers like the night.

I released the breath I'd been holding. Asher stepped up to Devin until their noses were almost touching. *Please don't*, I thought desperately. *Don't kill him anyway.* Slowly Asher extended his hand.

"Welcome to the Rebellion," he said. Devin brought his own hand up and shook Asher's. He looked like he was in shock.

"Thank you," he whispered. "I'll devote myself to your cause."

Raven cried out in pain behind him, and Devin turned and ran to where she was still crumpled on the ground.

"I'm so sorry," he said, kneeling beside her. "Raven, I never meant for this to happen." He looked around helplessly. "I can't heal you," he said. "I'll find somebody who can. I promise."

The last time I'd heard those words, I'd been attacked by a Guardian and a Rebel was trying to find me help. This time, the Rebel was Devin.

"I'll do it." I stood up. Everyone turned to look at me. It was the last thing I'd ever thought I'd volunteer for—and yet, it felt right. "Raven saved my life. I owe her." I had a feeling our lives were inextricably linked from here on out. Devin looked so grateful—and for the first time, his eyes softened.

"Thank you," he said, taking my hands. "Here. Like this."

He placed my hands on her. We closed our eyes, and for a moment, everything was still. Raven sat perfectly rigid while I summoned all of my powers of dark and light, everything I had been working to control. I felt something stir beneath my hands.

"Your eyes," Devin said, holding my gaze. "They're silver."

I could feel it. I looked down. Something silvery, light,

and quick was flowing from the wounds on Raven's back. The mercurial liquid streamed from her wounds, taking shape into something huge and fluttery. New wings were emerging where her old ones had been. But they weren't white, and they weren't black.

They were a glistening silver.

"You did it," Raven whispered, standing slowly and letting the feathers unfold behind her. "You really did it. I should—" She stopped herself just short of saying something snarky. She met my eyes and nodded, slightly. "Thank you. They're beautiful."

I had done it. I had gone from failing at restoring life to a tiny alpine flower to healing great, gaping angelic wounds. As if thinking the same thing, Devin caught my eyes. He looked so proud—happy, for the first time since we'd met.

Suddenly I felt something begin to push through my own back. I cried out and doubled over, reaching my hands behind me to feel what was happening. When I pulled them away, they were dripping—not with blood, as I'd feared, but with the same liquid silver. Devin's eyes grew wide.

"Skye," Asher said with wonder.

I saw the shadow my wings cast onto the little clearing

in the woods before I realized what was happening. My own wings, the same color silver as Raven's. As the rattle. As my eyes.

Asher stepped forward, with Ardith and Gideon close behind him, forming a V. "Raven, we can welcome you into the Rebellion, too. Skye, you'll officially join us now? We'll all fight against the Order together."

I looked around the woods. My friends surrounded me, watching to see what I would do.

"Come on, Skye," Asher said, offering a hand for me to take. He looked so hopeful, so sure that I would reach out and place my hand in his. The first breeze of spring ruffled his black hair, and he grinned. "Let's go."

Which is why my heart was breaking at what I was about to do.

I took a step back. "I can't," I said.

For a second, it looked like he hadn't heard me. He continued to hold his hand out to me, his eyebrows raising slightly in surprise. His dark eyes stirred, as if trying to process what I'd just said.

"What?" His voice was no more than a whisper.

"No," I said, louder this time. My heart was breaking into millions of shards of glass. My insides felt cut up from them. "My wings are silver, like my eyes—"

"Don't do this, Skye—" he pleaded, his voice cracking at my name.

"Asher, you know I have to. You've known this for a while now. I'm not a Rebel, and I'm not a Guardian. I don't think I was ever meant to be either. I need the balance of both in order to live without buckling under this power. I'm both and I'm neither. The dark and the light. I can't exist without the other."

"You can," he said. His voice sounded strange and sad and desperate. Were those tears in his eyes? I looked down, biting my lip and trying hard not to let my own tears spill over.

"I can't." I forced myself to keep saying the words I knew I had to say. "I have to finish what my parents started. I was born to do this—to start a new faction. I'm—I'm grateful to you. To both of you." Devin looked up and met my eyes. It felt so wrong to be facing both of them like this, almost like we were back on the roof of the school during my first lesson. Only this time, I wasn't going to learn what I needed to know from them. I was going to have to find it in myself. "We'll make our own rules," I said. "Maybe there is such a thing as fate, and all this is supposed to happen. But if that's true, my fate has always been to make my own decisions. My parents died trying to find a way for us all to live. I can't let them down."

Raven stepped up beside me.

"You and I have never quite . . . seen eye to eye." She paused, and I could tell it was an effort for her to be nice to me. "But our lives are connected now. I healed you; you healed me. Our powers run through each other. I think our wings have made that clear." She took another step toward me. "If I belong anywhere in this universe now, it's with you, Skye."

"I'll join you, too." I looked to see who was speaking and saw Ian step into the clearing. He looked so serious, so determined, and I knew instantly that we would be friends forever, our entire lifetime. He would fight beside me, I'd seen it with my own eyes. And if it would be anyone there beside me, it would be Ian. Loyal, observant Ian, always watching, noticing when something was wrong, just a step or two behind. A strange and sudden thought occurred to me, then. Could Ian be a Rogue, like Aunt Jo? A little bit alone, a little bit out of sync, and quick to notice angelic powers like my eyes—even if he didn't know what he was seeing? They both shared a particular hatred for Asher, that's for sure. A Rogue's hatred.

"I'm behind you one hundred percent, Skye," he said, moving beside me and Raven. "And I always have been.

I'll die fighting alongside you." He put his arm around me and grinned.

"So will I," said Aunt Jo. "I always said you should follow your own star. And I don't belong to either faction—the Rebellion or the Order. I've always been somewhere in between."

"Skye?" Asher said, and I turned to face him finally. He looked like he was fighting back something massive within him. My heart ached. In a perfect world, there would be no Order and no Rebellion. There would be no division of sides, nothing standing between us. But I knew I was making the right choice. "I love you," he said. His voice shook with effort. "I love you so much, it's like my whole life was just leading up to the moment I met you. And then as soon as I did, I lived in fear, every day, that you would be taken away from me." He looked down. "I just never thought you'd be the one to do it."

"I love you, too, Asher," I whispered. Somewhere, by the edges of the clearing, I could hear Cassie sigh, and the shards of my heart were breaking into smaller, sharper pieces. I felt like my whole body was breaking. But I had to stay strong. "I have to do this."

Asher's hand fell, finally, to his side, and hung there without purpose, as if its entire reason for being had suddenly been taken away. Beside him, Devin put a hand on his back. I was finally able to see all of the emotions in his eyes, everything he could now let himself feel. And beneath the concern, I saw something else. Hope. But was it hope for me? For the Rebellion? For the fate of the universe? Was he hoping I could save it—or hoping that there was still a chance for us now that he was free to love?

I couldn't think about those things just yet. They would have to wait. I had a mission now, of my own.

I looked at Ian and Raven and Aunt Jo. They stood on either side of me, hands poised at their sides, and for the first time, I felt purpose. I finally had a clear direction. I knew who we were and the journey we were about to embark on.

We weren't light, and we weren't dark. We were the in-between. We were something fractured and put back together again, better, stronger, illuminating the night.

Acknowledgments

HEARTFELT THANKS (AND HUGS) go to:

The team at Harper, especially Karen Chaplin, Andrea Martin, Barbara Lalicki, and Marisa Russell.

Colin Anderson and Erin Fitzsimmons, for your breathtaking vision.

Maria Gomez, for being a phone call away.

The readers, bloggers, booksellers, librarians, and teachers who supported *A Beautiful Dark*—and all of your wonderful emails, tweets, postcards, and messages!

Dark Days cohorts extraordinaire Amy Vincent, Kiersten White, and Amy Garvey, for being the best late-night-empty-Italian-restaurant-dinner-company a girl could have, and providing inspiration, support, and raucous, delirious, sleep-deprived laughter.

Anne Heltzel, Jess Rothenberg, Leila Sales, and Rebecca Serle, for rooftop wine, stoop coffee, cheese anytime, advice, tips, photo ops, horse-dancing, puns, panicked phone calls—I'm so glad we found one another.

My friends near and far—from Boston to Snug Harbor,

from Chicago to DC to San Fran to right down the block; from the booth at Heidelberg to the halls of Page to caaandyhouse to sharing a cubicle wall. Whether I take the subway, the B63, or the Bolt Bus to see you, thank you for reading, for cheering me on—and reminding me that life is meant to be lived (in addition to being written about). If I know how to write about friends convincingly, if I understand friendship *at all*, it's because of you guys.

And always, Jody and Lee Davies, Shelby Davies, Sandra and Mark Messler, and the Sigler clan. With so much love.

"I can't go with you."

The minute I said those words, there was no going back. There was no changing my mind.

A few months ago, I might not have been so sure. Ever since that icy night in January when I turned seventeen, life as I knew it had boiled down to this: I had to choose.

Between light and dark.

Between the Order and the Rebellion.

Between Devin and Asher.

Tonight, in these woods, everything changed.

Because I chose neither.

I could no longer pretend that I belonged on one side or the other. I wasn't a Guardian, and I wasn't a Rebel. I knew that now, with more clarity than I'd known anything in my life.

"Skye," Asher said. His eyes were pleading. "Don't do this." He looked between me and the group standing behind me, and then to Ardith, as if for help. "We need you." He paused. "I—"

He didn't finish the sentence, but he didn't have to. I knew what he was going to say.

The unsaid words twisted around my heart and squeezed tightly.

I need you.

And maybe he did. Maybe he needed me for my powers, so the Rebellion could win—or maybe to fight beside him, as we'd been planning.

But did I need Asher? My powers had surpassed his, as Raven had predicted they would. I didn't need his help anymore.

And did I need love? It was a new choice, a different choice. Between following my heart and starting on the path I finally knew I was supposed to take. It wasn't easy, but I knew the answer. I had always known.

The silence twisting around my heart snapped, and the pain flooded through me as I realized it.

I had to let him go.

Dusk was settling in the woods around us. To my left, Aunt Jo stood with her arms crossed next to my two oldest friends, Cassie and Dan. On my right, my friend Ian looked defiant next to fallen angel Raven, my former enemy, now linked to me in a way I didn't yet fully understand. And standing in front of me, facing me down, were the Rebels: Ardith and Gideon, Asher—and now Devin. All of them on the same side, for the first time. I couldn't see any Guardians, but that didn't mean they weren't there, lurking in the shadows.

Guardians stalk these woods.

"Skye, you don't have to do this." Asher's hands hung at his sides, where they'd fallen when I told him I was leaving the Rebellion. "Let's talk. We can figure this out."

"She made up her mind," Ian said, stepping forward. He had never trusted Asher, and disdain radiated off him. A light shone in his eyes. He had won. "We're starting a new group."

"Ian," I hissed. I put my hand on his shoulder and pulled him back.

Next to Asher, Devin looked up sharply. His blue eyes pierced mine, but he said nothing.

"I'm sorry if I made you think something else," I said. "But this is who I am. And this is what I have to do."

"You're just as cold-blooded as the Order," Ardith spat,

anger and betrayal clouding her eyes. "I knew we couldn't trust you."

"She's not. You know that," Devin said. "She's doing what's right. Doesn't the Rebellion believe in that? Even if they disagree with her cause?" It was the first time he had spoken since jumping from the Order. Ardith whirled on him, the starlight catching her long chestnut hair.

"Oh, look who feels right at home speaking up," she growled. "A Rebel for a whole minute and you've already found some *rules* to follow. You can take the Guardian out of the Order, I suppose—"

"Don't make me cut you, Ardith," Raven said icily. She ruffled her silver feathers, which glinted sharply in the fading light.

"It's no use arguing." Gideon had been silent, too. Even though his voice was low, we all heard him perfectly. "Whether it's now or on the battlefield. We're enemies now." His eyes grew cold and distant—the look of someone retreating into his horrible memories—memories he spent every day trying to forget. "We're going to war. Against each other."

Silence echoed across the woods as his words sunk in.

"Then that is how it has to be." Everyone turned to look at me, and I felt my hands balling into fists at my sides. All I could think was that I had to get home. To start figuring out what all this meant. What my future held now.

I swept past the group and toward the cabin, where the last remaining pieces of my childhood sat in a box in the attic, waiting for me to bring them home. I knew the Rebels were questioning my decision, but I didn't care. My friends would support me, even if the Rebels didn't. The reality was that I knew I never had a choice to begin with. This was *always* how it had to be—it's just that I hadn't realized it until now.

I tore through the woods to the place where my parents had set up camp once upon a time. The house was exactly as we'd left it that morning, but I saw everything differently now. It was like looking at a jigsaw puzzle that's been taunting you for months, watching the image suddenly snap into place and wondering how you never saw it there before.

I climbed the stairs to the attic, and would have taken them two at a time if I thought the rickety wood could handle it. There, in the corner, was the rumpled sleeping bag that Asher and I had shared the night before. He had been so patient with me while I figured out my powers, given me so much strength. His confidence in me alone made me feel like I could become as powerful as everyone said. Like I really could be the key to saving the universe.

But I couldn't give that same confidence back to him. I

couldn't fight by his side if it meant denying who I really was, my mother's daughter, with my mother's powers—a part of me that was just as much alive as my powers of the dark. He had to understand. He had to have known this day would come.

On the other side of the room, by the stairs, was the stack of boxes that I'd knocked into the night before, spilling their contents everywhere. In the darkness, I hadn't had a chance to go through them. But I knew who they belonged to.

My parents.

Last night, a small metal object had gone rolling across the floor. When I'd bent to pick it up, the ball of fire Asher held in his hands showed that I was holding a baby's rattle. The silver was dented and old, tarnished from disuse. But in the dim glow of the fire, I could just make out that it had once been engraved with something significant.

The letters *Sk.*

And beneath them, a string of numbers. My birthday.

As the rattle jangled softly in my hands, I realized that it wasn't just a childhood toy. It was a message. A *sign*.

Little silver bells, my parents used to sing me to sleep at night, as light from the moon cast shadows of branches and leaves on the walls. *When they ring, we'll know.*

I used to think it was just an old folk song, its gentle rhythm lulling me to sleep. But as I listened to the faint silver jangle in the dead of night, something clicked.

Silver, for my eyes. For the strange mix of powers that surged within me, stronger by the day. For the flashing wings that had finally grown in fits of stabbing pain from beneath my shoulder blades.

I always wondered what, exactly, the lyrics meant. *When they ring, we'll know.*

But last night I figured it out, as sharp and clear as the rattle's bell. When all the silver forces in my life converged, we'll know it's time. To fight.

It was the final sign I needed to have the courage to reject both the Order and the Rebellion. To start off on my own. Since turning seventeen, everyone in my life had tried to control me. But now it was time to take matters into my own hands.

I wrapped the rattle carefully in a T-shirt and packed it in my backpack. I opened the flaps of the box that had fallen on its side and began to sift through what was left. There had to be more clues. Something to tell me what I was supposed to do now.

The sun was beginning to set. As it aligned with the window, it cast an orange beam of light in my eyes. I stood

7

and raised an arm to shield them from the glare. Motes of dust swirled around me as I struggled to slide the window open, letting the fresh mountain air gust into the tiny room.

The sky was a pale, crisp blue, fading to a pinkish glow as the sun hovered above the jagged outline of the mountains on the horizon. I closed my eyes and the light swept across my nose and eyelids, touched the tops of the trees below. The world glowed on the other side. The light shone brightest at the center, seeping into darkness as I squeezed my eyes tighter. Dark and light. I was neither. I was both. I was all of it.

The sun was setting on one chapter of my life. But it was rising on the next. The world was waking up, and I felt like I was waking up with it.

"Planning on jumping?"

My eyes flew open.

I didn't have to turn around to know who was behind me. I'd heard his voice so often that it had become a living, breathing part of me, as real as the cells in my skin and the oxygen in my blood. He was repeating the very same words I'd said to him that moment on the roof of Northwood School, when I'd learned who I really was.

The child of a member of the Order and a Rebel angel who had broken away. The daughter of dark and light.

Except now I knew that there was more to this story than I'd ever dreamed possible. My mother wasn't just a Guardian, but a Gifted One who possessed the Sight. Now

I finally understood the visions I'd been having. They were glimpses of the future.

The breeze coming through the open window smelled like spring. Spring meant renewal. Well, maybe I could bring renewal to the world. For too long, two groups had vied for power over the world and the people who walked it: the Order, responsible for controlling human fate; and the Rebellion, who believed in the passion and chaos of a life messy and lived to the fullest. But neither group was perfect. Neither was right. I couldn't let the Order control human life forever, but a world controlled by the Rebellion would mean chaos and anarchy. I stood between them now. Maybe I did have the fate of the universe in my hands.

"You've been waiting for a chance to say that back to me, haven't you?" I asked, gathering the courage to turn around.

"You sort of gave it to me on a silver platter this time." I could hear the smirk in his voice, and I turned to face him.

"I'm not going to jump," I said. "Don't worry." He wasn't smiling. His lips didn't even twitch. "Even if I did, I could catch myself now. Wings and all."

In the fading light, his dark features began to blur, to fade along with the sun into the corners of the attic already cast with twilight shadows. He grabbed at an invisible speck of dust in the air, crushed it in his fist, looked away.

"Asher—"

"Don't."

"I'm sorry."

"You're sorry?" So many things burned in his coal-black eyes. Anger. Betrayal. If I looked deep enough, maybe even pain. Instead, I let my gaze drop to the warped planks of the wooden floor.

"I have to do this."

"I protected you, Skye. I devoted myself, every waking second, to keeping you safe from the Order."

"I know—"

"I gave you a family with the Rebels. I was ready to commit my life to fighting with you. Side by side."

"I—"

"A *team*."

"Me too, but—"

He looked up then, and that look sent lightning crashing through my heart.

"I loved you."

What was I doing? Not for the first time, I wondered if I was making the right decision. It was too hard. Shouldn't it be easier to follow your own star?

"I loved you, too," I said. I walked up to him, took his hands. They uncurled from fists, shaking ever so slightly in mine. "I still do."

"Then how," he said through clenched teeth, "can you leave me?"

The mountain wind blew between us. The sun sparkled through my eyelashes, catching tears.

"Because I have to do this. It's who I am. Can't I love you but not believe in what you believe in?"

"It'd be a whole lot better if you believed."

The corner of his mouth twitched, and I smiled, despite myself. "That's not funny."

"I know." He sighed, grabbed my hands in his, and pulled me closer. I let him wrap his arms around me, and I rested my cheek on his chest. "It's just that I really did think you were a Rebel. I thought we were in this together. For always."

I felt tears prick the backs of my eyes, and was glad he couldn't see. I forced them down.

"I wish that we could be," I said. "But it's impossible."

"Skye, you know I have to do the right thing, too— don't you? I have to go back to the Rebellion. We've fought so hard for this; I can't turn my back on them now. Ardith and Gideon are counting on me. I let them down, once. I can't do it again. It's not about the rules. It's not like the Order. It's about honor. It's about loyalty. I thought you understood that."

"Don't talk to me about loyalty," I said, my face growing hot with frustration. "I'm loyal to my family. To my friends. To my own blood." I took a deep breath. "So, I guess that means we're against each other now."

"Maybe." He looked thoughtful. "Maybe not. Looks can be deceiving. You of all people should know that." He took a step back, and lifted my chin so he could look into my eyes. He raised an eyebrow.

"Do you believe in us, Skye? That there could be a happy ending for us if we wish for it hard enough?"

I swallowed. Did I believe? My life was fine before Asher and Devin came into the picture. I had Aunt Jo and my friends and won ski races and got straight As, and that was enough. It wasn't exciting, it didn't make me *feel* anything, but it was safe, and it was mine. Now, I felt too much. And all it did was make things confusing. All I felt was the pain I'd been trying so hard to escape since my parents died.

It was the kind of life the Rebellion believed in.

But forming this new group, stopping this collision of Chaos and Order—that was a fight I couldn't afford to lose. No matter what I had to give up in order to win.

I closed my eyes, and when I opened them again I was crying.

"No," I said. "I don't."

Asher let go of me. He opened his mouth to say something, then closed it again just as quickly.

"I'm sorry," I whispered.

"I don't believe you."

"You have to."

He took my hands in his and gripped them tight. "Skye," he said fiercely. "Listen to me. When this is all over, when we've found a way to end this, we will be together."

I raised my eyes to meet his. "Then prove it."

It was a challenge. It was the very thing he'd yelled to me above the wind, the first time we'd raced each other.

I'll win!

Prove it.

He pulled me into him so fast I didn't see it coming, and I threw my arms around his neck and kissed him. He held on to me, tightly, as the sun dipped quietly below the mountains and the darkness rose to meet us and the wind blew in through the open window, gusting up under my wings, which had unfurled in Asher's arms, and lifting us both off the ground. It was the kind of kiss you read about in books, the kind they write songs about. A kiss that told the story of us. The whole messy, complicated story.

He let go of me, letting me fall, gently, to the ground.

"I will. And if you think I'm giving up on *that*," he said, brushing the hair out of my face, "you're crazy."

"That's no good-bye," I whispered, pushing down the lump welling in my throat.

"Nope. It's a promise."

Asher gave me one last look, a millennia of history contained within that one gaze. "See you on the other side," he said.

In a rustle of black feathers, he moved to the window.

Then he was gone. And everything went still. The bottom of my life fell out from beneath me. Just like that.

On shaky legs, I walked to the window and leaned my hands against the weathered sill. The night unfolded before me, a dark expanse of stars.

What have I done?

The floor creaked, and soon Cassie had walked up beside me.

"You okay, babe?" she said softly, putting a reassuring hand on my back.

"No," I said, wiping away a tear. "But I will be." I let my head fall onto her shoulder, and she wrapped her arms around me.

"I think what you're doing is incredibly brave," she said.

"That's not why I'm doing it."

"I know." She pulled away and looked at me, her green eyes sparkling. "You're doing it because it's right. And you won't have to go through it alone. I know your secret now, and nothing could make me leave your side."

"Not even Dan?" I asked hopefully.

"Not even Dan. Come on, he's not as important as my best friend!"

"You know, you really need to start making sure I'm not in the room before you talk about me," Dan said, coming up behind her. "I always hear you."

"You need to stop sneaking up on us then," Cassie replied blithely, waving him off.

"You guys have to get the bickering under control," Ian cut in, clapping a hand on Dan's back as he approached. "If we're going to work as a team now." His brown eyes found mine, searching. Ian, always comforting, always a friend, even when neither of us deserved it. "And Skye, Cassie's right. We're here for you. We're going to help you, whatever you need. We're in this together."

For a moment, I couldn't find the words to say what I was feeling. I looked around at my friends, my family, the only people I knew I could always count on. They were so loyal, dependable. As long as we were all together, I would never be alone. I'd questioned it once, but I knew I would never have to question it again.

"You guys are the best," I said, standing up. "I can't believe how far we've come since the night of my birthday. It seems like yesterday, but I feel like a different person now."

"You kind of are," said Cassie.

"But we still love you." Dan smirked. "Weird silver wings and all."

"Come on, Skye," Ian said. "Pack up. Let's go home."

I looked around at my friends and nodded.

"I'm ready," I said.

"For whatever's coming," said Dan.

"For the road ahead," Ian added.

"For a nap!" Cassie laughed.

"For all those things," I said. "And whatever else we're about to face."

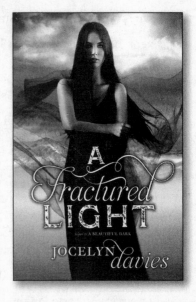